MISSION DE SURVIE

Peter DAVID est un écrivain prolifique : auteur d'une vingtaine de romans et scénariste de centaines de bandes dessinées, telles que des numéros de *L'Incroyable Hulk, Spiderman, Star Trek, Facteur-X, Serval*. Il a écrit plusieurs romans populaires de *Star Trek : La Nouvelle Génération*, dont *Imzadi*, *Strike Zone* et *Q-in-Law*, souvent placés dans la liste des best-sellers du *New York Times*. Il est aussi l'auteur d'un excellent roman de *Star Trek : The Rift*, et du premier roman original de *Deep Space Nine*. Parmi ses autres romans, citons *Knight Life* (une satire dans laquelle le roi Arthur, transporté dans l'avenir, fait campagne pour devenir le maire de New York), *Howling Mad* (l'équivalent loup-garou de l'*Entretien avec un vampire*, revu par les Monthy Pythons).

Peter David habite à New York avec son épouse, Myra (qu'il a rencontrée lors d'une convention *Star Trek*), et leurs trois enfants : Shana, Guinevere et Ariel.

Peter DAVID

STAR TREK® :
LA NOUVELLE GÉNÉRATION

STARFLEET ACADÉMIE

MISSION DE SURVIE

Traduit de l'américain par
Bruno Billion

Illustrations de
James Fry

POCKET

Titre original :
*Star Trek : The Next Generation
Starfleet Academy* ™ *# 3
Survival*

Publié pour la première fois en décembre 1993 par
Pocket Books, une division de Simon & Schuster Inc.,
New York, USA.

Loi n° 49-956 du 16 juillet 1949 sur les publications
destinées à la jeunesse : mai 1995.

ISBN 2-266-06273-5

A toutes les Nouvelles Générations de l'Univers

CHRONOLOGIE DE STARFLEET

2264

Lancement de la légendaire mission de cinq ans de l'*U.S.S. Entreprise*, NCC-1701, commandé par le capitaine James T. Kirk.

2292

L'alliance de l'Empire Klingon et de l'Empire Stellaire Romulien est dissoute.

2293

Le colonel Worf, grand-père de Worf Rozhenko, défend le capitaine Kirk et le docteur McCoy à leur procès, lors du meurtre du chancelier klingon Gorkon. Conférence de la Paix de Khitomer entre l'Empire Klingon et la Fédération. (*Star Trek VI : Terre Inconnue*, Pocket.)

2323

Jean-Luc Picard s'inscrit au programme standard de quatre ans d'études de Starfleet Académie.

2328

L'Empire Cardassien annexe la planète Bajor.

2341

Data entre à Starfleet Académie.

2342

Beverly Crusher (Howard, de son nom de jeune fille) entre à l'École médicale de Starfleet Académie pour huit années d'études.

2346

Massacre de l'avant-poste klingon sur Khitomer par les Romuliens.

2351

Les Cardassiens construisent une station spatiale en orbite autour de Bajor. Ils l'abandonneront bien plus tard.

2353
William T. Riker et Geordi LaForge entrent à Starfleet Académie.
2354
Deanna Troi s'inscrit à Starfleet Académie.
2356
Tasha Yar entre à Starfleet Académie.
2357
Worf Rozhenko entre à Starfleet Académie.
2363
Le capitaine Jean-Luc Picard prend le commandement de l'U.S.S. *Entreprise*, NCC-1701-D.
2367
Wesley Crusher entre à Starfleet Académie.

Un armistice est signé entre les Cardassiens et la Fédération.

Attaque des Borgs au point Wolf 359 : le lieutenant commander Benjamin Sisko et son fils Jake comptent parmi les survivants.

L'U.S.S. *Entreprise* détruit le vaisseau borg en orbite autour de la Terre.
2369
Le commander Benjamin Sisko prend le commandement de la station Deep Space Nine, en orbite autour de Bajor.

Sources : Star Trek ® Chronology, Michel Okuda et Denise Okuda.

*Dédié à
Shana et Jenny
mes toutes dernières fans ;
à Ariel
une future lectrice ;
et à Rose
qui s'occupe si bien
de tout ce petit monde...*

CHAPITRE PREMIER

Appeler ça une « ville » aurait été exagéré.

C'était un petit village. Aucun bâtiment n'avait plus de deux étages. De plus, la plupart étaient en ruines. Les habitations, percées de trous, n'avaient plus de toit, ou n'étaient que des tas de gravats.

Il n'y avait pas de mouvement dans les rues, car c'était l'heure la plus chaude d'une journée déjà étouffante. Les quelques habitants du village restaient enfermés pour échapper à la fournaise.

L'air était lourd dans le bâtiment réservé aux communications subspatiales. La construction avait été gravement touchée, mais c'était la première à avoir été réparée.

Le technicien délégué aux communications se moquait que la climatisation ne fonctionne pas ; dans le cas contraire, il aurait refusé de l'admettre. Sa peau à facettes était dure. Ses yeux, son nez et sa bouche se limitaient à des fentes sombres. Il portait l'uniforme d'un cadet de Starfleet et arborait l'expression de quelqu'un qui se pose des questions sur l'utilité de son travail.

Cela ne l'empêchait pas de continuer à surveiller les consoles de communication.

Il jeta un coup d'œil au chronomètre et soupira. Depuis cinquante-neuf minutes, il attendait désespérément une transmission subspatiale. Il n'y en avait eu aucune. A chaque heure pleine, comme le stipulait le règlement, il devait lancer un appel de détresse.

— Attention, dit-il en appuyant sur le bouton de transmission. Ici Dantar IV, qui appelle tout navire de la Fédération ou de l'Empire Klingon. Nous avons grand besoin de secours. J'insiste. Nous sommes dans une situation désespérée. C'est une urgence Code Un. Répondez, je vous prie, ou envoyez une équipe. Dantar, terminé.

Il coda le message et l'envoya.

La population de Dantar IV — passée de plusieurs centaines de colons humains et klingons à huit personnes —, avait été victime d'une attaque. L'assaut avait été repous-

12

sé, et l'ennemi détruit, mais à un prix terrible. La colonie était tellement ravagée qu'il s'était révélé impossible de rester sur Dantar.

Les navettes d'évacuation étaient pleines à craquer. Alors, huit braves s'étaient portés volontaires pour rester en arrière : cinq cadets de Starfleet Académie et trois cadets klingons. L'opérateur qui venait d'envoyer le message, Zak Kebron, faisait partie du premier groupe.

Zak appartenait à une race de guerriers appelés les Brikars. A cet instant, il réfléchissait à la mélasse dans laquelle lui et ses compagnons se trouvaient.

Ils étaient coincés sur Dantar depuis plus de deux semaines, attendant l'arrivée des secours. Mais personne n'était venu. Quand les colons étaient partis, ils avaient assuré les cadets qu'un navire passerait les prendre avant une semaine.

Ils n'étaient pas menacés... Pas encore, du moins. Bien que les colons aient vidé les réserves, il restait suffisamment de rations pour nourrir les huit volontaires pendant plusieurs semaines.

Il y avait un abri : deux bâtiments avec quatre murs et un toit encore en état. Même si ce n'était pas le grand luxe, cela leur suffisait.

Mais il fallait compter avec la solitude... et l'idée qu'une nouvelle attaque était possible. L'incertitude leur tenait compagnie.

Et s'ils étaient condamnés à rester sur Dantar plus de quelques semaines ? Et si les provisions venaient à manquer ? A quoi en seraient-ils réduits pour subsister ? Et à partir de quel point la survie pour la survie ne valait-elle plus le coup ?

C'étaient des questions difficiles, auxquelles Zak Kebron n'avait aucune réponse.

Mais il disposait de beaucoup de temps...

Il jeta encore un coup d'œil au chronomètre.

Les jeunes gens n'avaient même pas de preuves que leurs transmissions étaient reçues.

Un grand nombre des composants vitaux de la console de communications subspatiales avaient été pulvérisés ; certains étaient irréparables. Les cadets avaient bricolé la console du mieux qu'ils pouvaient. Mais il restait possible que leur signal soit si faible que même un satellite en orbite ne le recevrait pas.

Mais que pouvaient-ils faire de plus ?

Zak entendit des pas derrière lui. Il pensa qu'il était inutile de se retourner, mais la force de l'habitude l'emporta.

Il garda une expression neutre sur le visage

quand il vit entrer un grand Klingon à l'air féroce. Sa longue moustache, terminée par des embouts de métal, tremblait légèrement à chaque mouvement de sa tête.

Kodash.

— Je viens prendre la relève, dit le Klingon.

Zak savait pertinemment que Kodash le haïssait. Le guerrier faisait partie des trois émissaires klingons envoyés sur la colonie en même temps que les cadets de l'Académie. Puisque Dantar IV était un monde codirigé par la Fédération et l'Empire, des représentants des deux groupes avaient été dépêchés quand des disputes s'étaient avérées susceptibles de détruire la colonie. Les jeunes diplomates avaient réussi à calmer la situation, mais des assaillants non identifiés avaient fini par anéantir Dantar IV.

A présent, les cadets et les Klingons utilisaient tout leur *self-control* pour ne pas retomber dans les querelles qui avaient empoisonné l'atmosphère de la colonie.

Cependant...

Kodash n'avait pas rendu la tâche facile à ses camarades. Il n'avait fait aucun effort pour cacher son dédain pour Zak Kebron ; le Brikar avait affiché avec une grande fierté sa haine des Klingons.

Le cadet savait que sa Némésis avait une

bonne raison de se montrer. C'était l'heure où Kodash devait le remplacer aux communications ; un planning rigoureux avait été mis au point par le groupe.

Cependant...

L'irruption du Klingon exaspérait la frustration de Zak, son inquiétude qu'ils restent coincés sur cette maudite boule de glaise jusqu'à la fin de leurs jours.

Tout cela l'encouragea à dire :

— Pas de problème.

— Comment ça, « pas de problème » ? s'étonna Kodash.

— Je peux continuer encore un petit moment. (Zak lui fit signe de déguerpir.) Va t'occuper à autre chose.

Le Klingon avança.

Un instant satisfait, Zak se régala de voir les veines du front de Kodash pulser de rage.

Puis, doucement, le Klingon dit :

— Dégage.

Zak lui répondit de la manière la plus efficace. Il fit pivoter son siège pour lui tourner le dos.

Kodash craqua.

Un instant plus tard, le fauteuil fit de même.

Le Klingon savait qu'il ne pourrait pas éjecter le Brikar de son siège ; il était trop lourd. Aussi, il agrippa le dossier et tira de toutes ses forces.

Le fauteuil céda ; Zak roula sur le sol.

Kodash n'eut pas le temps de se réjouir de sa blague. Kebron se jeta sur lui, propulsé par la rage.

Cette bagarre n'était pas seulement le résultat de la haine existant entre les deux jeunes gens ; elle provenait surtout du sentiment d'impuissance qu'ils éprouvaient face à leur situation et à l'idée inquiétante qu'elle pourrait se prolonger indéfiniment.

Kodash n'eut pas le temps de s'écarter. Les deux combattants roulèrent sur le sol jusqu'à sortir de la salle.

Coinçant le Klingon sous lui, Kebron brandit le poing. Une main ferme l'empoigna, l'empêchant de frapper son adversaire.

— Non, Zak, ne fais pas ça.

Furieux, le Brikar ne se retourna même pas :

— Laisse-moi tranquille, Worf.

— Lâche Kodash, répliqua son ami.

Kebron se retourna :

— Cette histoire ne te regarde pas.

Le jeune Klingon ne relâcha pas sa prise sur le poignet du Brikar :

— Zak, tu n'accompliras rien ainsi.

Les autres cadets approchaient, suivis de près par le reste de la délégation klingonne.

Ils avaient entendu les bruits du combat et les cris. Dans l'air immobile de Dantar IV, les sons portaient loin.

Worf les fixa d'un regard qui semblait dire : *Laissez-moi faire.*

Kodash avait recouvré assez de souffle pour déclarer :

— Il m'a provoqué !

— Je n'ai provoqué personne, protesta Zak. J'ai parlé avec courtoisie. *Tu* t'es offusqué de ma politesse.

— Baisse le poing, gronda Worf, et nous discuterons d'une manière plus civilisée.

Quand ils s'étaient rencontrés, Zak n'aurait pas plus fait confiance au cadet nommé Worf qu'à un autre Klingon.

Avec le temps, il avait appris à apprécier son camarade de l'Académie, mais il était clair que ce sentiment ne s'appliquait pas aux congénères de Worf, qu'il avait toujours du mal à supporter.

Pourtant Kebron baissa le poing.

Il avait conscience de la désapprobation de ses camarades. Tania Tobias, la jeune spécialiste en ingénierie, l'observait en plissant les paupières. Sa chevelure blonde, d'habitude méticuleusement coiffée, était mise à rude épreuve par la chaleur. La jeune fille paraissait mille fois plus fatiguée que lors de leur arrivée sur Dantar.

A sa droite se trouvait Mark McHenry, souvent appelé par son surnom, « Mac ». Sa spécialisation en astronavigation ne lui était d'aucune utilité sur une planète déserte comme Dantar IV. Mac avait la fâcheuse réputation de passer son temps « dans les nuages », même si, en réalité, il restait conscient de ce qui l'entourait. Pour l'instant, le jeune rouquin était pleinement concentré sur l'instant présent.

Pendant que Kebron fixait les cadets, l'attention de Worf s'était portée sur les Klingons ; il voulait voir quelle allait être leur réaction.

Un des deux guerriers s'appelait Gowr. Le plus petit des trois envoyés, il était aussi de loin le plus fort. Il n'aimait ni les humains ni les Brikars, et considérait Worf avec un dédain visible. Le cadet était physiquement un Klingon, mais son esprit appartenait à Starfleet.

C'était une combinaison que Gowr trouvait déplaisante ; heureusement, il ne commandait pas la délégation.

Cette tâche revenait à la jeune Klingonne qui luttait pour contrôler le tempérament explosif de ses camarades.

Son nom était K'Ehleyr. Forte, fière et taciturne, quand elle parlait, c'était avec une grande confiance et la certitude d'avoir raison. Elle se fiait tant à ses capacités que la possibilité qu'elle puisse commettre une erreur ne lui venait jamais à l'esprit.

Bref, K'Ehleyr était tout ce qu'une Klingonne pouvait aspirer à devenir. Le respect qu'éprouvait Worf à son égard s'était métamorphosé au fil des jours. Déchiré entre son héritage klingon et son éducation terrienne, il lui enviait sa sérénité psychique et son assurance. Au fil des épreuves traversées par le groupe, elle avait toujours gardé son calme.

D'une certaine manière, cela inquiétait un peu Worf. Il commençait à se demander si le vernis d'impassibilité de K'Ehleyr n'allait pas finir par se craqueler sous l'effet de ses angoisses et de ses frustrations. Cette petite altercation risquait d'être l'événement qui la pousserait au-delà de ses limites.

— Kodash, qu'est-il arrivé ? demanda la Klingonne.

L'interpellé rajusta son uniforme, et répondit d'une voix furieuse :

— C'était l'heure de prendre mon service à la console de communications subspatiales. Le Brikar a refusé de me laisser la place.

— As-tu commencé le combat ?

— Non, c'est lui.

— C'est faux ! protesta Zak.

Le regard de K'Ehleyr se posa sur Worf.

Le cadet croisa les bras :

— Si Zak Kebron affirme qu'il n'a pas commencé, sa réponse suffit à me convaincre.

— Me traites-tu de menteur ? gronda Kodash.

La Klingonne se retourna vers son camarade :

— T'a-t-il frappé le premier ?

— Quelle importance ?

— Ça compte pour moi, Kodash. Le Brikar t'a-t-il frappé le premier ? Réponds-moi ! Oui ou non ?

— Non, mais...

— Fiche le camp, Kodash.

Le grand Klingon parut sur le point d'exploser :

— Comment oses-tu...

Lorsque K'Ehleyr reprit la parole, elle utilisa un ton plus doux. Tous savaient à présent qu'elle parlait moins fort quand elle était en colère :

— Fiche le camp, Kodash.

Le Klingon ouvrit la bouche pour protester, puis il la referma. Le regard de K'Ehleyr et le ton de sa voix avaient enfin fait leur effet. Il recula, foudroya une dernière fois Zak du regard, puis partit.

Worf entraîna Kebron loin du groupe :

— Tu n'avais aucune raison de le provoquer de cette manière.

— Quel est ton problème, Worf ? demanda le Brikar. Même K'Ehleyr s'est rangée de mon côté...

— Je ne suis pas K'Ehleyr, lui rappela son ami. Tu savais parfaitement que tes manières provoqueraient cette réaction de Kodash. Ne cause plus de tels problèmes dans l'avenir. C'est compris ?

Ensemble Worf et Zak avaient surmonté bon nombre d'obstacles. D'abord ennemis, ils avaient partagé leur chambre. Puis ils étaient devenus alliés. A présent, la force de leur amitié était mise à l'épreuve par les faits.

Le Brikar dut réfléchir longtemps avant de répondre. Finalement, il se contenta de dire :

— Oui.

— Bien, répondit Worf. J'espère ne plus avoir à revenir là-dessus dans l'avenir. A présent, si tu désires continuer ton travail de surveillance des communications, je ne te retiens plus.

Zak hocha la tête, puis il retourna dans le bâtiment.

Worf regarda les autres et dit :

— Je crois que vous avez des choses plus

importantes à faire que regarder deux imbéciles se disputer. Des objections ?

Les autres cadets acquiescèrent en silence. Ils retournèrent prestement au travail.

Ce fut seulement alors que le Klingon souffla. De tous ceux qui avaient assisté à l'altercation entre Zak et Kodash, seuls restaient K'Ehleyr et lui.

Ils demeurèrent un moment face à face en silence.

— Eh bien, dit enfin K'Ehleyr, ç'aurait pu être pire.

— En effet, concéda Worf. Nous avons eu de la chance.

Elle soupira ; pour la première fois en plusieurs semaines, le Klingon sentit chez elle une pointe d'incertitude.

— Worf, par Kahless, que va-t-il nous arriver ?

— Nous serons bientôt secourus.

— Tu le crois vraiment ?

Elle approcha de lui, et il lut de la tristesse dans ses yeux. La confiance qui se dégageait d'elle n'était pas nécessairement un bon indicateur de ses tourments intérieurs.

— Bien sûr que je le crois, dit Worf. Pourquoi en serait-il autrement ?

Elle massa sa crête nasale avec deux doigts :

— Parce que nous n'avons reçu aucune nouvelle depuis le départ des colons. Parce que nous risquons à chaque instant de nous entre-tuer. Worf, peut-être te fais-tu des illusions ?

— Je refuse de le croire.

Elle haussa les épaules :

— Si tu refuses d'admettre que le soleil est chaud, cela change-t-il la réalité ? Je ne le pense pas. L'univers n'attend pas ton approbation ; il est ce qu'il est. Crois ce que tu veux. Mais tu risques d'être déçu. L'illusion est un luxe qu'un chef ne peut pas se permettre.

K'Ehleyr se mit en mouvement pour s'éloigner, mais elle le regarda une dernière fois :

— Ton assistance scientifique, Soleta, n'est pas accourue pour assister au spectacle. Il est réconfortant de savoir que notre Vulcaine avait des choses plus importantes à faire.

Worf se contenta d'acquiescer. Il était inutile de révéler à la Klingonne que Soleta n'était pas en ville.

La Vulcaine était moins affectée qu'eux par le climat aride de Dantar, et ce, pour deux raisons : son monde présentait un climat à peu près similaire, et son corps disposait d'une variété de biomécanismes qui lui permettaient de mieux supporter l'environnement hostile de la colonie.

De plus, même à l'agonie, le stoïcisme vulcain ne lui aurait pas permis d'admettre qu'elle était en difficulté.

A cet instant, elle explorait le désert environnant. Elle prenait des mesures; elle menait des expériences. Bref, elle était...

Elle était en retard !

CHAPITRE
II

Le soleil de Dantar martelait le crâne de Soleta, mais elle ne le remarquait même pas. Son attention était rivée sur son tricordeur, qui lui fournissait des données intrigantes à grand renfort de « bips » électroniques.

Elle vérifia encore, histoire de confirmer que l'appareil fonctionnait. Ce qu'il lui apprenait était totalement inattendu.

Son plan originel était de prélever des échantillons de sol dans la perspective d'une éventuelle utilisation agricole. Mais la situation avait changé : son tricordeur avait intercepté un signal.

— Une balise, murmura-t-elle. Une espèce de balise.

Oui, il n'y a pas de doute.

Elle appuya sur son commbadge :

— Soleta appelle Worf.

Aucune réponse.

Elle fronça ses sourcils arqués et essaya de nouveau.

Une fois de plus, aucune réponse.

La chaleur avait-elle affecté la liaison ?

Peu probable.

Peut-être sa transmission était-elle brouillée ?

Cette idée l'intriguait... Une balise automatique qui parasitait les transmissions au hasard ? Ou encore — c'était une perspective plus inquiétante, du moins pour un être capable de concevoir de l'inquiétude —, une machine qui brouillait toutes les fréquences utilisées par les appareils de Starfleet ?

— Fascinant.

Deux options se présentaient à Soleta. Elle pouvait retourner à la colonie pour prévenir les autres et les ramener — la décision la plus prudente —, ou pousser un peu plus loin son enquête.

La Vulcaine savait que retourner à la colonie était une mauvaise idée ; la balise n'appartenait peut-être pas à une installation permanente, mais à un navire qui s'était récemment posé.

Ce pouvait être un allié ; dans ce cas, ils seraient sauvés.

Bien évidemment, il pouvait s'agir aussi d'un ennemi, qui essayerait de tuer Soleta dès qu'elle se montrerait.

Tant de possibilités lui venaient à l'esprit.

Mais celle qui pesait le plus sur sa décision, c'était qu'elle ne connaîtrait probablement jamais la solution de l'énigme si elle partait.

Une belle occasion scientifique ratée.

Le risque que sa curiosité ne soit pas satisfaite l'emportait sur son souci de sécurité. Coincée sur une planète avec des cadets débutants et des Klingons méfiants, et peu de chances d'être secourue, elle était *déjà* en danger !

Soleta avança lentement, utilisant comme abri les quelques rochers qui parsemaient le paysage.

Elle continua jusqu'à arriver au sommet d'une colline et s'immobilisa.

C'était un navire. Le métal blanc de sa coque brillait sous le soleil. Il s'était écrasé ; au vu des dégâts, il ne pourrait jamais redécoller. Ses stabilisateurs et ses propulseurs s'étaient désolidarisés de la coque. Ses ailes avaient été arrachées lors de l'atterrissage forcé. La Vulcaine estima que le vaisseau avait dû glisser dans le sable sur plus d'une centaine de mètres avant de s'arrêter.

Soleta reconnut immédiatement son origine. Si ses marquages et sa forme générale ne suffisaient pas à l'identifier, les traces de brûlure qui striaient la carlingue étaient reconnaissables.

C'étaient celles d'un barrage de DCA... Les effets du canon qui avait bravement défendu Dantar IV.

Il ne faisait aucun doute que Soleta venait de retrouver le vaisseau qui avait attaqué la colonie. Durant l'assaut, les tricordeurs avaient *identifié* un navire d'origine klingonne, équipé d'un armement de la Fédération. Cette combinaison avait provoqué de nombreuses disputes entre les colons, qui s'entre-accusaient de sabotage. La question du navire avait beaucoup préoccupé les cadets.

Soleta s'attendait à un problème. C'est pourquoi un fuseur était accroché à sa ceinture. Espérant qu'elle n'en aurait pas besoin, elle vérifia qu'il était chargé.

La Vulcaine approcha lentement du navire, sans quitter des yeux son tricordeur, qui cherchait des signes vitaux.

Aucun mouvement.

Il n'y avait personne à bord... Aucun être vivant, en tout cas.

Mais la balise fonctionnait toujours. Selon toute vraisemblance, elle avait été activée par quelqu'un après l'atterrissage en catastrophe. Ça impliquait qu'il y avait au minimum un survivant. A moins que le dispositif ne se soit mis automatiquement en route après l'impact ? Il aurait également pu être activé par une personne décédée depuis.

Tant de possibilités...

Soleta se glissa par une des ouvertures béantes de la coque et posa un pied sur le pont du vaisseau. Des rais de lumière solaire filtraient par les trous de la carlingue. C'était une chance. Bien qu'armée, la Vulcaine n'avait pas songé à emporter une torche.

Quand elle s'enfonça davantage dans le navire, les ténèbres remplacèrent peu à peu la lumière. Le grillage métallique du pont craquait sous son poids. Chaque bruit était amplifié.

Soleta manqua trébucher sur un cadavre.

Elle recula, surprise.

Sa vue s'accoutumait peu à peu à l'obscurité ; elle écarquilla les yeux.

Non, ce n'était pas un corps. La Vulcaine interrogea son tricordeur, qui ne lui apprit rien de plus. Alors elle remarqua le placard vide situé à sa droite, et elle comprit. C'était une sorte de scaphandre, utilisé en général pour effectuer des réparations dans le vide intersidéral. Il avait dû tomber du placard quand le navire s'était écrasé.

Elle réprima le vague embarras qu'elle éprouvait pour s'être laissé prendre.

Elle baissa les yeux sur son tricordeur, qui afficha une impulsion longue d'à peine un dixième de seconde.

Des signes vitaux.

Droit devant elle.

Qui que ce soit, l'ennemi était parvenu à approcher dans un silence total ; considérant l'acuité de l'ouïe vulcaine, ce n'était pas une tâche facile.

Par réflexe, Soleta recula d'un pas. Ce fut probablement ce qui lui sauva la vie.

Elle sentit un grand déplacement d'air devant elle.

Un poing.

Si la Vulcaine doutait encore de se trouver face à une entité hostile, elle cessa aussitôt.

Elle recula encore ; son assaillant la suivit. Alors elle bondit sur la gauche et dégaina son fuseur. Tandis qu'elle levait son arme, un bras s'abattit sur le sien, lui faisant lâcher prise. Le fuseur heurta le sol avec un bruit aigu.

Soleta jeta un coup d'œil dans la direction où son arme avait disparu, mais ce fut une erreur. Profitant de sa déconcentration momentanée, un poing s'abattit sur sa tempe. Des étoiles explosèrent dans la tête de la Vulcaine. Elle chancela, mobilisant toute son énergie pour rester consciente.

Son dos heurta une paroi du navire. C'était une bonne nouvelle ; dans les ténèbres qui l'entouraient, elle disposait au moins d'un point de repère.

Elle se concentra pour se calmer et ignorer la panique qui lui tordait les entrailles. Elle avait des problèmes... Mais elle saurait faire face jusqu'à ce que quelqu'un vienne à sa rescousse.

Avant que son assaillant puisse à nouveau la frapper, Soleta entra en action. Elle coinça le bras de son adversaire entre son genou et son coude.

Un instant, elle se trouva dans une position précaire, à la merci du moindre coup. Mais c'était un risque nécessaire, le temps que sa main valide trouve le support qu'elle cherchait.

Elle le trouva : l'épaule de l'assaillant.

La peau qu'elle sentit sous ses doigts avait la consistance du cuir ; elle était presque aussi dure que de la pierre. La sensation lui parut familière, mais elle remit son analyse à plus tard. La survie était la seule chose qui importait pour l'instant. Elle plaça ses doigts et son pouce sur l'épaule de son adversaire, comme on le lui avait appris, et serra.

Le combattant inconnu poussa une exclamation. Puis il chancela.

Et ce fut tout...

La prise vulcaine aurait dû le rendre aussitôt inconscient. Soleta recommença, cette fois en y mettant toutes ses forces.

Son ennemi s'écroula ; sa tête heurta une paroi. La Vulcaine ne parvint pas à se dégager à temps : elle tomba avec lui. Ils s'écrasèrent sur le sol. Dotée d'une imagination fertile, Soleta aurait pu penser que l'onde de choc s'était propagée sur toute la planète.

Pendant un long moment, aucun des deux combattants ne bougea. La respiration de la

Vulcaine était rapide et saccadée, mais toute son attention se concentrait sur son ennemi.

Il ne fit aucun bruit et ne broncha pas.

Il était inconscient.

Soleta réussit à se dégager et resta assise près du vaincu le temps de reprendre sa respiration. Elle se permit un sourire de satisfaction. Pour une Vulcaine, c'était un luxe, mais elle l'avait bien mérité.

Elle se releva, s'épousseta et rajusta son uniforme. Ensuite, elle réfléchit.

Que faire de mon agresseur ?

Dans ce navire, l'espace était des plus réduits. Elle tâtonna dans les ténèbres jusqu'à trouver une des jambes de sa « victime ». Puis elle tira l'être jusqu'au trou par lequel elle était entrée.

Grâce à la structure de la pupille vulcaine, munie d'une protection spéciale contre les changements brusques de luminosité, ses yeux se firent rapidement à la lumière de l'extérieur.

Soleta regarda son adversaire.

C'était exactement ce qu'elle avait pensé...

Dans son esprit, il ne faisait aucun doute que *quelqu'un* allait se sentir très mal quand elle reviendrait à la colonie.

CHAPITRE

III

Tania et Mac vérifiaient les niveaux d'énergie du générateur qui alimentait les quelques bâtiments encore en état. La jeune blonde leva les yeux en entendant Worf entrer. Il avait les mains jointes derrière le dos, comme toujours quand il faisait une inspection.

Fidèle à sa légende, il grogna :

— Rapport ?

Tania sourit :

— La même chose qu'hier, Worf. Et qu'avant-hier, et que le jour d'avant. Le générateur est opérationnel. Les niveaux d'énergie sont acceptables. Toutes les connexions sont en place. Il n'y a aucun problème avec les câbles. (Elle marqua une pause.) Tu t'attendais à autre chose ?

Il ne lui rendit pas son sourire.

— Je m'attends à ce que ton rapport soit précis. Rien de plus.

Elle hocha la tête :

— Très bien, Worf. Je comprends.

Il tourna les talons ; Tania le rappela :

— Oh, monsieur Worf...

— Oui ?

— J'ai remarqué en arrivant que K'Ehleyr était assise dehors, près du dortoir des Klingons. Elle semblait déprimée. Puisque vous êtes nos deux chefs, peut-être aimerais-tu lui parler pour savoir s'il y a un problème.

— Oh ? (Il sembla réfléchir à fond au sujet.) Très bien, merci de m'avoir informé...

— Pas de problème.

Worf sortit.

Mac paraissait s'intéresser à un graphique affiché sur un écran. Ça ne l'empêcha pas de lancer :

— C'était très gentil de ta part.

— Quoi ?

— De lui suggérer d'aller voir K'Ehleyr. Ce que je veux dire, c'est qu'il est évident que tu es folle de lui.

La mâchoire de Tania en tomba presque jusqu'à ses chevilles :

— Je te demande pardon ?

— Je disais qu'il est évident que...

— Oui, j'ai bien compris.

38

— Alors pourquoi m'as-tu demandé de répéter ? (Il leva les yeux vers elle.) Amnésique, peut-être ?

— Mac, je ne suis pas *folle* de Worf.

— Vraiment ?

— Oui. J'admets que je l'aime bien. C'est un excellent ami et un bon cadet — loyal, et... (Elle s'arrêta à temps.) Etre amoureuse de lui serait ridicule et déplacé.

— Vraiment ?

— Oui, vraiment. Alors arrête de dire ça.

— Très bien... Attends... Histoire d'être sûr. Dois-je cesser de dire que tu es folle de Worf ? Ou m'abstenir de l'adverbe « vraiment » ? Ou encore du mot « ça » ? La première solution ne me pose aucun problème. La deuxième, en revanche, pourrait être difficile à appliquer. Quant à la troisième, c'est purement impossible...

— Les deux premières suffiront bien, coupa-t-elle.

— Très bien. (Il reprit ses occupations, puis fit remarquer :) Je trouvais ça sympathique de ta part parce que, selon toute évidence, Worf est fou de K'Ehleyr.

— C'est *faux* !

Tania ricana comme si cette hypothèse était la plus ridicule qu'elle ait entendue.

— Vrai... En vérité ?

— Oui, en vérité.

— Très bien. Dans ce cas, je dois avoir les neurones perturbés.

— Qu'est-ce qui te perturbe, Mac ? demanda-t-elle patiemment.

— Eh bien, de la manière dont je vois les choses, tu trouves Worf plutôt séduisant. Mais tu penses qu'il serait plus heureux avec K'Ehleyr, alors tu fais de ton mieux pour cacher tes sentiments, et agir dans l'intérêt de notre ami klingon. Franchement, je trouve ça noble.

— Oui. Eh bien... (Elle s'éclaircit la gorge.) *Si* c'était ce que je veux faire, ce *serait* noble. Mais ce n'est pas le cas, compris ?

— Puisque tu le dis, Tania.

Un long silence suivit, puis Tobias sourit :

— Tu sais, Mac, pour un type qui ne paraît pas faire attention à ce qui se passe autour de lui, tu ne cesses pas de m'épater.

Mark leva la tête :

— Désolé. Tu disais ?

— Oublie ça.

— Très bien, répondit-il avant de se replonger dans son travail.

K'Ehleyr était précisément là où Tania l'avait dit, assise sur un bloc de pierre, à l'extérieur du bâtiment qui servait de résidence aux Klingons. Worf s'arrêta près d'elle et croisa les bras sur sa poitrine.

— Soleta est en retard, déclara-t-il. Elle m'a dit dans quelle direction elle comptait aller aujourd'hui. Même en admettant qu'elle se soit éloignée un peu plus de la ville que d'habitude, elle devrait être revenue. J'ai l'intention de partir à sa recherche.

— Tu as besoin d'aide ? demanda la Klingonne.

— J'ai une volontaire ?

— Tu me demandes de l'être ?

— Non.

— Dans ce cas, je ne suis *pas* volontaire.

Worf leva les yeux au ciel.

— Si nous partions tous les deux, dit-il, l'un de nous pourrait revenir au camp pour chercher de l'aide. En cas de problème, bien sûr...

— C'est vrai. (K'Ehleyr ménagea un moment ses effets.) Donc, tu me demandes de t'accompagner.

— Je ne fais que souligner à haute voix les avantages du travail en équipe.

— Très bien. (Elle se leva et épousseta son uniforme.) Puisque tu exiges ma présence...

— Je ne...

— *J'aimerais* t'accompagner, finit-elle d'une voix moins officielle.

Worf ne sourit pas, car ce n'eût pas été approprié. Il fut cependant amusé. Deux Klingons tellement enfermés dans leur carcan de fierté qu'aucun n'admettait avoir besoin de l'autre, ou simplement désirer passer un moment en sa compagnie.

Pourtant rien n'aurait été plus *approprié*.

Ils prirent la direction qu'avait suivie Soleta en quittant la colonie, et emportèrent avec eux du matériel simple comme des tricordeurs, des fuseurs (en cas de danger), et des gourdes pleines (dans l'éventualité, plus probable, où ils auraient soif).

De temps en temps, Worf tournait la tête vers K'Ehleyr, mais elle ne semblait pas particulièrement encline à entamer une conversation. Néanmoins, il décida d'ouvrir le feu.

— Pourquoi restais-tu assise ainsi dehors, tout à l'heure ?

— Starfleet recommande-t-il une manière de s'asseoir ?

Un coin de sa bouche menaça de former un sourire, mais il se retint :

— Non, c'était une façon de s'asseoir en accord avec les règlements de Starfleet.

— Bien, soupira-t-elle. Je ne voulais pas entrer à cause de Kodash. Il est furieux parce qu'il pense que je ne l'ai pas suffisamment soutenu lors de l'incident de cet après-midi.

— J'ignore si ça te fera plaisir, répliqua Worf, mais j'ai dit à Zak Kebron qu'il s'était mal comporté. (Il secoua la tête.) Il n'est pas facile d'oublier ses préjugés.

— Je sais.

Ils continuèrent de marcher.

— Ç'a été... plutôt frustrant pour moi, dit K'Ehleyr.

— Pour nous tous.

— Pas cette mission. Ma vie entière n'a été qu'une suite de frustrations.

Worf ne fit aucun effort pour cacher sa surprise :

— Je trouve ça difficile à croire.

— Vraiment ? Pourquoi ?

— Parce que tu sembles extrêmement capable. Parce que tu inspires le respect. Parce que...

— Tu ne comprends pas.

— Dans ce cas, explique-moi.

Elle soupira :

— J'ai du sang humain dans les veines, Worf.

— Vraiment ?

— Oui. Et j'ai passé chaque instant de ma vie à essayer de l'oublier. (Elle ralentit.) Je me suis toujours poussée au-delà des limites que s'impose un Klingon, parce que j'ai besoin de me prouver qu'une différence biologique ne fait pas de moi une tarée, mais une femme et une guerrière aussi capable qu'une autre Klingonne. (Elle secoua la tête.) Je dois te paraître ridicule.

— Tu penses que je pourrais trouver ça ridicule ? N'oublie pas à qui tu t'adresses, K'Ehleyr. J'ai été élevé par des humains. Même si mes parents adoptifs ont fait en sorte que j'honore et que je comprenne mon héritage klingon, j'ai dû me conformer aux critères de comportement des humains. Mon enfance n'a pas été une expérience facile.

— Ce qui veut dire... ?

— Ça signifie en clair que je me suis beaucoup battu. Mon père prétend qu'il a passé plus de temps à l'école à cause de moi que lorsqu'il était enfant, parce que mes professeurs le convoquaient souvent pour parler de mes « problèmes ». Dans l'Empire, tu étais une Klingonne avec du sang humain luttant pour rester digne de son héritage. Pendant ce temps, j'étais élevé sur Terre par des parents humains. Je trouve ça drôle.

— Je pense plutôt que c'est dommage, répondit K'Ehleyr. J'aurais voulu te connaître quand j'étais enfant, Worf. Je déteste l'avouer, mais tu m'aurais été d'un grand soutien.

— Toi aussi.

Ils s'arrêtèrent de marcher ; leurs regards se croisèrent.

Worf fut certain qu'il aurait dû dire quelque chose. Si seulement il avait pu savoir quoi...

Soudain, la Klingonne remarqua quelque chose à la périphérie de son champ de vision. Elle pointa un doigt :

— Regarde !

Les yeux de Worf suivirent la direction qu'elle indiquait. Il vit une silhouette féminine qui portait un lourd paquet sur les épaules.

Non, ce n'était pas un paquet.

Un corps !

— C'est Soleta ! s'exclama le Klingon.

Il se précipita à sa rencontre. Son tricordeur battait contre sa cuisse tandis qu'il courait, K'Ehleyr sur les talons.

— Tu vas bien ? demanda-t-il à la Vulcaine quand il fut à portée de voix.

— Evidemment.

— Qui est-ce ? demanda la Klingonne.

Soleta ne répondit pas sur-le-champ. Elle s'arrêta et attendit patiemment l'arrivée des deux Klingons, ajoutant une poignée de secondes pour qu'ils reprennent leur souffle.

— C'est notre assaillant, expliqua-t-elle. J'ai découvert son navire. Il m'a attaquée, et j'ai « titillé » son épaule. Ainsi s'est conclue notre première entrevue.

— Et tu l'as porté tout ce chemin ?

Elle dévisagea Worf :

— Tu fais montre d'un incroyable talent pour souligner l'évidence, aujourd'hui. Pourquoi donc ?

— Plus tard, répondit l'autre cadet. Est-il humain ? Klingon ?

— En fait, dit Soleta, ni l'un ni l'autre.

Elle laissa tomber le corps. Il roula sur le dos.

Les deux Klingons ne tentèrent pas de cacher leur stupeur. Quant à Soleta, soit elle n'avait jamais été surprise, soit elle était trop adepte du contrôle des émotions pour le montrer.

— Le visage de l'ennemi, dit-elle d'une voix neutre.

Ce faciès appartenait à un membre d'une espèce très familière, dont le nombre de représentants sur Dantar IV venait de doubler.

L'agresseur inconscient était un Brikar.

CHAPITRE IV

— C'est une ruse ! Je refuse d'y croire !
Zak Kebron faisait les cent pas dans les quartiers des cadets, donnant l'impression d'une tornade vivante. Il serrait les poings.

Ses camarades l'entouraient, un air compatissant sur le visage.

— Zak..., commença Worf, pour ce qui lui parut être la centième fois.

Mais le Brikar ne lui accordait aucune attention. Il se tourna brusquement vers Soleta.

— Comment as-tu pu faire ça ?

La Vulcaine garda un visage impassible, comme d'habitude :

— Je n'ai rien fait, Zak, sinon mon devoir de cadet de Starfleet, et me défendre pour survivre.

— Qu'aurais-tu préféré, Zak ? intervint

Tania. Que Soleta se fasse tuer pour épargner ta fierté ?

Un très court instant, il parut y réfléchir, puis il trouva l'idée ridicule.

— Que vais-je faire, à présent ? demanda-t-il d'une voix proche du gémissement. Depuis des semaines, les Klingons me surveillent. Ils regardent le moindre de mes gestes d'un air soupçonneux, et je leur rends la monnaie de leur pièce. A présent, nous découvrons l'identité de notre assaillant, et c'est un membre de mon peuple ? Ce n'est pas un humain, mais un...

Il s'interrompit, comme si une idée venait de lui traverser l'esprit.

— Qu'y a-t-il, Zak ? demanda Worf.

— Il ne peut pas être Brikar ! s'exclama Kebron. Son navire est intact !

— Il n'est pas intact, précisa Soleta.

— Je ne veux pas dire qu'il n'est pas endommagé, expliqua Zak. Il ne devrait plus rien rester. Selon le règlement de l'armée brikarienne, un pilote doit détruire son vaisseau s'il en perd le contrôle.

— Peut-être espérait-il le réparer ? proposa Tania.

— Mais il a été capturé, et son navire est toujours entier. Ce qui prouve qu'il ne peut pas être...

C'est alors qu'il se produisit quelque chose.

Un éclair de lumière intense éclaira l'horizon, attirant l'attention de tous les cadets. Ils se protégèrent les yeux pour ne pas être aveuglés. Quelques secondes plus tard, le phénomène fut suivi par un bruit sourd.

Une explosion.

Puis vint le vent, qui souleva la poussière et propulsa des graviers dans les rues désertes de la colonie.

Tous demeurèrent silencieux un long moment après que les effets secondaires de l'explosion se furent dissipés.

— Quelque chose comme ça, Zak ? demanda Worf.

Kebron ne répondit pas.

Worf entra dans le bâtiment des communications subspatiales, où le prisonnier brikar avait été conduit. Il était encore inconscient. Soleta avait employé tant de force pour pincer sa peau insensible qu'il resterait dans cet état un certain temps.

K'Ehleyr, Gowr et Kodash se trouvaient là aussi. Le cadet les entendit parler en klingon tandis qu'il approchait. Quand il entra dans la salle, ils se turent.

Les deux mâles regardèrent Worf avec un mélange de suspicion et de dédain. L'expression de la jeune femme demeura prudemment neutre :

— Ta Soleta a fait du bon travail.

— Elle sait être efficace, acquiesça Worf. Kodash n'était pas d'humeur à écouter des compliments :

— Ce Brikar est inconscient, certes, mais il n'y a aucune raison de ne pas interroger l'autre.

— Je suppose, gronda le cadet, que tu fais référence au cadet de Starfleet Zak Kebron.

— Bien sûr !

— Il n'a rien à te dire, car il ignore tout de cette affaire ; il est furieux du comportement inqualifiable d'un membre de son peuple.

— Pour l'amour de Kahless, ouvre les yeux, Worf ! rugit Gowr, suivant l'opinion de Kodash, comme à son habitude. C'est une conspiration ! Kebron travaillait avec lui ! Il est...

— Il n'est pas suspect dans cette affaire, rétorqua Worf.

— Tu ne vas pas me dire...

— Si, Gowr. Je vais te le dire, et tu m'écouteras... Il me semble que vous vous faites des idées. J'ai essayé jusque-là de faire montre de patience. Je pensais que c'était crucial pour le bon déroulement de cette mission. J'avais expliqué l'importance de la tolérance à mes camarades ; à l'exception de la bagarre avec Kodash, ils m'ont écouté.

52

« Je commence à croire que ma retenue vous a conduits à me sous-estimer... A *nous* sous-estimer. Et à vous faire croire que vous pouviez disposer de nous comme vous le vouliez. Ce n'est pas le cas. »

K'Ehleyr s'adossa à une console.

— Je suppose que tu as un message à nous communiquer ? dit-elle d'un air particulièrement détendu.

— Deux, la corrigea Worf. Primo, je veux qu'il soit clair que nous ne sommes pas faibles, et que nous ne refuserons pas un combat. Secundo, Zak Kebron ne devra pas être inquiété à cause de l'origine de notre prisonnier.

— Mais il...

— Il ne devra pas être inquiété, répéta le cadet en articulant chaque syllabe. Aucune remarque pernicieuse, aucune insinuation, aucun sous-entendu. Pas même un regard de travers. Il n'est pas responsable de cette situation ; il est même plus touché que nous. Et je ne tolérerai pas que son inquiétude soit aggravée par des remarques. Est-ce clair ?

Un long silence lui répondit.

— Complètement, dit enfin K'Ehleyr.

Gowr releva la tête, comme pour protester. Mais il croisa le regard de son chef, et se ravisa. Kodash ne broncha pas.

Le prisonnier brikar reprit conscience.

Immédiatement, l'attention des quatre Klingons se porta sur lui.

Le guerrier gémit et secoua la tête. Par réflexe, il voulut se gratter le crâne, mais il ne put bouger les mains. Cet état de fait provoqua d'abord chez lui une réaction de surprise. Puis il comprit qu'il était attaché.

Il rugit : un cri de rage inarticulé plutôt impressionnant.

Les Klingons parurent amusés.

— Mieux vaut que tu gardes tes forces, dit K'Ehleyr. Ton énergie sera mieux employée à répondre à nos questions.

Le Brikar leva la tête, remarquant la jeune Klingonne pour la première fois. Son regard fit le tour de la salle, s'arrêtant plus particulièrement sur le grand Klingon qui portait un uniforme de Starfleet. Apparemment, la combinaison l'étonna.

— Je ne vous dirai rien, cracha le prisonnier. Où est la Vulcaine ? J'ai un compte à régler avec elle.

— Tu n'es pas en position de le faire, répondit Worf. Brikar, tu n'as pas l'air de comprendre les règles fondamentales des négociations.

— C'est vrai, Worf, constata la Klingonne d'une voix presque triste. Il nous annonce qu'il ne dira rien, et qu'il exige quelque chose en retour...

— Oh, nous lui donnerons quelque chose. Surveillez-le pendant que je vais chercher les autres. Et alors, ami... (il s'agenouilla pour être au niveau du visage de l'extraterrestre)... je t'assure que tu en auras plus que tu n'en avais demandé.

CHAPITRE
V

Le Brikar était assis ; Gowr et Kodash l'avaient relevé. Il lançait des regards furieux alentour.

Zak l'observait à quelques mètres de distance.

Les autres se tenaient près de lui ; ils le jaugeaient prudemment. Kebron semblait avoir retrouvé son calme. Quand il avait enfin accepté de voir les choses en face, il était entré dans une telle fureur que les cadets avaient craint qu'il ne tue le prisonnier s'il se trouvait face à lui. A présent, il était relativement calme...

Trop calme, pensait Worf.

Il semblait presque plus facile de contrôler le Brikar quand il était en rage : là, il faisait penser à un volcan prêt à exploser.

— Qui es-tu ? demanda Zak.

L'autre Brikar ne répondit rien.

Le cadet répéta sa question, cette fois dans sa langue natale.

Sans succès.

— Je suis Zak Kebron, du clan Kebron. A quel clan appartiens-tu ?

Toujours rien.

— Je t'interroge officiellement sur ton rang et ton statut dans la société brikarienne. Refuser de répondre m'autorise à t'imposer un duel à mort.

— Alors, défie-moi ! répondit le prisonnier. Tue-moi si tu le peux. Tu n'auras pas davantage de réponses, et je n'aurai plus à écouter les gémissements d'un chiot de la Fédération qui prétend être un véritable Brikar.

Worf lança un regard à Kebron ; il restait parfaitement immobile. On aurait cru que les mots l'avaient traversé sans le toucher.

— Tu es un terroriste, dit Zak après un court silence. Un terroriste et un pirate. Une disgrâce pour les Brikars.

— Si tu espères que je confirme ton opinion sur moi, tu risques d'attendre longtemps, le défia l'autre. Tes insultes ne sont que du vent, Kebron. A présent, cesse de m'importuner. (Sa grosse tête pivota vers Soleta :) En revanche, petite Vulcaine, j'ai des comptes à régler avec toi. Je t'assure que je ne t'oublierai pas.

— Les éléphants ont bonne mémoire, lança Tania.

Worf fit un signe à K'Ehleyr. Elle le rejoignit, un peu à l'écart des autres.

— Le Brikar semble déterminé à ne pas coopérer, fit observer le cadet.

— Ce n'est pas une surprise.

Soudain, ils entendirent un grand bruit derrière eux. Ils firent volte-face.

Soleta, Tania et Kodash faisaient tout leur possible pour éloigner Zak du prisonnier. Celui-ci gisait au sol, renversé par un coup de poing de son compatriote.

— Tu oses me qualifier de traître ! hurla Kebron. C'est toi le renégat !

— Je suis ce que je suis, Kebron, cracha l'autre Brikar. Pas un fantoche, comme toi !

La Vulcaine essayait de calmer Zak. En lui parlant doucement, elle le conduisit dans un coin de la pièce. Kebron tenta à plusieurs reprises de tourner la tête vers le prisonnier, que Gowr et Mac relevaient. Mais Soleta, d'une main ferme, l'obligea à la regarder.

— Ecoute-moi, Worf, dit K'Ehleyr à voix basse. Je sais ce que tu vas dire, mais c'est folie que vouloir procéder de cette manière. Laisse-nous le prisonnier une heure et il parlera.

— Non.

— Une demi-heure, alors. (Elle sourit :)

59

Nous apprendrons tout ce qu'il sait. Il nous suppliera de le laisser parler.

— Non, répéta Worf, plus fermement.

— Dans ce cas, que comptes-tu faire ? Continuer ainsi en espérant qu'il s'ennuie assez pour nous fournir des renseignements ? Bon sang, Worf ! S'il en avait eu la possibilité, la Vulcaine serait morte ! Si on lui en laissait l'occasion, il en serait de même pour nous ! Cette créature ne mérite pas un traitement spécial. Pourquoi protèges-tu ce chien ? Quel genre de Klingon es-tu ?

— Je suis un cadet de Starfleet. Mes camarades m'ont nommé chef du groupe. Je refuse de recourir à la torture. Pas tant que nous disposons d'autres moyens.

— Il n'y en a pas d'autres !

A leur grande surprise, Mac vint se placer entre eux. D'une voix de conspirateur, il souffla :

— J'ai un plan terrible.

Worf le dévisagea avec des yeux pleins d'espoir :

— Oui ?

— C'est un plan tellement génial que personne n'y aurait pensé !

— Et quel est-il ? demanda K'Ehleyr.

— Quel est-il quoi ? fit Mark.

Worf essaya de ne pas perdre patience :

— Le plan génial, quel est-il ?

Le rouquin pointa un doigt sur Soleta :

— Elle peut le faire.

— Faire quoi ?

— La fusion mentale. Soleta est particulièrement douée en matière de contact télépathique. C'est pourquoi elle est si utile pour calmer les gens qui l'entourent. Une fusion mentale est plus difficile, mais elle en est capable.

Les deux Klingons échangèrent un regard. Puis ils fixèrent Mac.

— Depuis quand es-tu expert en techniques mentales vulcaines ? demanda Worf.

— Depuis que j'ai lu un article sur le sujet il y a trois ans. (Il plissa le front et se gratta le menton.) A moins que je ne l'aie écrit. Laissez-moi réfléchir...

— Aucune importance. Soleta !

— Je sais ce que tu vas me demander, dit la Vulcaine. J'ai entendu... la suggestion de McHenry. (Elle toisa son camarade et, bien que son visage demeurât impassible, son regard ne semblait pas très amical.) Worf, je préférerais une autre option.

— Je suis ouvert aux suggestions, déclara le chef des cadets. Selon K'Ehleyr, nous n'avons pas d'autre solution que la torture. Trouves-tu cela acceptable ?

Elle soutint son regard un instant, puis baissa les yeux.

— C'est une question inutile. Tu sais que je considère cette pratique comme particulièrement répugnante.

— Soleta, je ne veux pas te forcer...

Elle releva la tête ; son regard était dur et implacable.

— Tu ne pourrais pas. Même si tu étais commandant d'un vaisseau, un ordre de cette nature ne serait pas légal.

Worf ne dit rien.

La Vulcaine parut se concentrer. Normalement, elle n'éprouvait aucune difficulté à s'exprimer ; pourtant, elle semblait chercher ses mots.

— La fusion mentale n'est pas une technique facile à maîtriser. Il faut de nombreuses années de pratique. Mes professeurs, sur Vulcain, me considèrent comme un prodige. Ils disent que j'ai une disposition naturelle pour la télépathie. Néanmoins, je suis loin d'avoir confiance en mes capacités. Pour la fusion mentale, l'état d'esprit de l'« opérateur » est un facteur crucial.

— As-tu peur ? demanda le Klingon.

— Peur ? (Soleta secoua la tête.) Bien sûr que non.

— Nous avions oublié... fit remarquer

K'Ehleyr avec un brin de sarcasme. Les Vulcaines ne s'encombrent pas l'esprit avec des émotions comme la peur.

Soleta répondit sans la regarder.

— L'absence de peur est une chose, K'Ehleyr. Elle ne signifie pas, cependant, que je sois privée de l'instinct de survie. La situation idéale, pour une fusion mentale, est celle où les deux participants sont volontaires. C'est une forme de communion.

« L'utiliser pour un interrogatoire équivaut à fracasser le crâne d'une personne avec un marteau. C'est possible, mais ce n'est pas la fonction première de cette technique, et les conséquences risquent d'être terribles pour les deux partis. Le Brikar a une forte personnalité. Un télépathe accompli pourrait faire ce que vous désirez, mais ce serait difficile. Pour une novice... »

Cette fois, elle leva les yeux vers la Klingonne :

— Si j'utilise la fusion mentale pour glaner des informations, je me mets dans une situation dangereuse et je risque de violer l'esprit même de Vulcain. Mais si je tourne le dos, et si je te laisse lui soutirer des renseignements par la torture, je deviendrai complice de ta brutalité.

« Voici le choix qui m'est imposé. Je veux

que tu le comprennes. Je souhaite que vous le compreniez tous les deux. »

Worf se contenta de hocher la tête. Il n'y avait rien de plus à dire.

CHAPITRE VI

Soleta regarda une dernière fois le visage enragé de son assaillant avant de fermer les yeux, comme si elle espérait que les réponses à ses questions étaient inscrites à l'intérieur de ses paupières. Puis elle adopta un rythme de respiration profond et régulier.

Quand elle rouvrit les yeux pour regarder le Brikar, le prisonnier y lut quelque chose qu'il n'apprécia pas.

— Eloignez-la de moi ! déclara-t-il.

Soleta ne l'entendit pas, ou elle se moqua de ce qu'il venait de dire. Elle approcha lentement de lui, comme si elle évaluait sa taille. Le Brikar ignorait ce qui allait se passer. Il lança un regard apeuré aux Klingons, puis aux cadets.

— J'ai dit : éloignez-la de moi !

La Vulcaine sembla se concentrer. Sa

respiration ralentissait. Son regard était rivé sur le prisonnier.

— Dis-nous ce que nous voulons savoir, Brikar, dit Worf.

— Va te faire voir !

Soleta n'était plus qu'à quelques centimètres de lui. Le pirate la regarda d'un air incertain :

— Je n'ai pas peur de toi, Vulcaine !

Les mains tendues vers son visage, les doigts écartés, Soleta semblait ne plus voir le prisonnier. A vrai dire elle paraissait contempler quelque chose au-delà de son crâne, comme si elle pouvait regarder à travers sa tête.

Le Brikar était solidement attaché à un siège. Il lutta pour se débarrasser de ses liens.

En vain.

— Eloignez-la de moi ! cria-t-il de nouveau.

Mais son regard croisa celui de Soleta.

Il était implacable.

Il voulut l'intimider avec la flamme de ses yeux, mais ça ne fonctionna pas non plus.

La Vulcaine plaça ses doigts de chaque côté du visage du Brikar. Il sursauta, comme s'il avait reçu du courant électrique. Il voulut reculer la tête, mais il n'arrivait plus à bouger, devenu la victime sans défense du regard pénétrant de Soleta.

Doucement, d'une voix à peine audible, elle murmura :

— Nos esprits se rejoignent...

La bouche du Brikar remua. Il voulait dire « Non », mais les mots ne sortaient pas de sa gorge.

— Tes pensées sont miennes, continua Soleta. Tes pensées sont miennes ! Je sais tout ce que tu sais.

Le prisonnier écarquillait tant les yeux que Worf eut l'impression qu'ils allaient sortir de leurs orbites.

— Je suis... Soleta, dit la Vulcaine.

Elle lança son esprit à l'assaut, abattant peu à peu les barrières mentales que son adversaire dressait. Elle devait s'ancrer dans son cerveau avant de pouvoir apprendre ce qu'elle désirait savoir. Pour cela, il fallait procéder avec prudence.

— Je suis Soleta. Je suis...

— So... Soleta, dit le Brikar.

— Je suis Soleta, répétèrent-ils ensemble.

— Nous... sommes Soleta, continua la Vulcaine. Nous sommes Soleta.

Il voulut résister, mais il lui fallut quelques instants seulement pour répéter.

— Nous sommes Soleta.

— Nous sommes... (Cette fois, elle ne termina pas sa phrase pour l'obliger à la finir à sa place.) Nous sommes...

— Soleta, souffla Mac.

Tania lui fit signe de rester silencieux.

Le Brikar résistait toujours, mais la Vulcaine persévéra.

— Nous *sommes...*

— *Nous sommes Baan*, cracha enfin le prisonnier.

Soleta chancela.

Se procurer cette simple information semblait avoir exténué la cadette. Mais elle prit une grande inspiration et rassembla ses forces. Ses doigts appuyèrent plus fort sur les tempes du prisonnier ; il aurait certainement fallu les briser pour les arracher du visage de Baan.

— Nous sommes venus sur Dantar parce que... commença la Vulcaine.

— Nous avions... une mission.

Baan avait les yeux ouverts, mais il ne voyait plus personne dans la pièce.

— Et quelle était cette mission ?

La bouche du prisonnier trembla.

— *Et quelle était cette mission ?* répéta Soleta.

L'émotion qui faisait hésiter sa voix trahissait son stress.

— Base... secrète...

Worf étouffa un juron. Il se tourna vers K'Ehleyr, qui semblait aussi surprise que lui.

— Demande-lui où elle se trouve ! gronda le Klingon.

Soleta ne répondit pas ; elle n'avait pas entendu son ordre.

— Pourquoi ? demanda-t-elle. Pourquoi les attaques ? Pour...

Alors elle se mit à répondre elle-même. Ses doigts commencèrent à trembler. Ses paupières étaient si douloureusement closes que des larmes coulèrent sur ses joues. Quand elle ouvrit à nouveau la bouche, elle parla avec l'accent épais du Brikar. Baan articulait les mots, mais ils sortaient des lèvres de la Vulcaine.

— Les Brikars.... veulent des privilèges... expansion coloniale illimitée... Menace... quitter la Fédération... des années de planification... établi... établi....

Soleta marqua une pause. Elle prit une profonde inspiration qui lui arracha un cri. Worf voulut intervenir, mais Tania et Mac le retinrent par les bras.

— Je ne te le conseille pas, fit McHenry.

Tania acquiesça :

— Si tu l'arraches à la fusion mentale, ce pourrait être dangereux pour elle. C'est un peu comme un plongeur qui remonte trop vite à la surface. Elle serait victime d'un équivalent mental de la maladie des profondeurs.

Soleta cria presque le mot « établi », comme s'il s'était agi d'un bouchon qu'elle eût voulu éjecter.

— Etabli... des bases secrètes près des frontières de la Fédération. La principale se trouve sur Dantar IV... L'entrée est...

La Vulcaine fut prise de convulsions ; elle hurla. Voir Soleta, qui d'habitude contrôlait parfaitement ses émotions, crier comme si on lui arrachait l'âme était une chose horrible.

C'en fut trop pour Worf. Il se libéra de ses camarades, courut jusqu'à Soleta, puis brisa son contact avec le Brikar.

Les mains de la Vulcaine restèrent crispées, les doigts tendus. On eût dit qu'elle ne réalisait pas que la fusion était interrompue.

— Elle ne respire plus ! s'écria Zak Kebron.

En effet.

Soleta était paralysée, comme si son corps s'était éteint.

Worf l'allongea sur le sol et lui tira la tête en arrière pour libérer la trachée.

Le Brikar prisonnier, pendant ce temps, recouvra un semblant de lucidité. Il semblait sortir d'un cauchemar.

Worf se pencha sur Soleta ; il s'aperçut que ses yeux cherchaient les siens.

— Worf...

— Je... tu avais cessé de respirer...

— J'étais en transe, l'informa-t-elle. Je respirais à un rythme bien plus lent que la normale pour sortir de la fusion mentale. Un contact aussi profond ne se brise pas comme ça.

— Oh...

Il ne trouva rien d'autre à dire.

Se redressant, il aida son amie à se relever. Elle se passa les mains sur le visage pour finir de recouvrer ses esprits, et sentit de l'humidité sur ses joues. Elle réussit à cacher sa surprise.

— Je... n'ai pas pleuré ?

Tania secoua la tête.

— Un simple réflexe. Tes paupières étaient tellement crispées qu'elles ont activé tes glandes lacrymales. Ce n'est qu'une réaction biologique, rien de plus.

Soleta hocha la tête :

— Je n'en doutais pas.

Une fois rassurés sur l'état de santé de leur amie, l'intérêt des cadets se porta sur Baan.

Le prisonnier regardait Worf, Zak et les autres, mais son expression avait perdu beaucoup de sa superbe.

Kebron fut le premier à rompre le silence :

— Salutations, Baan. C'est agréable de savoir à qui on s'adresse.

— Tu nous as dit pratiquement tout ce que nous voulions savoir, l'informa Worf. Une seule question demeure : vas-tu coopérer pour la suite ?

— Quelle différence ça fera ? cracha Baan.

Mais sa remarque manquait d'assurance ; le Klingon se demanda si le prisonnier ne se souvenait pas des détails de son interrogatoire. Pour l'instant, Baan était vulnérable ; il fallait en profiter pour finir de lui tirer les vers du nez.

— Il n'y en a aucune pour moi. Après tout, nous connaissons l'existence de la base secrète. Nous sommes au courant de ta mission : provoquer la fuite des colons pour obtenir un accès plus facile à cette installation.

Le Klingon ne faisait que supposer, en se fondant sur ce qu'ils avaient appris. Mais Baan n'en savait rien. Son expression désespérée confirma à Worf qu'il ne s'était pas trompé.

Il poussa son avantage :

— A présent, tu peux nous révéler le reste de ton plein gré, si tu le désires. Sinon, nous demanderons à Soleta d'entrer à nouveau dans ta tête.

C'était du bluff. Worf avait déjà décidé qu'il ne ferait plus subir cette torture à sa camarade vulcaine.

Mais Baan l'ignorait.

Soleta aussi. Par bonheur, elle était vulcaine, et donc formée à garder ses sentiments pour elle. Son visage resta vide d'expression. Elle semblait parfaitement capable de pénétrer de force dans l'esprit du Brikar pour en extraire, comme un dentiste, les informations souhaitées.

Worf se pencha vers le prisonnier ; le Brikar put respirer son haleine. Il indiqua Soleta d'un signe de tête.

— Parleras-tu avant que je lui demande de s'occuper de toi ? Si tu t'obstines, nous obtiendrons les informations dont nous avons besoin. Et ton cerveau sera définitivement grillé ; tu n'auras pas plus d'intellect qu'un yucca. C'est à toi de décider, Baan de Brikar. Choisis bien.

Les Brikars ne transpiraient pas. Dieu merci, car Baan aurait été trempé de sueur.

Le Klingon haussa les épaules.

— Comme tu veux. Soleta ?

Il lui fit signe d'approcher. Elle n'hésita pas et vint, les doigts tendus. Elle semblait prête à lui ouvrir le crâne pour lui prendre son cerveau.

— Très bien ! s'écria le prisonnier. Très bien ! Eloignez-la de moi !

Worf arrêta la Vulcaine :

— Soleta, ce ne sera pas nécessaire.

A sa propre surprise, elle réussit à prendre un air déçu.

— Tu en es sûr ?

— Pour l'instant.

Elle entra dans son jeu.

— Il ne faut pas me tenter ainsi, Worf. Tu sais que les occasions de m'amuser sont peu nombreuses. Et je n'ai vidé personne de ses connaissances depuis *si longtemps* !

Les Vulcains ne mentaient jamais. D'ailleurs, Soleta avait dit la vérité. De fait, peu de choses la rendaient heureuse, car « plaisir » était un mot trop fort pour ceux de sa race. Et puisque la jeune fille n'avait jamais vidé *personne* de ses connaissances, elle n'avait fait qu'exagérer la vérité.

Mais elle avait parlé avec une telle sincérité que le Brikar en trembla.

Ce n'était pas le cas de Tania, debout derrière Baan. Elle avait mis ses doigts dans sa bouche pour ne pas rire, et ses épaules s'agitaient spasmodiquement tant elle était amusée. Mark McHenry, qui n'avait pas tout suivi, fixait Soleta avec de grands yeux étonnés. Zak tournait le dos ; il était impossible de voir sa réaction.

Worf garda un visage impassible.

— S'il ne coopère pas, je t'autoriserai à... (il marqua une pause pour trouver les mots adéquats) faire de lui ce que bon te semble.

— Merci, Worf.

Elle s'inclina et reprit sa place.

— Je vais coopérer, je le promets ! s'écria le Brikar.

— Bien.

Worf croisa les bras et patienta.

Baan soupira :

— Tout ce que vous avez dit est vrai. Ma mission consistait à faire fuir les colons. Mon navire a été spécialement conçu pour cette opération ; il utilise de la technologie klingonne, mais aussi l'armement de Starfleet. Nous voulions nous débarrasser des colons par tous les moyens possibles. En revanche, nous refusions de lancer un assaut à grande échelle, car nous craignions d'attirer l'attention de la Fédération sur nos activités avant d'être prêts.

« Oui, il ý a une base secrète. A l'époque où nous l'avons établie, la colonie n'existait pas encore. L'arrivée des colons a compliqué les choses. Puisque seul ce secteur de Dantar est habitable, il était logique de construire notre QG dans la région où, malheureusement, les Klingons et la Fédération ont choisi d'installer leurs hommes.

« L'entrée de la base est cachée sous le bâtiment qui abrite les générateurs centraux. J'ai essayé de ne pas bombarder ce secteur lors de l'attaque. Hélas ! l'accès au complexe ne peut être obtenu que grâce à un transmetteur spécial qui se trouvait à bord de mon vaisseau. Il a été détruit quand je me suis écrasé. Après quelques vaines tentatives pour le réparer, j'ai lancé un appel de détresse. C'est à ce moment-là que la Vulcaine est arrivée. »

— Cette base, demanda Worf. Que contient-elle ?

— De l'armement. Tout ce qui permettrait de transformer Dantar IV en relais stratégique, en particulier pour des opérations de commandos.

— Et de l'équipement de transmission subspatiale ?

— Bien sûr, fit Baan.

— Quelle puissance ?

— Enorme. On pourrait envoyer un message dans la Galaxie Andromède si on le voulait.

— Nous pourrions surtout appeler de l'aide, dit Tania à voix basse. Faire parvenir un S.O.S. au cœur de la Fédération...

Worf hocha la tête.

— Comment entrer ?

Baan le regarda, méprisant :

— Tu es sourd, Klingon ? Je t'ai déjà expliqué : avec un transmetteur qui ne fonctionne plus.

Tobias avança.

— Comment marchait-il ?

— Sur une bande de fréquences spéciale, avec un code prédéterminé.

— Connais-tu le code ?

Le Brikar secoua la tête :

— Non, mais je peux vous mener à l'entrée. Si vous réussissez, je vous accompagnerai même à l'intérieur.

Le fils Rozhenko le regarda d'un œil soupçonneux :

— Tu sembles bien impatient de nous aider, tout à coup.

— Je n'ai aucun désir de passer le reste de mes jours sur cette maudite planète.

Le Klingon eut l'air de ne pas le croire.

— Qu'est-il arrivé aux colons ?

— Ils sont partis. Tu étais là. Tu l'as vu par toi-même !

— Mais nous aurions dû avoir la visite d'un navire de secours. Ce n'est pas le cas. Que leur est-il arrivé ? Le sais-tu ?

Le Brikar haussa les épaules.

— Ils sont peut-être tombés dans un trou noir. A moins qu'ils n'aient été déchiquetés par une tempête magnétique ? Ou encore ont-ils été capturés par les Romuliens ? Tout est possible. Je n'ai aucune idée de leur sort. Si ce n'est pas la réponse que tu espérais, c'est ton problème, pas le mien.

— En effet. Puisqu'il en est ainsi, Baan, je

pense que tu resteras ici un bon bout de temps. Tu seras libéré uniquement quand nous aurons réussi à pénétrer dans la base secrète, à envoyer un message de détresse et à obtenir des secours.

— Tu es un imbécile ! s'écria le prisonnier. Vous n'entrerez jamais dans le complexe sans mon aide ! C'est folie que refuser ma proposition !

Worf grimaça :

— Si ce n'est pas la réponse que tu espérais, c'est ton problème, pas le mien.

Le Brikar grogna.

Comme si la présence de Baan n'avait plus d'importance, Worf fit signe aux autres de le suivre dehors. K'Ehleyr ordonna à Gowr de garder le prisonnier. Quelques instants plus tard, tout le monde était réuni devant le bâtiment. Certains se montrèrent incapables de contenir plus longtemps leur excitation.

— C'est génial ! s'écria Tania. Si nous arrivons à trouver cette base secrète, nos efforts n'auront pas été vains.

— Ne t'emballe pas, dit Worf. D'abord, il faut localiser le complexe. Ensuite, il faut y entrer.

— Voilà qui ne m'inquiète pas outre mesure, répondit la jeune blonde. Après tout le temps que nous avons passé à nous ronger les sangs et à croire que nous ne pouvions pas agir, ça nous changera. C'est exactement le genre de défi qu'il faut pour nous remonter le moral.

— Au travail, dans ce cas.

Elle le salua, un geste moqueur, car cette tradition militaire était lettre morte dans Starfleet. Elle fit signe à Mark de la suivre ; ils disparurent dans le bâtiment où Tania accomplissait d'ordinaire son travail d'ingénieur.

Worf se tourna vers Soleta :

— Tu vas bien ?

Sans Baan pour les observer, il était inutile de prolonger la mascarade.

Elle hocha la tête.

— Je me sens... rétablie. Ne t'inquiète pas, Worf. Ce n'était pas l'expérience la plus agréable de ma vie, et je n'ai aucun désir de recommencer. Mais je survivrai.

— Je n'en doutais pas, répondit-il avec un demi-sourire.

Zak Kebron, pour sa part, restait à l'écart. Il ne prêtait qu'une attention distraite à ce qui se passait, car son esprit bouillait encore de rage. Quand Worf approcha de lui, le Brikar parut redouter le dialogue qu'il sentait venir.

— Toutes les choses que Baan raconte sur l'hostilité grandissante des Brikars envers la Fédération... commença son camarade.

N'ayant aucun talent pour la diplomatie, Zak mit les pieds dans le plat :

— Tu veux savoir si elles sont vraies. Et si c'est la vérité, tu désires savoir pourquoi je n'en ai jamais parlé ?

Worf hocha la tête.

Kebron soupira. Il remarqua que K'Ehleyr et Kodash se tenaient à proximité. Il aurait voulu les chasser, passer sa frustration sur eux. Mais quel objectif cela aurait-il servi ?

— J'en avais entendu parler. Mais tu dois comprendre : mon peuple aime jacasser sur beaucoup de choses. Oui, il y a eu des sentiments antifédérationnistes, mais il y a aussi des sentiments antiklingons, antiromuliens, et ainsi de suite. Les Brikars sont agressifs, et ce ne sont pas des apôtres de la tolérance. Tu dois le savoir.

— Je m'en étais rendu compte, admit sèchement le Klingon.

— Cela étant, je n'avais aucun moyen de deviner que ce sentiment générerait un authentique courant d'opinion... Sans parler de bases secrètes et d'autres choses dans ce genre.

K'Ehleyr avança.

— Néanmoins, tu reconnais que cela te mets dans une fâcheuse posture sur le plan de la sécurité.

Zak la dévisagea.

— Vraiment ? demanda Worf.

— Oui, vraiment. Kebron appartient à une espèce connue pour son hostilité.

— Que suggères-tu ? demanda Zak. Que je me constitue prisonnier pour partager une cellule avec Baan ? Cela servirait-il tes projets ?

— Je ne faisais que remarquer...

— Ce que nous savons déjà, la coupa Worf. Tu ne suggères pas sérieusement qu'un Brikar soit pénalisé pour les actions d'un autre ?

— Non, répondit la Klingonne. J'ai une idée, et j'aurai accompli mon devoir en la communiquant au reste du groupe. Si tu penses que le prisonnier est digne de confiance, ton opinion a la priorité. Après tout tu es le chef !

— Merci. (Il se tourna vers Kodash.) Désires-tu participer d'une manière ou d'une autre à cette conversation ?

Un instant, le grand Klingon ne répondit rien.

Zak se prépara à une repartie sanglante. Il était certain que son « camarade » se moquerait de lui parce que c'était un Brikar qui les avait attaqués.

Et Zak ne pourrait rien faire pour le contredire.

Il attendit.

— Tu dois te sentir humilié que ce soit un membre de ton peuple qui nous ait attaqués, souffla Kodash.

Kebron serra les poings.

— Sachant comment je me sentirais à ta place, je suis heureux de ne pas y être...

Puis il fit demi-tour et partit.

Zak n'arrivait pas à le croire. C'était tout ? Il dévisagea Worf, totalement sidéré.

— Je crois qu'il était sincère, dit le Klingon. Pas toi ?

CHAPITRE VII

Jamais les cadets n'avaient éprouvé le besoin de sonder l'intérieur du bâtiment des générateurs avec un tricordeur. A présent, ils avaient une bonne raison de le faire.

Mark McHenry traversa lentement la salle, comme un ancien prospecteur d'eau armé d'une baguette de sourcier. Il lisait minutieusement les indications du tricordeur.

Le générateur avait été coupé lors du départ des colons. Il fallait découvrir la présence de particules d'énergie accélérées ; dès que Mac les aurait détectées, la base secrète serait localisée.

Ses camarades l'observaient avec attention. Aucune parole n'avait été échangée depuis quelques minutes ; certains retenaient même leur souffle.

Enfin, Mark hocha la tête.

— Il y a quelque chose, en partie caché

par un champ de distorsion. Mais je crois tenir la solution. Attendez.

Il continua de sonder la pièce, brandissant son tricordeur comme un bouclier. Finalement, il s'arrêta devant un des générateurs géants.

— Alors ? demanda Worf.

McHenry désigna un point sous le générateur.

Les cadets gémirent.

— Tu plaisantes ! fit K'Ehleyr.

McHenry plissa le front.

— Je ne crois pas. Pourquoi ? Ai-je dit quelque chose pour te faire rire ?

Tania se massa les tempes.

— Non, Mac. Rien... Worf, Zak m'a aidée un jour à transporter un appareil de ce type, mais il était deux fois moins grand.

Kebron avança et fit craquer ses phalanges :

— Dans ce cas, il faudra que je travaille deux fois plus dur, non ?

Quand les générateurs avaient été installés, des grues s'étaient révélées bien utiles pour les transporter. Hélas ! toutes les machines avaient été détruites pendant le raid. Cela ne découragea pas le Brikar, qui approcha de l'énorme générateur cylindrique.

— Tu es sûr de ne pas avoir besoin d'aide ? demanda Worf.

— Aucun problème.

Zak se plaça face au générateur, plia les jambes et saisit la machine à pleines mains. Il tenta de la soulever.

Elle refusa de bouger.

— Puis-je te suggérer de faire levier ? dit Worf.

Il serait allé aider Zak, que celui-ci le veuille ou non. Mais il était parfaitement conscient de la fierté que ressentait le Brikar dans des instants pareils. Kebron se moquait de soulever le générateur. Il voulait montrer qu'il était *capable de le faire.*

Zak grogna en signe d'acquiescement, puis il tourna le dos au générateur. Il le saisit une nouvelle fois et essaya de le faire basculer sur ses épaules.

Le métal grinça ; l'appareil bougea.

Kebron serra les dents. A présent qu'il avait réussi à soulever la machine, il ne fallait pas perdre l'équilibre.

Ses muscles tremblaient sous l'effort ; il ferma la bouche pour éviter que des gémissement échappent à ses lèvres.

Le générateur bougea encore, et encore.

Alors le Brikar perdit l'équilibre. Le générateur menaça de lui échapper.

Worf se précipita pour l'aider, mais Kodash le précéda. Il vint se placer près de Zak pour supporter une partie du poids.

Cela permit au Brikar de trouver une meilleure prise. Kodash ne s'écarta pas ; il aida Kebron à soutenir le poids du générateur.

Histoire d'assurer le coup, Worf vint prendre place de l'autre côté. Une heureuse initiative, en fait, car le générateur commençait à basculer.

Ils restèrent ainsi pendant quelques instants. Le Brikar produisait l'effort principal ; les deux Klingons faisaient en sorte que la machine ne glisse pas.

Zak les regarda.

— Merci, grommela-t-il.

— Il n'y a pas de quoi, répondit diplomatiquement Kodash.

Puis il adressa à Worf un regard qui semblait dire : *Tu vois, je peux être poli quand il le faut.*

Ils attendirent un instant de plus, pour s'assurer que le générateur était en équilibre sur le dos de leur camarade. Alors le puissant Brikar fit quelques pas, Worf et Kodash à ses côtés. Les autres cadets et les Klingons, prudents, s'écartèrent de son chemin. Personne ne voulait risquer de recevoir un générateur sur le pied.

— Attention, dit Worf.

— Je... fais... attention, gronda Zak.

Il plia les genoux, puis laissa glisser l'appareil. Il heurta le sol avec un bruit sourd qui résonna dans tout le bâtiment.

— Beau travail, Zak, le congratula Worf.

Kodash ne fut pas aussi aimable, mais il hocha la tête, impressionné par la force du Brikar.

— Merci, répondit Kebron.

Mark McHenry ne perdit pas de temps. Il alla se placer à l'endroit dégagé par ses camarades, toujours armé de son tricordeur.

— C'est bien ici.

Sous lui, il n'y avait qu'un sol métallique d'apparence solide. Worf vint le rejoindre.

— Tu es sûr ?

— Positivement. C'est là que se trouve...

Il marqua une pause et fronça les sourcils.

— La base secrète, soupira Tania.

— *Oui !* C'est ça ! La base secrète est là-dessous. (Il s'arrêta encore.) Je suppose que nous pourrions cesser de l'appeler « base secrète ». Après tout, nous l'avons trouvée, non ? On pourrait l'appeler « la base trouvée » ?

— Si tu veux, dit Worf avec un sourire. Tania, découpe une ouverture.

La jeune fille était prête. Armée d'un laser, elle s'accroupit sur la zone qu'avait indiquée McHenry, puis régla l'outil sur l'intensité la plus faible. Elle ne voulait pas risquer d'endommager quelque chose qui pourrait leur être utile plus tard.

Le laser perça la plaque de métal avec un sifflement strident.

Tania procédait lentement, prête à éteindre l'outil si le matériau lui opposait une trop grande résistance. Ce ne fut pas le cas. Le rayon découpa la plaque sans problème. Au bout de quelques minutes, Tobias avait percé un trou rond assez grand pour faire passer tout le monde... En supposant qu'il y ait vraiment quelque chose sous le bâtiment.

Worf approcha avec une barre à mine ; quelques secondes plus tard, il avait soulevé le cercle de métal et regardait dans le trou, bientôt imité par les autres.

Ils virent une cavité profonde de plusieurs mètres, au fond de laquelle se trouvait un panneau constellé de diodes multicolores. Le tout était rivé à la grosse écoutille qui occupait le fond du puits.

— C'est ça, souffla Tania.

— Un fuseur l'ouvrira sans problème, proposa Worf.

Soleta secoua la tête.

— Ce n'est pas une bonne idée.

— Pourquoi ?

— Parce qu'il est probable que la base secrète...

— La base *trouvée* ! la corrigea Mac.

Elle l'ignora :

— ... soit protégée. Si nous tentons d'entrer de manière trop violente, nous risquons d'activer un système d'autodestruction. Nous n'aurions plus rien. Pire, si le dispositif d'autodestruction est assez puissant, nous serons morts.

— Donc, nous devons agir avec prudence.

— C'est toujours une bonne idée, dit la Vulcaine.

— Très bien. Tania...

— J'ai compris... Mac, donne-moi ton tricordeur.

— Pour de bon ? Ou c'est seulement un emprunt ?

— Un emprunt.

Il lui tendit l'appareil, rassuré de savoir qu'elle le lui rendrait.

Tania se pencha au-dessus du trou et régla le tricordeur.

— Ça devrait marcher, dit-elle en pianotant sur le petit clavier.

Quelques secondes plus tard, l'appareil émit un sifflement strident.

Soleta se boucha les oreilles et recula.

— Que fais-tu ? demanda Worf.

— Je crois avoir reconnu la technologie utilisée, expliqua Tobias. Le tricordeur génère ce qu'on appelle un « signal poignée-de-main ». Il fait savoir à la serrure qu'un dispositif électronique désire entrer en interface avec elle. C'est la méthode qu'on utilise pour raccorder un tricordeur à un ordinateur.

— Tu obtiens quelque chose ? demanda Mac.

— Pas pour l'instant. Je vais changer de fréquence.

Elle appuya sur une touche ; le bruit se modifia légèrement.

Aucune réponse.

Elle essaya, encore et encore.

A la cinquième fréquence, il se passa quelque chose.

Les diodes du sas se mirent à clignoter plus rapidement. Une série de signaux sonores parvint au tricordeur.

Par réflexe, Worf se prépara à une explosion. Ce ne fut pas la peine. Après une trentaine de secondes, le silence revint.

Tania referma son tricordeur.

— Je l'ai.

— Le code d'accès ?

— Non, admit-elle. Mais j'ai l'ensemble des signaux qu'ils utilisent pour le codage. C'est un peu comme si, sur une fourchette de cent nombres, j'avais obtenu la certitude que le code se situe entre un et dix.

— Et maintenant ? demanda K'Ehleyr.

La jeune blonde se sentit un instant supérieure à la Klingonne. C'était agréable.

— Maintenant, vous me donnez une heure pour relier le tricordeur à un commbadge. Ensuite, nous aurons peut-être un moyen de quitter cette fichue planète.

— Tu peux le faire, Tania, dit Worf. J'ai confiance en toi.

— Merci, Worf. C'est gentil.

CHAPITRE VIII

— C'est une insulte ! grogna Gowr. Je devrais faire partie de l'expédition !

Il fulminait dans la salle des transmissions subspatiales, à quelques mètres du prisonnier brikar. Il pointa rageusement un doigt en direction de Baan.

— Pourquoi dois-je le surveiller ? Qu'un des crétins de Starfleet le fasse ! S'il y a du danger dans la base...

— Je me soucie surtout du danger que représenterait le prisonnier s'il s'échappait, coupa K'Ehleyr.

— Je ne vais pas m'évader, grogna Baan. Où irais-je ?

— Tu entends ? gronda Gowr. Il dit qu'il ne va pas s'échapper !

— Et tu le crois ? (La Klingonne secoua la tête :) Gowr, bien sûr qu'il va tenter de s'évader !

— Que Kodash le surveille ! Ou encore toi !

— Gowr, j'ai décidé que c'était ton travail pour une seule raison. (Elle posa une main sur son épaule.) Tu es le seul en qui j'ai confiance.

— Comment ?

— Selon moi, cette tâche est très importante, et je l'ai confiée à la seule personne que j'en estime capable.

Gowr soupira ; il savait qu'il s'était fait rouler.

— Comme tu voudras, K'Ehleyr.

— Bien. (Elle prit la direction de la porte.) Nous comptons sur toi, Gowr.

— Oui, oui, je m'en occupe.

Dès que le Klingon eut tourné le dos, Baan se remit à l'ouvrage. Il continua de faire en sorte que ses liens se desserrent, en appliquant une série de pressions légères sur la corde.

Il guettait le moment propice de passer à l'action...

CHAPITRE
IX

Le panneau arrière du communicateur ouvert, ses circuits avaient été raccordés au tricordeur. Du coup l'appareil émettait une série de sifflements stridents.

L'opération durait depuis un moment.

Les Klingons et les cadets de Starfleet étaient éparpillés dans la pièce, assis ou debout. Essayant par tous les moyens de ne pas paraître ennuyés, ils réussissaient fort mal.

Tania demeurait imperturbable. Analysant les signaux transmis par le communicateur, elle les comparait aux renseignements fournis par le tricordeur.

Enfin, Zak Kebron exprima à haute voix ce que les autres pensaient tout bas :

— Tania, nous perdons notre temps.

Tobias ne se retourna même pas :

— C'est ta grande expérience de l'électronique qui parle, Zak ? Ou tu commences juste à t'impatienter ?

— Je ne comprends pas, intervint K'Ehleyr. Tu disais que tu parviendrais à ouvrir cette porte.

— Tania sait ce qu'elle fait, affirma Worf. J'ai confiance en elle.

Il n'était pas convaincu, mais il jugeait important de se montrer solidaire de sa camarade.

— Merci, Worf, répondit Tania, se demandant s'il était sincère et soupçonnant qu'elle n'apprécierait pas la réponse à cette question. Ce qui se passe, au cas où vous ne comprendriez pas, c'est que le communicateur essaie toutes les combinaisons d'ouverture possibles. Le problème se résume ainsi : selon mes estimations, il y en a environ quarante-deux mille neuf cent vingt-cinq.

Quelqu'un poussa un gémissement ; certainement Kodash.

— Par les dieux, murmura K'Ehleyr. Il faudra plusieurs jours pour toutes les tester.

— Pas vraiment, expliqua Tania. Nous travaillons à haute vitesse. Nous avons déjà éliminé plus de huit mille combinaisons. Il y en a encore pour un petit bout de temps, mais...

Soudain ils entendirent un grincement.

Ils sursautèrent, surpris par le son que

commençait à émettre la porte. Quelque part sous le sol, résonna le bruit d'un mécanisme qui n'avait pas fonctionné depuis longtemps.

— Reculez ! hurla Worf.

Ils obéirent. Un instant, le cadet klingon se demanda à quelle distance ils seraient certains d'être en sécurité. Si Tania avait déclenché le système d'autodestruction, cette question n'avait probablement plus d'importance.

— Tout va bien ! s'écria Tobias. Tout va bien !

— Comment le sais-tu ? demanda K'Ehleyr.

— C'est mon travail.

Le sas s'était ouvert, et quelque chose en sortait. Les cadets, sidérés, fixèrent la plate-forme constellée de diodes qui venait de s'élever.

Elle s'arrêta et attendit.

— On dirait un ascenseur primitif, fit remarquer Soleta.

— Il est peut-être primitif, grommela Tobias, mais il fonctionne. C'est le principal.

— Très bien, dit Worf. K'Ehleyr, Soleta, Zak, Kodash et Tania m'accompagnent. Mac, tu restes ici pour surveiller notre progression. Nous serons en contact par communicateur.

— Ne t'inquiète pas, Worf, tout se passera bien, l'assura McHenry.

— J'en suis sûr. En route, cadets.

Le Klingon désigna la plate-forme à ses compagnons.

— Car en vérité, continua Mark, qu'est-ce qui pourrait nous arriver de pire ? Périr ? La mort serait une grande aventure.

Tous le regardèrent avec des yeux ronds comme des billes.

— C'est Peter Pan qui a dit ça. *Peter Pan* est ma biographie préférée.

— *Biographie* ? (Tania le regarda d'un air incrédule.) Mac, c'est de la fiction.

— Vraiment ? Tu en es certaine ?

— Oui !

— Hum, voilà qui remet en question bon nombre de mes convictions. Je vais devoir réfléchir.

— C'est cela, l'interrompit Worf. Mais n'oublie pas ton devoir.

— Pas de problème.

Rozhenko fut le premier à poser le pied sur la plate-forme. Il s'assura que l'ascenseur était assez solide pour supporter son poids. Comme rien ne se passa, il fit signe aux autres de le rejoindre.

Il n'y avait pas beaucoup de place.

— Et maintenant ? grogna Kodash, coincé entre Worf et Zak.

Avant que quelqu'un puisse lui répondre, le sol trembla sous eux. Avec un vacarme de mécanique rouillée, l'ascenseur s'enfonça dans les profondeurs de la base secrète.

— Je vous l'avais bien dit, fit Tania.

Mark McHenry les regarda descendre. Dès qu'ils eurent disparu de son champ de vision, il appuya sur son commbadge.

— McHenry appelle Tobias. C'est un essai.

— *Nous t'entendons, Mac. La fréquence d'appel reste ouverte.*

— Bien. Tania, j'ai une question...

— *Vas-y.*

— Je suppose qu'*Alice au Pays des Merveilles* n'était pas un guide touristique non plus, alors ?

— *Quoi ? répondit Tobias. Qu'as-tu dit ?*

— Oh, rien. Aucune importance. Je veux dire, qui serait assez idiot pour penser ça, hein ? Ou qui aurait des parents s'amusant à lui raconter pareilles foutaises ?

— *Certes*, dit Tania, qui n'avait rien compris à ce qu'il racontait.

— Bien. C'est... ce que je pensais. Tenez-moi au courant de l'évolution de votre mission.

— *Sans problème.*

McHenry s'assit et secoua la tête :

— Papa, maman, si je me sors de cette aventure, vous devrez me fournir un certain nombre d'explications.

CHAPITRE
X

Tania éternua violemment, soulevant un nuage de poussière.

— Je suis désolée.

K'Ehleyr eut un sourire condescendant.

— Oui, j'imagine que, pour certains, la poussière doit être trop...

Alors elle sentit son nez la démanger. Elle plissa le front et, incapable de se contrôler, partit d'un fabuleux éternuement.

Un nouveau rideau de poussière, plus important, s'éleva.

— Désolée, grommela la Klingonne.

— Aucun problème, dit Tobias.

Cette réaction allergique était compréhensible. Il était même étonnant que personne d'autre ne soit victime de crises d'éternuements. La base secrète des Brikars n'était pas particulièrement bien entretenue.

Les sols et les murs étaient décorés de

mosaïques compliquées. Sur les parois, une succession d'images montrait des Brikars en diverses situations de combat. Worf remarqua des représentations, plus petites, de Klingons, de Gorns, et d'autres races. Des couloirs étroits se croisaient dans toutes les directions.

Sous ses pieds, le Klingon nota la présence d'une série de grilles, disposées par intervalles de trois mètres. Mais il n'avait aucune idée de leur utilité.

— Ces mosaïques, expliqua Zak, racontent l'histoire de Brikar. Celle-ci, par exemple, parle de la Bataille d'Eldins'aar.

— Qui ? Quoi ? demanda Tania.

— La légende dit qu'Eldins'aar — un puissant guerrier — a affronté seul une horde d'ennemis pour défendre une ville peuplée de femmes et d'enfants dont tous les mâles avaient été massacrés. Eldins'aar a combattu pendant douze jours et douze nuits. Le sol était tellement gorgé de sang qu'il resta rouge à jamais. Les Plaines d'Eldins'aar portent le nom du héros.

— Nous avons des légendes similaires, fit K'Ehleyr. Nous parlons de Kahless l'Inoubliable...

— Qui a combattu son frère, Morath, pendant douze jours et douze nuits, parce que celui-ci avait manqué à sa parole, continua Worf.

La Klingonne le regarda d'un œil intéressé.

— Il est agréable de constater que tu es versé en histoire.

— Bien sûr que je le suis. Kahless a toujours été mon héros. J'essaie de prendre exemple sur lui.

— Moi aussi, répondit K'Ehleyr.

Kodash, qui mesurait l'épaisseur de la poussière sur un mur, hocha la tête.

— Il est intéressant d'observer, fit Zak, que nous partageons des philosophies similaires.

Le grand Klingon leva la tête.

— J'espère que tu ne n'impliques pas, Brikar, que nous pourrions tous devenir amis.

Prenant un air dédaigneux, Kebron répondit :

— Ne sois pas ridicule.

— Ça suffit ! coupa Worf. Tania...

Elle scruta son tricordeur et secoua la tête.

— Des traces d'énergie partout autour de nous. J'ai du mal à les localiser précisément.

— Très bien. Nous allons devoir explorer.

— Faudra-t-il nous séparer ? demanda Soleta.

Le cadet klingon réfléchit un instant.

— La seule raison de diviser nos forces

serait de gagner du temps. Je ne suis pas particulièrement pressé. Restons ensemble.

— Logique.

— Je suis ravi que tu m'approuves.

Dans la salle des communications subspatiales, Gowr essayait de rester éveillé. Il entendit un bruit derrière lui et sursauta.

Il fit pivoter son siège pour voir le prisonnier brikar...

Et constata, à son grand soulagement, que Baan était toujours attaché à la chaise, les mains derrière le dos.

— Quelque chose ne va pas ? demanda le Brikar.

— Rien. Rien du tout.

— C'est dommage. Tu sais, je crois que bientôt quelque chose ne va pas aller.

Il ferma la bouche, puis cracha à la figure de Gowr. Le projectile visqueux atterrit avec une rare précision, sur le front du Klingon.

Furieux, Gowr se leva en s'essuyant le visage.

— Espèce de maudit bâtard de Brikar ! s'écria-t-il.

Il brandit le poing, prêt à frapper le prisonnier à la tête.

Mais Baan para le coup.

Il fallut un instant pour que Gowr comprenne ce qui était arrivé : la main gauche de

Baan était libre ; elle serrait le poignet du Klingon dans un étau implacable.

Le Brikar brandit son autre main. Les liens pendaient toujours à son poignet. D'un geste brusque, il les enroula autour du cou de Gowr.

Le Klingon tenta de se libérer.

En vain.

Baan saisit l'autre extrémité de la corde et serra. Gowr était coincé. Il tenta désespérément de résister à l'étreinte du Brikar.

Sans résultat.

Baan tira un peu plus sur la corde.

— Tu aimes ça, Klingon ?

Il était clair que Gowr ne l'entendait plus. Ses yeux roulèrent dans ses orbites ; sa tête bascula en arrière. Son corps devint plus pesant.

Baan serra encore quelques instants pour s'assurer que son ennemi était bien mort. Puis il laissa tomber le cadavre sur le sol.

Une fois ses mains libres, quelques instants lui suffirent pour délier ses pieds.

Il abandonna les cordes, la chaise et le corps de Gowr, puis prit la direction du bâtiment des générateurs.

Worf s'arrêta devant une porte et appuya sur la commande d'ouverture. Le panneau de métal coulissa pour laisser entrer le Klingon.

Derrière lui, Tania émit un sifflement admiratif.

— Je suis impressionnée.

La pièce dans laquelle ils pénétrèrent n'était pas grande, mais elle était pleine. Worf ne reconnut pas la plupart des objets. Pourtant leur fonction était évidente.

C'étaient des armes.

Et des armes à l'aspect dangereux.

Worf prit un fusil et le souleva. Son canon était le plus grand qu'il ait jamais vu. Il devait avoir une puissance incroyable.

— Solide, dit-il. Bonne fabrication, bien équilibré.

— Vous faites un couple charmant, railla K'Ehleyr. Range-le.

Worf obéit à regret, pensant qu'il repasserait par ici avant leur départ et qu'il s'approprierait une des armes.

Ils ressortirent. Il y avait une intersection un peu plus loin devant eux. Se fiant au hasard, ils décidèrent de continuer tout droit.

Mark McHenry surveillait le déroulement de la mission, ce qui ne lui semblait pas bien difficile. Sa situation n'allait pas tarder à changer...

Il sentit l'ombre qui bondissait sur lui plus qu'il ne la vit.

Si fasciné par des choses sans importance

que puisse être l'esprit de Mark, jamais il n'était lent quand un danger le menaçait. Prendre conscience d'une présence derrière lui l'obligea à analyser le problème en un quart de seconde.

Il savait que ce n'était pas Gowr, parce qu'il surveillait le prisonnier et qu'il n'aurait pas abandonné son poste sans raison.

Ce n'était pas non plus une équipe de secours, car elle se serait annoncée en entrant, avec une déclaration du genre : « Bonjour, nous sommes de la Fédération ! Il y a quelqu'un ? »

Il savait aussi que ce n'étaient pas ses camarades, car tous se trouvaient dans la base secrète — pardon, *trouvée.*

En procédant par élimination, ce ne pouvait être que Baan. Le Brikar avait dû se libérer et réduire Gowr à l'impuissance. Il s'apprêtait à faire la même chose à McHenry.

Mac tenait à sa tête. Au fil des années, il avait appris à l'aimer, et il n'avait aucune intention de la perdre.

Tout cela passa dans son esprit en un clin d'œil.

Le cadet entra immédiatement en action. Il plongea, sentant quelque chose fendre l'air à l'endroit où s'était trouvé son crâne l'instant d'avant.

Alors il roula au sol pour tenter de mettre

le plus de distance possible entre lui et le Brikar. Puis il appuya sur son commbadge :
— McHenry appelle Worf !

Dans la base, Worf activa son communicateur :
— Ici Worf. Qu'y a-t-il, Mac ?
Avant que McHenry puisse répondre, le Brikar frappa. Heureusement, le coup ne fit que frôler la tête du cadet.

Il était néanmoins suffisant pour l'assommer. Mark s'écroula.

Baan admira son travail avec un sourire satisfait. Il décida qu'il pourrait tuer l'humain plus tard.

Ce qui urgeait, en revanche, c'était de répondre à Worf. La voix impatiente du Klingon sortait du commbadge de McHenry :

— *Mac, je répète, qu'y a-t-il ?*

Essayant de gagner du temps, le Brikar agit d'instinct. Il approcha sa bouche du communicateur, puis murmura, imitant la voix de McHenry :

— J'ai oublié.

C'était certainement la chose à dire, car Worf se contenta de soupirer :

— *Si ça te revient, contacte-nous. Worf, terminé.*

— Oui, Worf, terminé, murmura Baan. Worf, Soleta, et vous tous... Pour vous, tout sera bientôt terminé... pour de bon.

CHAPITRE
XI

— Que voulait Mac ? demanda Tania.

— Qui peut savoir !

Worf secoua la tête.

Soleta avait entendu le bref dialogue entre les deux cadets. Elle approcha du Klingon :

— Il avait quelque chose de bizarre.

— Bien sûr, comme toujours. Il vit dans un monde à lui.

— Non, Worf, insista la Vulcaine. J'ai détecté un changement dans sa voix. De plus, même si je suis la première à admettre que le cerveau de Mark McHenry ne fonctionne pas toujours logiquement, nous contacter, puis oublier la raison de son appel...

— Semble un peu fort, conclut Tobias, même pour lui.

Worf regarda ses deux camarades. Les autres avaient pris de l'avance ; K'Ehleyr fit demi-tour.

— Que se passe-t-il ?

— Je n'en suis pas sûr, répondit Worf. Mais j'ai l'intention de le savoir. (Il activa son commbadge.) Worf appelle McHenry.

Baan était penché sur l'assemblage tricordeur-communicateur qu'avait créé Tania, et il avait jeté le commbadge de Mark dans un coin.

Le Brikar entendit la voix de Worf, mais il était trop occupé à reproduire le code d'ouverture de la porte.

Il connaissait la fréquence d'activation des serrures. Bien évidemment, il avait fait en sorte de ne pas révéler cette information aux cadets. Par bonheur, la Vulcaine n'était pas parvenue à lui tirer le renseignement de la tête.

Il connaissait également les signaux permettant de mettre en route les systèmes de secours, les pièges et les dispositifs de sécurité du complexe. Il était temps de s'en servir.

Il entendit à nouveau la voix insistante de Worf. Baan ne voulait surtout pas faire une chose susceptible de mettre la puce à l'oreille de ses adversaires avant que son piège soit prêt. Après tout, il avait réussi à imiter l'humain ; il y parviendrait encore. Ce Worf n'était qu'un Klingon facile à berner.

— Ici McHenry. Qu'y a-t-il ?

Zak et Kodash ne s'intéressèrent pas à la conversation qui se déroulait derrière eux. Ils continuèrent leur chemin et découvrirent une salle dont le mécanisme d'ouverture ne fonctionnait pas parfaitement.

— Tu veux savoir ce qu'il y a dans cette pièce ? demanda le Brikar.

— Bien sûr.

Zak réussit à glisser ses gros doigts dans l'interstice existant entre les deux panneaux de la porte. Dès qu'il fut prêt, Kodash l'aida à forcer l'ouverture.

Lorsque Kebron jeta un coup d'œil à l'intérieur, il se retint de hurler de joie.

— Nous y sommes...

En effet. Au contraire du reste du complexe souterrain, la console des communications était très moderne.

— Nous l'avons trouvée ! s'écria Kodash. K'Ehleyr, nous l'avons trouvée !

Puis il entendit Worf crier quelque chose à propos de problèmes.

Alors se fit entendre un grondement.

Kodash et Zak échangèrent un regard, troublés, et reculèrent. La porte se referma.

— Par Kolker, qu'est-ce que c'est ? demanda Zak.

Quelques instants plus tôt, Worf parlait dans son commbadge :

— Mac, tu vas bien ?

— *Bien.*

Le Klingon regarda les autres, puis il dit :

— Mac, parle-moi de *Peter Pan.*

Il y eut une hésitation :

— *Pardon ?*

— Parle-moi de... *Peter Pan.*

La communication fut coupée.

Worf réfléchit à la vitesse de l'éclair :

— Le Brikar est libre. Nous sommes en grand danger. (Par pur réflexe, il dégaina son fuseur et appela les autres par-dessus son épaule :) Zak ! Kodash ! Des problèmes ! Rappliquez !

Le sol se mit alors à trembler.

— Que se passe-t-il ? demanda Tania.

A mesure que le grondement augmentait, ils éprouvèrent de plus en plus de difficultés à garder leur équilibre.

Kodash et Zak couraient dans leur direction.

Très logiquement, ce fut Soleta qui comprit la première. Elle dit simplement deux mots, dont la terrible signification échappa tout d'abord à Worf.

— De l'eau !

Baan posa le commbadge, puis il l'écrasa

sous son talon, un sourire épanoui sur le visage.

Le Klingon l'avait piégé, il devait l'admettre. Mais c'était trop tard. Le Brikar avait réussi à mettre en service le système de sécurité. Le roulement qu'il entendait sous ses pieds lui indiquait que les cadets et les Klingons ne lui poseraient bientôt plus aucun problème.

A présent, tous entendaient le grondement, qui devenait peu à peu un véritable rugissement. Worf regarda à gauche et à droite, cherchant quelle direction prendre. Il serrait son fuseur, mais il ne savait pas où le pointer, ni même quoi viser.

A cet instant, elle déferla sur eux.

Une lame de fond apparut à chaque extrémité du couloir. Ils eurent à peine une seconde pour réagir ; ce ne fut pas suffisant. L'eau les atteignit avant qu'ils puissent bouger. Ils furent renversés, puis soulevés par la vague. La force du courant était telle que Worf perdit son fuseur.

La vague les poussa comme des fétus de paille vers sa sœur. En quelques secondes, les couloirs — malgré des plafonds à plus de cinq mètres du sol — furent inondés. Très vite, il resta moins d'un mètre entre l'eau et la voûte. Comme le niveau montait régulièrement, l'issue était facile à deviner : la noyade...

Les cadets tentèrent de nager, mais ils n'arrivèrent à rien car l'eau était trop forte. Ayant l'impression d'être emportés par un torrent, ils furent aspirés sous la surface, puis propulsés comme des marionnettes contre les parois de métal.

Worf se débattit, tentant de trouver une prise quelque part.

Il heurta quelque chose.

Il ne savait pas ce que c'était, mais il réagit instinctivement et s'agrippa comme s'il s'était agi d'une bouée de sauvetage. Il lui fallut un instant pour s'apercevoir que c'était un corps. Incapable de voir à qui il s'accrochait, il songea à lâcher prise.

Worf ne voulait pas prendre le risque d'entraîner quelqu'un dans sa course folle. Mais la personne semblait l'encourager à s'arrimer.

Utilisant son sauveteur inconnu comme une échelle, le Klingon remonta vers la surface, centimètre par centimètre. L'eau menaçait à chaque instant de l'emporter.

Il sortit enfin la tête à l'air libre et se retrouva nez à nez avec K'Ehleyr.

— Dépêche-toi ! s'écria-t-elle.

Worf découvrit qu'elle était suspendue à un conduit courant au plafond. Il saisit le tuyau d'une main, et lâcha sa bienfaitrice.

L'eau leur arrivait au menton ; le niveau continuait de monter.

— Une idée ? demanda-t-il.

— Oui. Si j'avais su que nous mourrions aussi tôt, je n'aurais pas gâché les moments passés ensemble.

Worf tenta de se hisser un peu plus.

— Nous n'allons pas mourir.

— Tu es optimiste.

— Non, je sais quoi faire, dit-il en jetant des coups d'œil alentour.

— Une greffe de branchies ? railla K'Ehleyr.

— Ici, dit-il avec un signe de tête. Tu te souviens de cette porte ?

— Quelle porte ? Elle se trouve sous l'eau !

— C'est l'arsenal. Si je réussis à...

— Tu es fou ! Tu ne parviendras pas...

— Ecoute ! coupa Worf. Je peux rester ici et tout t'expliquer, mais nous serons noyés avant. Ou je peux essayer de nous tirer de là ! Tu continues à te plaindre ou tu me donnes un coup de main ?

K'Ehleyr glissa, mais se rattrapa in extremis.

— Pourquoi pas ? Je n'ai rien d'autre à faire aujourd'hui.

— Très bien ! Allons-y ! Un, deux et trois !

A trois, il plongea.

K'Ehleyr le suivit sans trop se faire d'illusions sur leurs chances de survivre.

Mais tant qu'à mourir, autant être avec lui...

Soleta, Tania et Kodash se débattaient contre les éléments, luttant désespérément pour garder la tête hors de l'eau. Zak demeurait invisible. La force du courant avait diminué, mais le niveau augmentait toujours.

La Vulcaine commençait à couler ; Tania comprit qu'elle ne savait pas très bien nager, ce qui semblait logique, sachant que Vulcain était une planète désertique. La natation ne devait pas être une occupation courante sur ce type de monde.

La blonde voulut appeler Soleta, mais elle but la tasse.

La Vulcaine disparut sous les flots. Kodash, alourdi par son armure, coula à son tour.

Le courant manqua de pousser Worf plus loin que la porte qu'il essayait d'atteindre. Mais ses doigts saisirent le chambranle de métal.

K'Ehleyr passa devant lui. Prenant appui sur un bras et une jambe, il réussit à la rattraper au tout dernier moment.

Sous l'eau, tout était silencieux. C'était un peu comme flotter dans les profondeurs de l'espace. Par bonheur, ici, ils ne devraient pas s'inquiéter du choc de la décompression.

Le seul danger était de se noyer.

Par gestes, Worf parvint à expliquer à sa compagne qu'elle devait actionner la commande d'ouverture de la porte. Un instant, il se demanda avec horreur s'il n'existait pas un système de blocage des serrures en cas d'urgence. Si c'était le cas, ils ne reverraient jamais la surface, car les poumons du Klingon étaient sur le point d'exploser.

K'Ehleyr tendit la main contre le courant. Ses doigts se trouvaient à quelques centimètres du tableau de commande. Worf la poussa de toutes ses forces ; sa main s'écrasa sur le bouton.

La porte s'ouvrit.

Worf, K'Ehleyr et l'eau s'engouffrèrent dans l'arsenal. La salle se remplit en quelques secondes. Avant d'être à nouveau submergés, les deux Klingons profitèrent d'un instant de répit pour remplir leurs poumons d'air.

A l'Académie, les cadets effectuaient des manœuvres en apesanteur au cas où ils se trouveraient sur une planète à gravité plus faible que celle de la Terre ou dans un navire privé de gravité par une panne.

Ces leçons s'avérèrent utiles.

Worf cala ses pieds contre une paroi et se propulsa dans l'environnement aquatique. Il traversa la pièce et s'empara du fusil qu'il avait examiné un peu plus tôt.

Même sous l'eau, il remarqua le regard interloqué de K'Ehleyr.

A quoi cela va-t-il lui servir ? devait-elle penser.

Il n'était pas exactement en position de s'expliquer.

Il espéra seulement que son plan marcherait, et que les autres survivraient assez longtemps pour en bénéficier.

Tania était ballottée comme une barque pendant une tempête. Sa tête frôlait dangereusement le plafond.

Soudain, son pied droit heurta quelque chose.

C'était une sorte de plate-forme sur laquelle elle allait pouvoir se tenir, ce qui lui permettrait de résister au courant et de garder la tête hors de l'eau.

Une seconde plus tard, Soleta apparut près d'elle. Puis ce fut au tour de Kodash. Ils avaient de l'eau jusqu'au menton, et ils devaient basculer la tête en arrière pour respirer, le front contre le plafond en mosaïque.

— Comment... ? réussit à dire Tania.

Elle parvint à baisser la tête, et aperçut quelque chose.

Tobias devina une silhouette humanoïde imposante. Elle-même se tenait sur sa tête, et l'être supportait les pieds de ses camarades sur ses bras tendus.

Elle sut immédiatement qui c'était.

Alors elle releva la tête pour respirer.

— Zak ! C'est Zak !

Soleta, qui crachait toujours de l'eau, parvint à acquiescer. Kodash secoua la tête ; malgré le rugissement du torrent, Tania l'entendit murmurer :

— Sauvé par un Brikar. Jamais je ne survivrai à cette honte !

« Sauvé » n'était pas le terme qui s'appliquait à la situation. Apparemment, Kebron pouvait retenir assez longtemps sa respiration ; ça valait mieux, car son corps de pierre ne lui permettait pas de nager. Mais Tobias savait qu'il ne pourrait pas rester éternellement ainsi.

Au rythme où le niveau de l'eau augmentait, leur numéro d'équilibristes ne les aiderait pas longtemps.

Worf avançait dans le couloir inondé, tenant son fusil hors de l'eau. K'Ehleyr nageait derrière lui. Elle leva les yeux vers le plafond et remarqua qu'il n'y avait plus de poche d'air. La fin était proche.

Et son compagnon s'amusait avec une arme !

Quelle idée a-t-il donc en tête ?

Son camarade évoluait près d'une des grilles métalliques du sol. Il visa.

A cet instant, la Klingonne comprit son plan.

Worf appuya sur la détente.

Un puissant rayon disrupteur jaillit du canon de l'arme. Le cadet eut à peine le temps de remercier Kahless que le fusil n'ait pas été électrique. Dans ce cas, K'Ehleyr et lui seraient morts électrocutés. Mais le recul, à cause de la loi de l'action et de la réaction, le projeta vers le haut avec une telle force que sa tête heurta le plafond.

Il ne s'était pas trompé : la grille faisait

partie d'un système de drainage. Dans des circonstances ordinaires, l'eau serait restée en place suffisamment longtemps pour noyer les intrus. Puis les drains se seraient ouverts automatiquement pour l'aspirer dans des réservoirs, sans doute ceux qui avaient alimenté le piège.

En faisant exploser une des grilles, Worf avait accéléré le processus.

Accroché à un tuyau courant au plafond, le cadet klingon observa la suite des événements. Au début, il n'y eut aucun signe indiquant qu'il avait accompli quelque chose de positif. Puis le liquide, sous lui, commença à tourbillonner.

K'Ehleyr.

Où était K'Ehleyr ?

Un instant, l'esprit de Worf fut envahi par l'image de la Klingonne entraînée dans les systèmes d'alimentation souterrains.

Il allait lâcher prise et plonger pour la sauver quand il vit une main jaillir du centre du tourbillon. K'Ehleyr luttait contre le courant ; elle perdait la partie. Dans quelques secondes, elle disparaîtrait.

Elle était trop loin pour que Worf l'attrape, mais ce détail n'allait pas l'arrêter. Il tendit le fusil, crosse en avant. Elle parvint à s'en emparer.

— Accroche-toi ! hurla le cadet.

K'Ehleyr réussit à empoigner l'arme avec l'autre main, et Worf la hissa. Sa tête jaillit de l'onde tumultueuse. Elle cracha de l'eau pendant quelques instants, reprit sa respiration, puis sauta pour attraper le tuyau auquel le cadet était accroché.

— Ça... ça marche ! dit-elle.

— Peut-être pouvons-nous encore accélérer le processus, gronda Worf.

Il plongea l'arme sous l'eau et l'orienta pour viser plus loin dans le couloir. Il espérait que sa mémoire photographique serait assez précise pour qu'il touche une autre grille.

Ce fut le cas. Un autre tourbillon naquit ; le niveau de l'eau baissait.

Le Klingon visa dans une autre direction et tira. Un troisième siphon apparut. L'eau menaçait sans arrêt de les entraîner, mais les deux camarades tenaient bon.

— Tu as réussi ! s'écria K'Ehleyr.

— *Nous* avons réussi, corrigea-t-il, essayant de paraître modeste.

Il n'y parvint pas vraiment.

La Klingonne le scruta un instant. Puis elle l'embrassa.

Worf n'en revint pas.

— Pourquoi donc ?

Elle sourit et répondit :

— Pour *me* faire plaisir.

Tania ne comprenait plus rien. L'instant d'avant, elle luttait pour trouver de l'air ; le suivant, le niveau de l'eau avait considérablement diminué.

Il descendait encore.

Quelques minutes plus tard, Kodash, Soleta et elle purent *descendre* de Zak. Il leur sourit.

— C'était agréable, dit-il. Je peux rester ainsi pendant plus longtemps, si vous voulez.

— Je ne crois pas que ce sera nécessaire, répondit Soleta.

— Venez, fit Tania. Il faut retrouver Worf et K'Ehleyr, pour nous assurer qu'ils vont bien.

— Ils sont tous les deux klingons, rappela Kodash. Ce simple fait leur garantit d'avoir survécu.

— Mais avoir du soutien ne fait pas de mal, non ? fit remarquer le Brikar.

Le grand Klingon ne répondit rien.

Worf et K'Ehleyr attendirent que le niveau de l'eau ait suffisamment baissé — afin de voir où se trouvaient les trous d'évacuation —, avant de se laisser tomber au sol.

Ils atterrirent dans une gerbe d'eau, accroupis comme des panthères. Leurs vêtements étaient trempés, et leurs cheveux collés contre leurs tempes et leur nuque.

Mais ils étaient en vie.

— Nous devons retourner à la surface, dit Worf. Il s'est passé quelque chose de grave. (Il mit son fusil en bandoulière.) Mais nous allons régler le problème au plus vite. En route !

Baan n'aimait pas la tournure des événements.

Provenant du sous-sol, il avait entendu ce qui ressemblait à une décharge de disrupteur. Puis il avait capté l'écho de quelque chose qui ressemblait à l'écoulement d'une grande quantité d'eau.

Non, il n'aimait pas ça du tout.

— Qu'est-ce qu'ils font ? grogna-t-il.

Il entendit alors un gémissement à l'autre bout de la salle du générateur.

Mark McHenry avait repris connaissance. Il se massait la nuque et tentait de recouvrer ses esprits.

— Vous avez tout gâché ! hurla le Brikar.

Mac, les idées encore confuses, ne trouva rien à dire.

Le soldat avança vers lui, l'air menaçant, les poings levés.

— S'ils réussissent à remonter, ils ne trouveront que ton cadavre !

Il y eut un léger bruit derrière le Brikar. Il voulut se retourner, mais son attention fut attirée par McHenry, qui dit :

— Tu vas être frappé par-derrière.

Baan, furieux, retroussa les lèvres :

— Quelle ruse pathétique vas-tu inven... ?

Alors il fut frappé par-derrière, comme annoncé.

Il s'écroula, terrassé par le coup qui avait touché un point vital de son système nerveux.

Il voulut se relever, mais un coup de pied lui ébranla le crâne.

Il eut à peine le temps de voir l'expression enragée de Gowr.

Baan n'eut pas l'occasion de se défendre. Il éprouvait quelques difficultés à accepter que le Klingon soit toujours en vie, que les cadets aient survécu... Bref, que tout soit allé de travers. Tout cela, combiné à l'assaut de Gowr, l'avait anéanti mentalement et physiquement.

Quand il sombra dans l'inconscience, il en fut presque soulagé.

Gowr le frappa encore, histoire de s'assurer qu'il était bien K-O. Il se tourna vers Mac :

— Tu vas bien ? demanda-t-il d'une voix rauque.

Mark hocha la tête :

— Et toi ?

— J'ai déjà été mieux, admit le Klingon, massant son cou là où la corde avait laissé une marque. Heureusement, la biologie des Klingons est très compliquée. Nous avons certains systèmes organiques de « secours » dont les non-Klingons ignorent l'existence. Nous y veillons : c'est plus pratique pour surprendre nos ennemis. Nous ne mourons pas si facilement.

— Tu m'en vois ravi...

Ils entendirent un bruit de machinerie. Quelques secondes plus tard, le monte-charge apparut, portant un groupe de cadets trempés jusqu'aux os. Worf bondit le premier, disrupteur au poing. Les autres avaient également pris des armes dans l'arsenal. Ils étaient prêts à la bataille, voire à se jeter tête baissée dans un piège s'il le fallait...

Les pauvres s'attendaient à tout, sauf à la vision d'un Brikar inconscient aux pieds de Gowr et de Mark.

— Salut, les gars, dit Mac. Avez-vous lancé l'appel de détresse ?

Tous échangèrent des regards.

— Non, répondit Worf.

— Alors, qu'attendez-vous ? Je n'ai pas envie de moisir ici plus longtemps !

Worf regarda K'Ehleyr. Elle haussa les épaules.

— Nous nous mettons tout de suite au travail, dit le cadet klingon.

— Il est temps, répondit Mark McHenry.

CHAPITRE XII

Tout le monde était installé autour de la table de conférences. Tous regardaient le capitaine Taggert, commandant du *Repulse*. Le navire — qui avait récupéré les cadets plusieurs heures plus tôt, après avoir reçu l'appel de détresse — venait de mettre le cap sur la base Stellaire 3. Une fois arrivés, les jeunes gens seraient transférés sur un autre vaisseau qui les ramènerait sur Terre, à Starfleet Académie.

— J'espère que vous n'allez pas être déçus, commença Taggert en caressant sa barbe poivre et sel. Mais vous l'avez manquée.

Worf plissa le front et échangea des regards avec les autres. Il prit la parole au nom du groupe :

— Manqué quoi, monsieur ?

— La guerre entre Brikar et la Fédération.

Il y a eu quelques escarmouches durant les dernières semaines. Mais, pour résumer, la Grande Alliance que les Brikars avaient cru fonder — l'union de plusieurs espèces hostiles à la Fédération — a été dissoute.

— Pourquoi ne suis-je pas surpris ? murmura Zak Kebron. Si je vous racontais les exploits des imbéciles qui dirigent notre planète, vos cheveux se dresseraient sur vos crânes.

— Je n'en doute pas, monsieur Kebron. En tout cas, votre gouvernement a contacté la Fédération pour résoudre le conflit par des moyens « pacifiques ». Les négociations sont en cours, mais elles seront longues. Les Brikars prétendent disposer de *biens* à offrir contre des concessions territoriales.

— Quels biens ? demanda Worf.

— Des prisonniers, dit Taggert. Des innocents qui voyageaient dans l'espace et qui ont été capturés par les navires brikars.

Les Klingons et les cadets échangèrent aussitôt un regard.

— Les colons, fit Soleta.

— Le professeur Trump, ajouta Tania, se rappelant l'instructeur blessé qui était parti avec les habitants de Dantar IV.

— C'est exact, confirma le capitaine. Nos services secrets rapportent que tout le monde est en excellente santé. Les Brikars savent que des prisonniers morts ne leur seraient d'aucune utilité. Nous devrions pouvoir négocier leur libération sans problème. De plus, considérant l'important stock d'armes brikariennes et le prisonnier dont nous disposons — grâce à vous —, nous aurons davantage d'arguments à avancer.

Il y eut un long silence, puis Taggert reprit :

— Sachez que je suis impressionné par la manière dont vous vous êtes acquittés de cette mission imprévue. Mes félicitations et mes commentaires seront envoyés à l'Académie et à l'Empire Klingon. (Il écarta les mains.) Ce sera tout. Vous pouvez disposer.

Une voix retentit dans le commbadge du capitaine :

— *Monsieur, Chafin à l'inter. Le croiseur klingon* Azetbur *vient de sortir de l'espace de distorsion. Il va récupérer nos jeunes amis de l'Empire.*

— Bien reçu. (Il se tourna vers les Klingons.) Vous feriez mieux de prendre vos affaires et d'aller en salle de téléportation. Il ne faut pas faire attendre votre peuple.

K'Ehleyr hocha la tête, puis lança un coup d'œil aux cadets de Starfleet. C'était le moment propice pour un discours passionné, ou pour se congratuler.

— Au revoir, dit simplement K'Ehleyr.

Les trois Klingons se levèrent et quittèrent la salle.

Les cadets échangèrent des regards étonnés.

Worf resta immobile. Il avait tant de choses à dire à K'Ehleyr qu'il ne savait par où commencer, ni même s'il *devait* commencer.

Il s'aperçut que Tania l'observait, comme si elle lisait ses pensées.

Quelles que soient les émotions qui faisaient rage dans son esprit, elle choisit de les garder pour elle.

— Cours-lui après, idiot !

Les Klingons entraient en salle de téléportation quand K'Ehleyr entendit une voix familière l'appeler. Gowr et Kodash s'arrêtèrent ; la Klingonne leur ordonna de continuer, puis elle se tourna vers Worf.

Il resta immobile, ne sachant quoi dire.

— Hum... quelle est ta prochaine mission ? demanda-t-il enfin.

— Je vais demander à être mutée dans les corps diplomatiques qui se chargeront des négociations entre les Brikars et la Fédération.

— Toi ? Diplomate ?

Elle plissa les yeux, mais sembla amusée :

— Ne suis-je pas un parangon de diplomatie ?

— Tu es une force de la nature, K'Ehleyr. Implacable. Si tu as choisi une carrière d'ambassadeur, je ne doute pas que tu enfonceras la diplomatie dans la gorge de ceux qui ne seront pas d'accord avec toi.

Elle éclata de rire. Puis, soudain sérieuse, elle ajouta :

— Worf, viens avec nous.

Il leva un sourcil étonné.

— Tu n'es pas un des leurs, ajouta-t-elle. Tu es un *Klingon*. Essayer de t'acclimater à leur monde est du gaspillage. Chez eux, tu seras toujours un étranger. Avec nous...

— Je serai un Klingon parmi des milliers d'autres.

— Jamais ! L'Empire Klingon aurait tant à t'offrir. Et je...

Elle s'arrêta. Un instant, elle parut presque empruntée. Puis elle s'obligea à reprendre un air impassible.

— Il n'est pas trop tard.

Worf soupira :

— Je me suis engagé dans une voie, K'Ehleyr. Je dois continuer mon chemin.

— Tu n'as aucun doute ?

— J'aurai toujours des doutes, mais je les surmonterai.

Elle le dévisagea et ajouta :

— Peut-être es-tu en cela un vrai Klingon.

Elle voulut monter sur la plate-forme de téléportation ; Worf l'arrêta d'une main sur l'épaule. Ils se regardèrent.

Trop de choses les séparaient...

— Bonne chance, K'Ehleyr. Affronte bravement tes ennemis, et meurs avec honneur. Je pense que nous ne nous reverrons pas.

— Bonne chance à toi, Worf. Affronte bravement tes ennemis, et meurs avec honneur... (Elle marqua une pause, et sourit :) Je pense... que tu te trompes.

Elle fouilla dans son sac et en sortit une petite statue, qu'elle lui tendit. Il reconnut immédiatement ce qu'elle représentait : Kahless l'Inoubliable luttant contre Morath.

— Regarde-la quand tu auras l'impression d'oublier qui tu es.

Puis elle disparut dans une gerbe d'étincelles.

Worf demeura dans la salle de téléportation jusqu'à ce que le scintillement de l'onde porteuse s'estompe.

Alors, à pas lents, la statuette serrée contre son cœur, il partit retrouver ses amis.

Les cadets de Starfleet.

Sa famille !

Achevé d'imprimer
par Maury-Eurolivres S.A.
45300 Manchecourt

Imprimé en France
Dépôt légal : Mai 1995

SIX KEYS

Meg Garcia

ISBN: 978-1-61244-572-4
Library of Congress Control Number: 2017906328

Printed in the United States of America

Published by Halo Publishing International
1100 NW Loop 410
Suite 700 - 176
San Antonio, Texas 78213
Toll Free 1-877-705-9647
Website: www.halopublishing.com
E-mail: contact@halopublishing.com

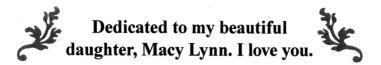

**Dedicated to my beautiful
daughter, Macy Lynn. I love you.**

Mommy

Contents

E

My name is Megan. I'm a married, twenty-six-year-old mother of four. I'm starting to have this eerie nightmare that I used to have when I was seventeen. I need to understand it, so I'm writing this story in hopes of finding someone who can help.

Normally, when someone has vivid nightmares or night terrors, it's due to some sort of trauma, or deep emotional issues. That would make having these night terrors valid. Not in my case. My parents are still married to this day, I have never had a split or broken home, and nothing tragic has happened in my life or in the lives of any close ones.

I have two siblings: an older sister and a younger brother. I've lived a pretty normal, suburban life-style. The only odd thing in my life are my parents' occupations; my mom is a registered nurse, and my dad is a detective, but to say that's odd is still a stretch. The only "odd" thing about their occupations are the hours that they work.

The background of my daily teenage life was simple. I had always been the weird one out of the family. It was like if they all went left, I couldn't help but go right. Being different never bothered me, though, and I almost thrived on it. I was sort of getting my own special attention without having actual attention. I had always been kind of a loner when it came to even my extended family. Within my group of friends, however, I was the complete opposite. With them, I was known as a social butterfly, who was loud and energetic and always trying to make them laugh. For being considered as an introvert around my family, I still felt loved and accepted, and they always embraced my so-called "weirdness". As a family of five, we were all so different, but we have always remained close.

I've always been an avid reader. What peaked my interests were horror, true stories, history, and conspiracy theories. The fear of history repeating itself and the unknown has always intrigued me. A 5'2" and 103lbs fearless, little girl was a good definition of me. Usually when something unexplainable happened or any conflict arose – whether it involved me or not – I ran straight into it. I imagined myself as some sort of an invincible force or some shit like that.

My parents' house had two things that creeped me out. In one of the living rooms, there was a giant bay window that reached from floor to ceiling. I always hated that window. It felt like I was a fucking animal in the zoo, exposed in my habitat for all the world to see. The other thing was the creaky floorboard in the doorway of my parents' bedroom. My siblings and I avoided going in there, because stepping on that board would vibrate the entire upstairs floor, sending chills throughout our bodies.

Like I have said before, my family was close. We never ate at the dinner table, and we didn't really "hangout" together a lot, but every day after school, we would all just sit together and talk for hours about our days. Afterwards, we would disperse to our own spaces and not see each other for the rest of the night.

At seventeen years old, life was good. I had my getaway bedroom, and I would get to spend every night texting with my high school sweetheart and all my friends before bed. Everything was perfect... until the nightmares started happening.

I'll never forget the first night it happened. The first dream I had of... him... will forever be imbedded in my memory.

I was on my new razor cell phone with my boyfriend playing the "no you hang up first!" game. When I saw his white face behind the chair in my room. I wasn't startled really, just confused. It was as white as a sheet of fresh computer paper. The eyes on the face were completely closed with wrinkles around the eyes that resembled fragments of old mascara crumbling off his non-existent eyelashes. His lips were muttering something. I put my boyfriend on mute and tried to see if I could hear what this pale face was saying. Nothing, my room was abnormally quiet. When I tried listening, it felt as if my ears had shut off. It started to give me a headache, so I unmuted my boyfriend. As soon as I looked at my phone to push the button, the face had disintegrated into nothing. Maybe my eyes were playing a trick on me? There is no possible way there could be anyone in my room.

Not much later the conversation still carried on about his so-called dreams and aspirations, I suddenly felt completely out of it. Now... this wasn't normal for me. Normally I couldn't focus on anything when talking to him. He always had my one-hundred percent attention. This time... I just couldn't. No matter how hard I tried, it wasn't there to me. I found his voice to be utterly obnoxious. I even put my phone down to go get something to drink, just to get a moment of clarity.

As I went back upstairs to pick up on this pointless conversation, I contemplated to myself. Why didn't I freak out? Why didn't I tell my boyfriend? And then I really started dissecting the incident… where the fuck was that light coming from?!

Ready to start investigating, I told my boyfriend that my mom was calling me downstairs so I had to go. Before he could even mutter an Okay, I snapped my phone shut.

Okay, so my room was pitch dark. My phone light was on my face. It only had enough light to shine a small portion of my cheek. So, that's voided. Maybe the moon? My bedroom was the only one upstairs that faced the back of the house, so at night the moon light shined the brightest in my room. For that reason, I had a full shade that I could pull down at night so I could sleep. The moon would peek through the cracks of the shade. It never eliminated the problem, but it did the job.

I stood in front of my window and tried to follow the trail of the moonlight with my hand. The light never held to my chair. Now before you think the moon possibly moved depending on the time span between seeing the face and my investigating. I carried that exact thought as well. I followed the light for the next two nights seeing exactly where is goes. It does reach my chair, but not as bright as it needs to be to illuminate the face as bright as it was.

I completely blocked it out of my mind. I never told anyone about it. I want to say about four or five nights had passed with nothing out of the ordinary. My boyfriend was trying to tell me about what he wanted to do to speed up his car, and I just couldn't stand it. I rushed him off the phone saying I had a biology final to study for. In all honestly, the sound of his voice just annoyed the hell out of me. Plus, *The Exorcist* was on TV. I just wanted to watch it before bed.

Trying to watch the movie my phone was just flooding with text messages about weekend and Valentine's Day plans. I didn't even care at that point. I silenced my phone and flipped it over so the damn notification light would stop flashing in my face.

This movie never scared me. I've seen this movie so many times, I can quote every single line. But one scene in particular had scared the living shit out of me. There is a scene that has this white scary face in the background. It's just a quick flash, and then it's gone. I instantly had that dropping sensation in the pit of my stomach, and suddenly started feeling nervous. I just rode out the feeling, and finished the movie.

When the movie was over, I turned off the TV, set my alarm on my phone, still ignoring all my recent texts. All I wanted was to fall asleep. I was so fucking tired I could barely keep my eyes open. I was staring at the clock dimly lit on my phone, 2:03A.M. Fuck I've got to be up in four hours. I take my glasses off and bury my face into my pillow. Now I don't know what possessed me, as scared as I was, to open my eyes and look at my chair. There it was… the face…

Trying to justify what I was seeing was all in my head, my body felt frozen. My glasses are off, and I just watched a scary movie, my eyes are playing tricks on me. Just fall the fuck to sleep. I rolled over, and slowly drifted into sleep.

For what felt like a blink of an eye, I found myself looking at my ceiling. My body felt heavy. I couldn't breathe, and my hands were constricted to my bed, as if someone was holding them down. My chest slowly felt pressure rising from my hips. I look down my body and see something dark. I follow the darkness up with my eyes. It's on me. This fucker was hovering over the entire top half of my body. Muted by fear, all I can do is stare at this pale face asshole. His eyes were still closed, it looked human. He had a young adults facial structure. The only unhuman thing about him was the non-pigment in his face and how deep his features sunk into his face. I tried to wiggle my wrists free from his grasps, but I couldn't break free. So much for thinking I was fucking invincible.

Focusing on his face, it felt like hours had gone by. I tried studying everything I could about this man/thing that was on me. All black clothes I think? White skin, black shaggy hair. I, I think I feel a warm heavy drip of liquid dropping on my stomach. Is this man/thing oozing? Taking me a minute, I had noticed his eyes were open. Staring at me. His deep black lifeless eyes were staring right through mine. I felt like he was burning the back of my fucking head. I started to choke out a pathetic scary movie cliché questions. "What do you want? Who are you?" This thing leans into my face and hisses, "Time to play."

All the sudden I woke up from what I think could only be a nightmare. Thank God it was over. I noticed that I'm drenched in sweat. Which is odd for me because I'm always cold, even in ninety-degree weather.

Trying to shake it off, I sneak downstairs to the garage to steal one of my parent's cigarettes. I make it downstairs. My body felt so heavy. I heard a car outside pull into my driveway. My dad's off work, that means it's 5:30A.M. I rush as quiet as I can upstairs so I don't have to talk to him. I just felt the way that my face must have looked he would have instantly known something was wrong with me. The family already thought I was a little off, and I was OK with that, but I didn't want to add any more fuel to that fire. Plus, I felt crazy myself, I couldn't even tell if it was all in my head, or real.

I slipped back into bed, wide awake. All I could think about was that voice, and what he said. "Time to play." What the fuck would that even mean? I tried not to get myself worked up. Distracting myself, I went through all the texts I ignored last night, and half assed replied to every one of them.

That day at school the bell rang for first period. I always sat with a group of friends that I worked at the movie theatre with. One of my friends was going to a concert that night, but still had no one to cover her shift. She barely looked at me. Everyone could tell I was a little out of it. Out of nowhere I volunteered. That's all I had said for the day. My body just felt shut off. I was extremely exhausted, but I was avoiding my room like the plague.

I knew work tonight was going to be jam packed, because it was Thursday. Parents always took their kids to the movies on Thursdays so they don't have to feel guilty for ignoring them over the weekend. I don't care though, I just want to keep busy.

Walking into work, I brace myself for being called the Mexican Coraline by customers. After laughing off the seventy-ninth Coraline look alike joke, I try to see the end of the ticket line. It stretches out the door. I keep telling myself to just get through this, three buttons, give change, direct them to the location of the theatre, just ignore the jokes. I'm allowed one shitty attitude night. I can make it through these five hours on a shit mood. Maybe.

Mentally pushing myself through, I check to see if the line had gone down any. There he is… eyes locked on it… I choked out, "holy fucking shit. How? Why? Is he real? If he's real how did he break into a cop's house?"

"Um, excuse me?" There was a woman standing in front of me with her three sticky toddlers staring at me.

"Auditorium eleven, it'll be on your right. Enjoy the sh-show."

"Are you alright? You look a little pale?" her face looked concerned. I say nothing and pointed in the direction of her theatre. If another person tries to have another conversation with me I will snap. I need to focus.

Selling ticket after ticket, I keep eye contact with this thing. I can't look away because I'm fearful he'll disappear. I'm going to make this fucker stand face to face with me, then I'll ask him what kind of sick game is he trying to play! At least that's what I hope will happen. What realistically will happen is I will curl up in fear and cry like a fucking bitch baby. I wonder if anyone else can see him…

The line dwindles to twenty people… the noise in my ears begin to muffle, my eardrums aching… seventeen… my palms become sweaty, and my vision becomes cloudy…

focus Megan!... twelve… money starts sticking to my fingers, I'm fumbling trying to make change… six… all I can hear are his boots clanking on the floor, moving with the line his smirk turns into a demented grin… three… he's right on me… can anyone else see him? I'm trying to stand my ground, but my knees are shaking, I look like I should piss or something… one… standing in front of me. Black shaggy drenched hair, white face, black sunken eyes. Mesmerized by his face he towered over me. I couldn't look at anything else but his eyes. Opening my mouth, I blurt out "who are you?!"

Interrupted by another woman, looking at me the exact same way as the one before. Where did he go?

"Are you alright, Miss?" I blink uncontrollably, trying to focus on my dried-out eyes.

"Um, yeah, how can I help you?" in the back of my mind I'm screaming. Terrified. Where'd he go? How can he just disappear like this? I stared at the asshole the entire fucking time. I looked into his eyes. Smelling his wet, irony smell. I talked. Could it be possible I was hallucinating?... all I know is I'm not going to school tomorrow. I'm going to fake stomach cramps and just sleep all day. That's what I need. A good night's sleep. I'm just exhausted.

The next morning, I con my mom into letting me stay home. I slept all day. A good eleven hours. After being awake for a bit, I instantly regretted sleeping that long. I was too groggy talking with my family, so I went straight upstairs to my room to go back to bed. By the time, I finally woke up it was about ten at night. Awesome. Movie marathon I guess.

Forty minutes into the first movie I can feel my eyes dropping un-voluntarily. Surprised, I just decided to roll with it and pass out.

After what felt like a second, I woke up and saw that my door was wide open. I heard the floor creek and felt the vibration underneath me... "Mom?"

A sly whisper replied, "Megan...." Scared shitless, I already knew who it was. It was him, and he's started his 'game'. I shot up out of my bed to see if I could catch him. Nothing. I hear my name again. "Megan..." this time the sound was creeping up from the family room. I hurry to the upstairs loft and look down hissing into the dark, "where are you?!". No response. This went on for about another ten minutes. Searching through the house for him. It was like playing cat and mouse, I just wasn't sure if I was the cat, or the helpless mouse. His whispers started to feel more cowardly the more his game progressed. My fear turned into annoyance. "Come out you coward!". I waited in the middle of my downstairs. I quit, "you win.".

Heading upstairs I couldn't help but wonder if I was going crazy... but there have been so many things going on all at once, how can I be? I get back into bed, feeling stupid. If he's real, he is all parlor tricks to just get a scare.

Sleep finally took over my body. Suddenly I awoke feeling a huge rush of chills run up my spine. I opened my eyes. I found myself standing in my parent's living room, looking out my parent's giant window. How in the hell?

I tried to move, but my body was immobile. I tried screaming for my Mom, but no sound could come out. I prayed my Dad's squad car would pull up into the driveway. It never did...

My thoughts in that moment were, I'm going to die. This is how it ends. My thoughts were interrupted by feeling something heavy in the air behind me. Hearing nothing, I remembered this silence was the exact same I felt at the theatre. He was close. I could feel it. I tried doing and thinking whatever I could to wake up. The thick air finally filled up the entire living room, making it barely possible to breathe. Then, there he was. I could feel him. His mouth was in my ear. He was right behind me. He whispered softly "Megan".

All I could do was shut my eyes. After a few seconds, I could belt out a scream. The sound left my lips and I felt myself falling out of bed. My skin was crawling. I've never had a nightmare that vivid before… Was it really a nightmare? From that night on I kept my TV on all night. Either MTV or Nick at Night. Always something happy, used as background noise.

After a while, I ended up breaking up with my boyfriend. I isolated myself from my friends. Kept quiet. Night-time was like clockwork. The incident was always the same. I could feel when it was coming. Every now and again, it would have subtle changes. Sometimes I was already in front of the window. Other nights I was searching for him and walked myself to the window. Very few times I could see him out the window across the street just staring at me and give me a devious smile, followed by the whisper. The way he said my name felt like bugs crawling out of my ear. I would randomly feel it throughout the day. Wherever I was, it didn't matter. I took that as a sign that his presence was near.

One night I was able to get a good look at all of him instead of his face. To this day, I wish I hadn't… I saw that his black long sleeve shirt was torn and soaked with blood. I tried to examine the wound as quick as possible before the thick air took my breath. Dirty black boots, dark jeans. Who was the guy?... he looked like he was standing out in the rain, water dripping all over him. But there was no rain. I noticed something new. The letter E… it looked as if the letter E was carved into his pale stomach. What is the E for? The whisper took longer than usual. Was he waiting for me to find the letter on him as a clue to his game? When the whisper came, I was finally back in bed, itching at my ear. This time I didn't go back to sleep. All I could think about was the letter E. And what kind of meaning was it, and who was the E for?

I tried to do some research on the "E" figure. But, I didn't know how to even go about searching something like this? Creepy pale faced wet man spirit with the letter E? Too difficult, I gave up. I decided to lean towards me going insane, and losing grip on reality. That was oddly more comforting. Eventually… it'll go away.

It never went away. It stayed a normal routine from age seventeen to twenty. When I turned twenty, I moved out of my parent's house. I stopped seeing him when I was awake. My mood changed. I felt well rested and relief that maybe it was just the house.

For six years, I visited my parent's house quite regularly. Even stayed there overnight every now and again. Nothing happened. Everything was peaceful, until about a month ago…

I'm starting to have the exact same dream again...
Only difference is I'm standing in my own family room,
facing my window. Staring out at him into the woods in my
backyard. When I wake up, I'm not in my bed like before.
I wake up standing in my living room. I'm starting to think
there is something more to this than just in my head... I
need to figure this out. For my family... Because as my old
friend and I were back at it again, the smile grew wider on
his face... I knew... this was only the beginning...

The Nanny

(Narrated on YouTube by <u>Through the Abyss</u>)

Growing up, I had always wanted to be a dad. Sadly, my wife, Alicia and I had been told by doctors that conceiving a child was not an option for us. Not being able to have a child of our own had been one of the hardest battles in our marriage to overcome. There were times in our marriage that I was so sure that we would end in divorce, but we never did. Our love grew stronger instead. We both had advanced in our careers and traveled to every destination we could ever dream of. My wife and I had the most adventurous life with nothing tying us down… It was all bittersweet.

The first three years of our marriage were phenomenal. We didn't think that life could get any better. Life proved us wrong.

Alicia fell ill for about a month. Tired of being bedridden, she was finally convinced that she needed to go get checked out. I took the afternoon off to go along with her. After her basic checkup, the doctor came into the exam room, his lips twitching, trying to hold back a smile.

"Looks like you're pregnant, Congratulations! Let's get you down to ultrasound and get a look at baby." the doctor said, releasing his grin.

We were utterly stunned by the news. The only thing we could manage was a blank stare. We followed the doctor down to ultrasound, moving slowly, giving us time to process what was happening. That moment we were walking down the hallway, everything felt so surreal. When we entered the room, Alicia was instructed to lay on the bed. She seemed nervous so I wrapped my arms around her, bringing her close. I could tell by the look on her face she didn't know how to react because of me. I realized, me being stunned, my silence is probably being misconstrued. I had to say something.

"Now we've done it all, Babe." I whispered in Alicia's ear. Tears began to flood in her eyes, she squeezed my hand and kissed the tip of my nose, silently expressing how thrilled she was. After completing the procedure, the doctor handed us the pictures. It was so surreal to see our little baby for the first time. To think we would never have a biological child, and now there we were, looking at our little creation.

After leaving that first doctor's appointment, Alicia obsessed over the well-being of the baby. She bought every pregnancy and baby book ever written. She even quit her job so she could solely focus on caring for the baby.

Eight grueling months of anxiously waiting, our son, Braxton was born. His over worrying mother couldn't leave his side. Knowing he was going to be our one and only child, I couldn't blame Alicia for being terrified of everything around us. From the dangers within the house to the cruelties of the outside world, she was determined to keep Braxton safe from any harm. It took her about a year, when Braxton was at the stages of walking and talking, to realize that she might want to return to work. Alicia missed doing hair. I supported anything she wanted to do; she had sacrificed everything when we got pregnant with our son, and I felt like I owed the world to her.

For Alicia to be able to go back to work without worry, we decided the best decision for our son was to hire an in-home nanny after his second birthday. We posted a few ads and called different nanny services for recommendations. From scheduling interviews to trial runs with our son. We had gone through twenty-six interviews, and Alicia didn't deem any of them even moderately acceptable. The whole nanny process became such a blur. I was ready to throw in the towel on the entire thing.

My body crashed into a level of exhaustion that turned my mind hazy. Alicia went back to work part time. She scheduled her hours opposite of mine so our son never had to go to a baby sitter. We lived a hectic lifestyle at that time, Braxton in his "terrible twos" and there were never-ending interviews for a nanny. Running on fumes, I took it upon myself to take a personal day on Monday to relax at home with my family.

Later that Monday afternoon while Braxton was napping, there was a knock at the door. Alicia and I looked at each other puzzled. A second series of knocks followed. I answered the door. It was a woman, she was there for the in-home nanny position. Letting her in, my wife and I were scrambling to try to pick up the living room and smooth over our bedhead. We both apologized for the mess and letting the interview slip our minds. Claire was her name.

She was so sweet, instantly making us comfortable with the situation. She had such a beautiful tone to her voice. Alicia mentioned it was like Claire was singing a soft melody every time she spoke. We had to have her for Braxton. My wife and I felt like she was such a warm-hearted person, and she met all of Alicia's specific requirements.

Life started to fall back into place. Braxton instantly formed a bond with Claire. Those two even had their own little special language. My wife and I could always go to work with ease, knowing our son was left with the best care. In the evenings, we would return home, and spend quality time with our little family while Claire helped with dinner and household chores. Although that was never in her job description, Claire insisted on helping with other household duties so Braxton could spend as much quality time with us as possible.

Claire was with us for a month, and our everyday schedule continued smoothly. Alicia and I decided to have a couple of our friends over for dinner and drinks. None of our friends had children, so after having our surprise baby, our social life dwindled. Our friends still loved Braxton, but hanging out with a kid wasn't exactly at the top of their list.

Setting up for our guests was so easy with Claire around. She helped Alicia make dinner while Braxton helped me set the table. After everything was ready, Claire took him upstairs for movie night.

Dinner, games, and a lot of drinks later, we started babbling about the "parent life". We began bragging about how amazing and nurturing Claire was, how it was so easy for her to fit into our family, and how much Braxton loved her. That led to our friends asking a lot of questions out of genuine curiosity: "Is it weird?" "How old is she?" "Where did you find her?"

Answering these questions should've been a breeze; Alicia and I had a talent of finishing each other's sentences. But as we both tried to describe Claire, we discovered that our answers weren't adding up.

I described Claire as a woman in her late-twenties who dressed homely and had blonde hair with fair skin. I had assumed that Alicia was the one that set up the interview with Claire. But I couldn't believe Alicia's description of Braxton's amazing nanny. Claire in her eyes was a woman in her mid-fifties, she had short brown hair and tan skin. She looked very well put together. Alicia then claimed that she thought that I had set up the interview with Claire.

The way my wife looked at me after comparing our nanny terrified me to the core. I am supposed to be the man and protector of my family, and I was sitting there in complete disbelief. I failed my family. Paralyzed, we were unable to process our discovery. How was this even possible? We turned our eyes towards our friends, their faces portraying skepticism and fear. Wondering if we were out of our fucking minds, we shot out of our chairs, Alicia and I followed quickly. We rushed as fast as we could upstairs to Braxton's room.

I flung his door open, they were both gone... Alicia immediately dropped onto the floor, sobbing and calling out to our baby boy. I wanted to comfort her, but I just couldn't. Our friends and I ran throughout the upstairs floor, checking all rooms, closets, and windows. There was no sign of them. We double-checked downstairs to see if there was a way Claire could've secretly escaped but still nothing. All windows and doors were locked. Nothing was missing, just Braxton and Claire. It was as if they disappeared into thin air.

We trusted Claire with our precious son. She had to have planned this, she had to. Gaining our trust, breaking down every guard we had just to snatch him at the perfect moment when we were at our most vulnerable. How did she escape unnoticed?

I fumbled frantically in my pocket, trying to pull out my phone to call the police. When they arrived, the police officers were stumped on how could this happen. There were no physical signs of an escape; the most we could do was file a report. Doing that just made us sound even crazier. None of our information for the police was valid, because we were describing two completely different people. They immediately assumed we were suspects. Honestly, I even began to question my own sanity.

Alicia continues searching for Braxton. Calling the police daily, waiting for information about Claire to surface. I'm just trying to hold onto my sanity, and grasp the fact that I had the world… and lost it to whoever – or whatever – Claire was.

The Mutt

Once upon a time, a guy fell in love with a girl. Two years of pure bliss, the guy decided to surprise the girl with a key to their brand-new condo, they moved in together living happily ever after. THE END... or so I wished. My life used to be perfect, but now, I sit here, alone.

My name is Doug. I lost my girlfriend, Emma, about a year ago; eleven months and fifteen days to be exact. That night was the biggest regret of my life.

October fifteenth was the day that I surprised Emma at work with the closing papers and the keys to our brand-new condo. She was a second-grade school teacher, so I got to surprise her while she was supervising lunch. The entire lunch room was cheering for us after I dramatically surprised her. Filled with excitement we packed up and moved in that day.

While we were moving our boxes around and unpacking, we couldn't help but be flirtatious with each other. Every time she passed by me, her fingertips would graze my back, sending chills throughout my entire body. I sometimes can still feel her fingertips ghosting along my skin. I miss her touch.

Moving everything had us working through the night. We had tired playful banter to keep us going. From what would go where and whether to get a cat or dog. Emma loved bringing up the pet discussion. She would hint how she wanted both. Emma was an animal lover; if she had it her way, she'd have a million random animals as her pets.

After a few weeks, we adjusted living together, and established our regular home routine. At night, Emma would sit on the couch and FaceTime her mom, lasting from fifteen minutes to an hour. I never minded it. I would enjoy a cigarette on the balcony while she chatted with her mom, afterwards, I would close all the curtains and make sure all the windows and doors were locked.

Our bedroom window faced the front of the building we lived in. It had a decent view. It wasn't as beautiful as the back-balcony view, but it was still nice. Through the front bedroom window, there was a main road and a sidewalk that was dimly lit by a streetlight. We had a dark shade to go over this window to ensure our privacy. That shade would be the last thing I closed before lying down.

We would lay down in bed around 9:30 every night. That time of night the streets were always quiet, sidewalk bare, the streetlight on, and maybe an occasional car would pass by. But there was one night I went to close the shade, and the quiet normal street looked different. The night sky looked like a starless black bottomless pit that swallowed the moon; the streetlight eerily illuminated one portion of the sidewalk, resembling a spotlight, and under that spotlight sat a dog. A large, mutt-looking dog with what I assumed to be dirt caked through its fur was sitting alone, staring at me. Not just in my general direction, but staring directly into my eyes. This mutt gave me an off-putting feeling, as if there was something he was waiting for. I pulled the shade down quickly, startling Emma. As I got into bed, she could tell I was a little shaken up. She curled her body into my chest and didn't overwhelm me with questions of what was wrong.

"I love you, Dougy," she whispered to me. Dougy... I used to always give her shit for calling me that, but in that particular time, it brought me comfort.

The next three nights, the dog was still there, frozen in place. I woke up numerous times throughout the nights to see if the damn thing would eventually run off. It never did. In the mornings, I would try to go for a run to see if I could scare it off, but that stupid mutt was always gone by the crack of dawn.

The fourth night was odd. When I looked out of our bedroom window, I expected to have the normal stare down with the mutt. But this time, there was no dog; there was a man in its place. He appeared to be a shorter, slender, homeless bum. His beard strangely resembled the dog's fur. Trying not to make eye contact, I nonchalantly snapped the shade shut. The way that bum looked put an uneasy feeling in my stomach. I lay in bed, restless. I wanted to get up and try to take my mind off these weird incidences, but there was no way I could do that without waking Emma. If I told her what I had been seeing, she would think I was just being paranoid, and laugh it off.

On night five, I wondered what was waiting for me out there. Man, dog, cat, woman... hell, it could even be all of them!

I put my cigarette out on the balcony and headed inside. I noticed that Emma wasn't sitting on the couch having her regular night conversation with her mother. This got my heart pounding, and immediately thoughts were running through my mind of every dreadful scenario I would find her in.

"Emma!" I desperately called out. I ran through the living room and through the kitchen, frantically looking for her.

"Bedroom, babe," she yelled out to me. Following the sound of her voice, I rushed to our room to see that Emma was staring out the window.

"Why aren't you talking to your mom?" I asked nervously.

"She's not feeling well. Mom texted me goodnight and that she'll call me tomorrow on my lunch break. Babe, come over here. Look at this," she said with her eyes glued to whatever was outside. I didn't want that fucking mutt or bum looking at my Emma the way they looked at me. *Please, let it be something stupid*, I thought to myself. My feet felt like the roots of a tree trying to be pulled from the soil as I dragged my them slowly out of fear to the window.

"Are you okay? Why are you so pale? Please tell me you aren't getting sick, too?" she questioned innocently, looking at me worried as I stood behind her. I took in a deep breath and swallowed, trying to think of an excuse.

"No, no, honey. I'm just exhausted," I replied. I looked out the window, fearful.

"Look at that dog! He looks so cold and helpless! We need to help him," she said. My eyes widened, feeling as if they popped right out of my head. I had to quickly come up with a liable excuse.

"No!" I blurted out, "He probably has fleas or even rabies!" She was instantly pissed at my reaction.

"Doug, that is a life out there that needs help, our help. How can you go to bed turning that poor pup away like that?" she argued, furrowing her eyebrows.

Trying not to be a dick about the situation, I thought to myself that I finally had the perfect excuse to figure out why this dog was staring like this without her thinking I was insane.

"Ok, I'll go get him," I sighed.

"You are an amazing man, Dougy, thank you," Emma murmured, kissing my cheek as I slipped on my robe. I kissed her lightly, barely brushing my lips across her forehead before I made my way to the door. If I had known that was the last time I'd ever get kiss her, I would've made it count. I should have made it fucking count!

My feet started feeling heavy again. What if this dog attacked me? What if the bum came back while I was still out there? I should've taken something to protect myself. Or would that have seemed threatening? Maybe it was just a normal dog? Whatever, fuck it.

I got to the street, I looked back at our window to see Emma just waiting there, looking like a kid on Christmas morning. She wanted a dog. Her face looked so cute, she was just incredible. Turning towards the dog, it continued to stare directly at me. My body trembled more and more with every step I took.

"Hey buddy, are you hungry?" I asked as calmly as I could. When I got within three feet of the mutt, it ran off. I contemplated running after it, but I decided that it was too cold, and I didn't want to make the effort. *He'll be back; fucker always came back*, I thought. As I stood under the streetlight and looked out into the darkness, I was suddenly at ease. The fear I had coming up to this mutt was so anticlimactic. It was almost comical that I, a grown man, was so afraid of a stray dog, for Christ's sake. I wondered if he was even staring at our window. Maybe I had just misinterpreted the stare. What was a staring mutt going to do anyways?

As I was about to head towards our building, I looked up at our window, expecting to see Emma, standing there. The peace I had felt drained from my body, as if shards of ice shot through my veins. I stood underneath the streetlight, there he was, standing at my own window. The bum. He winked at me, and suddenly, it was like I had tunnel vision; all I could think of was that I needed to run, and I sprinted as fast as my legs could carry me. I had to get to her.

"Emma! Emma! EMMA!" I screamed out disrupting the silent night. I mentally kicked myself for not grabbing a weapon. But I needed to get to her as fast as I could.

My lungs were burning by the time I sprinted to our bedroom, but it didn't matter. Since I was feeling lightheaded, I had to stop and rapidly blink away the black splotches that clouded my vision so I could focus. On our bed was Emma, dead. Drenched in blood, scratches all over her body, so deep as if a vicious beast used her as a toy, her throat looked like it had been torn out. That must be why I never heard any screams...

"NO! Where are you, you son of a bitch!" I demanded furiously. I ran all over the condo and searched everywhere.

Eventually, my rage subsided enough that I was able to fully process that Emma was gone, I felt a sob creeping in my throat. I ran back to her, the horrific scene forever embedded in my memory. I sat next to her and pulled her bloody, lifeless body into my arms. How could this have happened to such a loving, innocent, perfect woman. I was only gone for a couple of minutes! I brushed some of the hair that was matted to her face, and wiped the blood away from her forehead as I sobbed for my dear Emma, the love of my life.

I had to call the police. They needed to get here as soon as they could before that monster would get too far. When the police officers arrived, I sat on the couch, covered in Emma's blood. They checked everything and felt the need to ask me the same questions a million and one fucking times. I told them everything, from the first night I saw that fucking mutt to now. They needed to stop questioning me and go search for the bum!

"Look for the dog, too! He's connected to the bum!" I added, feeling numb all over.

"This is pretty cut and dry here. Take him down and get a confession," I heard one of the detectives say while I was still trying to explain to them every little detail I could remember. Appalled by his disgusting mindset, I felt myself snap. All I could see was red. I lunged at the detective and instantly got taken down and handcuffed. Thrown into the back of the squad car, they read me my rights and arrested me for attempting to assault that detective. None of them understood how crazy it was for them to even think I could harm Emma!

Sitting in the back of the car, I looked out the window, remembering her smile, her smell. That was when I saw it. That fucking bum was walking that mutt down the street! I screamed for the police officer that was with me to get him. He rolled his eyes at me and turned his back to me, completely ignoring my plea. As the officer started to drive, I looked back at the bum, and he winked at me! Just like how he winked at me right before he killed the love of my life! And that cop was taking *me* to jail and completely ignoring the real killer, who was walking free right in front of him!

They'll see. I'll be out and find that fucking monster and bring him to justice. For my Emma! That's the least she deserves! They'll see!

Eleven months and fifteen days later, I still sit here with all these psychotic fuckers around me. I'm not insane. I know what happened. I will find him. I will kill him and that mutt of his. For my Emma. I will be out soon, my love, I promise.

A Friend

The rumors around school about Lynn Grayson's suicide are starting to get out of control. I didn't know her very well. She was quiet and mostly kept to herself. I can't say I was either nice or mean to her. When I heard about her "incident", I felt sadder for her parents than I did for her. How can a girl kill herself a day before her eighteenth birthday? It just doesn't make sense; Lynn must have really hated herself.

I live on the same street she used to live on. While driving home in my mom's silver Escape and blaring my music, I'd always pass Lynn, who always walked with her head down. She had frizzy, mousey hair, and she would wear the same pair of skinny jeans and grey, zip-up hoodie every day. I almost wanted to invite her to my house and see if she wanted to borrow some clothes or, at the very least, let me try to help fix her hair. But I honestly never cared enough to actually try, so I would just drive by and avoid eye contact as much as possible instead.

The drive home from school today will be weird. I won't have to avoid Lynn anymore. Am I going to miss that? Taking pity on a girl I don't care to say anything to? That's fucked up. At least this will give me a chance to finally scope out her house without looking like a total creeper.

As I slowly drive by her house, I notice tire tracks from the driveway stretching to the street; the trash can is lying on the other side of the driveway, and the trash is spread out throughout the lawn. I couldn't help but park the car on the side of the road and intently stare at the trash. Maybe I could see something bloody? Or possibly a crumpled-up suicide note? Nah, that's stupid. Why would Lynn's parents throw something like that away? I turn down my music and roll down the passenger side window so I can thoroughly scan the trash, I hear a phone ding. Using the sound to guide my eyes, I find an iPhone among the spilled contents. A perfectly working iPhone just going off in the yard. That's strange. Whose phone is it? Could it be Lynn's? Should I...? No, that'd be awful... Screw it! I sprint out of my car, snatch the phone, and rush my ass straight home.

I arrive home, toss my mom's keys onto the counter and hurry up the stairs with the phone. I throw it on my bed and stare at it as curiosity continues to surge in my head... Is this Lynn's phone? Or maybe it belongs to one of her parents? There's only one way I can find out. Should I look through it? That would be so wrong to do. I should just take it down to my mom and have her give it back to Mrs. Grayson.

Fuck that. I can't return it just yet. I need to know! The phone is right there in front in me, so it'd be a waste not to peak through it, right? I sit on my bed, unlock the phone (luckily no passcode), and start scrolling through it. I quickly learn that the phone belonged to Lynn. Honestly, I'm a bit creeped out, because it's not every day that you hold a dead girl's phone but whatever. I find that there are zero contacts, no extra apps, and no call history. Hmm, that's odd. Next, I check out the text messages and find that there are only two conversations with two different numbers. I decide to open the one with the most texts and begin to read:

Unknown: *Happy early birthday, Lynn.*

Lynn: who is this?

Unknown: *A friend.*

Lynn: I have no friends

Unknown: *Now why is that, doll?*

Lynn: because.......

Lynn: because I don't want any

Unknown: *I know that can't be true.*

Lynn: how do you know me?

Unknown: *I live close by. I want to be your friend.*

Lynn: then tell me who you are

Unknown: *Now, where's the fun in that? Gotta guess!*

Lynn: I have no idea.....

Unknown: *Well, until you start guessing, let's talk. What are you up to?*

Lynn: watching a movie.... dreading my birthday

Unknown: *Why is that, doll?*

Lynn: my parents are trying to get me to do something with my "friends", but when I tell them no, they'll try to do something with me and tell me to invite a friend, and then they'll bring my cousin, who's 14.

Lynn: ... and to add to my pathetic life, my cousin even hates me... she thinks she's too popular for me.

Unknown: *Why aren't you popular?*

Lynn: I just have a lot of anxiety, and I'm just weird.... and that's ok, I guess.

Wow, that's sad, Lynn. That must suck that you had to talk to a stranger just to feel relevant.

Unknown: *So why don't you just fake sick?*

Lynn: yeah and then have my mom check on me every 2 seconds? I'm good.

Unknown: *I love this part of the movie. Poor Fern. She just wants to be loved.*

Lynn: are you watching Jawbreaker??

Unknown: *Yup! One of my favorites!*

Lynn: me too! that's so weird. I'm watching it right now, and I'm at the exact same part!!

Unknown: *Well, that's weird! See? Meant to be friends right here!*

Unknown: *=)*

Lynn: I still don't know who you are though......

Red fucking flag, Lynn! Block the number! Nobody even watches that stupid movie!

Unknown: *Ready to guess who I am?! :) You can ask a question, and then I'll ask a question! It'll be like a game! :) :)*

Lynn: still drawing a blank... are u a girl?

Unknown: *Getting warmer!!*

Lynn: ok... are you in high school?

Unknown: *Kind of... okay, my turn.*

Unknown: *Why do you have anxiety?*

Lynn: because I'm too afraid of rejection and failure. I can't even take a test in the classroom.

Unknown: *What's wrong with the classroom?*

Lynn: I get too scared... I don't want to be the last one to finish the test and have everyone wait for me to finish. they'll stare... so I go to an isolated room so I can take it.

Holy shit... I had no idea... I thought you were just special needs or something!

Unknown: *That sucks. Why don't you just kill yourself?*

Lynn: well that's fucked up for a FRIEND to say.

Unknown: *Do you at least like your new phone?*

Lynn: how did you know I got a new phone?

Unknown: *I told you I live close by :)*

Lynn: how close?

Unknown: *You should really clean out your trash can... It smells like ass in here.*

Lynn: what the fuck!!? who the fuck is this??

Unknown: *I already told you, doll. A friend :)*

Lynn: you aren't my goddamn friend!!! I'm going down to get my dad! you sick fuck!

Unknown: *Go ahead. Your dad's downstairs right now, cooking dinner. Hey! Wouldn't it be tragic if he had a little accident?*

Lynn: you have no control

Unknown: *How would you feel about having your father's blood on your hands? Would it make you want to kill yourself? Ooo! That sounds enticing!*

Lynn: NO! no friend of mine would stalk me and threaten to murder my dad and tell me to kill myself! Where are you?! Do you have cameras or something??

Unknown: *Okay, okay, no killing Dad... But let's play a game!*

Lynn: I don't want to play with you!! Leave me alone.

Atta girl! Wait... why am I cheering on a dead girl?

Unknown: *Watch your head, sweetheart. The peanut butter container is about to fall.*

Unknown: *LOL! Stop hiding in the pantry before your mom thinks you're crazy and has you committed!*

Lynn: ARE YOU FOLLOWING ME!?

Unknown: *In a way... Okay, game time. Who knows you better than yourself?*

Lynn: no one

Unknown: *Yes.*

Lynn: how is this a game??

Unknown: *It's a guessing game, doll. Check my text details... Look at my number.*

KNOCK, KNOCK.

"Jess? Did you put gas in my car?" Jesus Christ, my fucking mother!!

"Yes, Mom! Please leave me alone! I'm doing homework!"

Lynn: this isn't possible... how do you have the same number as me?!

Unknown: *Come on! Guess! That's the fun part!*

Lynn: how do you have the same fucking number?? this has to be a prank!

Unknown: *No prank, my dear.*

Unknown: *Now... back to killing yourself!*

Lynn: NO! I love myself! yeah, my life sucks now, but it'll get better! things can only get better

Unknown: *See, I wanted to believe that, I still want to believe that. But...*

Lynn: but nothing! just leave me alone!

Unknown: *I can't. I'm apart of you, Lynn.*

Lynn: NO! no part of me wants to do this. you don't scare me! I'm going back to my room and deleting this conversation. DO NOT TEXT ME AGAIN!

Unknown: *Bad idea, Lynn. You can't escape me.*

Lynn: hitting play on my movie. lying in bed. goodbye, you fucking psycho!

Unknown: *No, you're not.*

Lynn: what the fuck!? is this a suicide note!? I didn't write this! where did this come from!?

Unknown: *Now, do you want to choose how you do it, or do I have to?*

Lynn: no, please don't make me do this. I don't want to die.

Unknown: *Boohoo! You're going to make me choose. No fun!*

Lynn: just choose to leave me alone... I'll do better! I'll be more optimistic! don't do this to my parents! I do NOT want to die!

Unknown: *Just pick up the blade. Fade into the black. Join your other half, Lynn.*

Lynn: mom & dad, sorry, I love u guysyhjkm

Oh, my god! Who killed her?! Is she crazy?! Oh, my fucking GOD! I don't even know what to think right now...

Ding, ding. Who's trying to text me now?!

Unknown: *Hello, Jess.*

Jess: Who is this?

Unknown: *A friend =)*

A Lucid Dreamer

My name is Anne. I work as a journalist for my local town's newspaper. It's not my dream job, but it pays the bills. I have no children, and no man. It's just me and my dog, Izzy. Not having such a demanding, exciting personal life makes my work life much more difficult. My boss has me dedicate all my time to work. It literally consumes all my life, making it impossible to have a social life, but I guess I don't mind. It is what it is.

Having this lifestyle gives me the freedom to cover more intricate stories, so I'm not stuck with weather, horoscopes, or daily boring stories. I cover global issues, outlandish conspiracies, politics, etc. Today the boss man wants me to cover something that would be fun and appealing to our readers... the analysis of lucid dreamers. Yay...

I have always been what would be described as a 'lucid dreamer'. A lucid dreamer is a person that is aware that they are dreaming and can control what is going on in their dream unconsciously. Now, I'm not sure if I believe in all that mumbo jumbo. Dreams are dreams, and the reason they happen the way they do, is because of your own thought process, period. There is no rhyme or reason. People that focus on proving the supernatural, and "abilities" are just a joke to me. I control what I dream, period. Covering this story almost puts a bad taste in my mouth. I have no idea how I am supposed to write this article without being biased.

The local coffee shop is one of my favorite places to do my work. Other than being a coffee addict, I feel like I can get social time in just being around people. I walk around the coffee shop with my notes to get a feel of what one's interpretation of lucid dreaming means to them. Six out of ten people don't even remember their dreams, and the other four agreed that dreams are just dreams. Old memories that just replay while your imagination transforms it into something unrealistic. All people are different, so to think that one would have control of what they're dreaming is just imagination, no one has control over what they are dreaming, because the brain is asleep. When I mentioned lucid dreaming, they had no idea what I was talking about. This article is going to be an absolute waste of time.

Reaching out to authors who have who specialize in these topics, one contacted me. Her name was Mary. She has published quite a few novels about lucid dreaming, dream analysis, and many more about her claiming to be a medium and a palm reader. Mary's latest novel was about demonic possession. In my opinion, this woman must be out of her damn mind.

Mary had agreed to an interview with me for my article. Due to distance, we set up a conference call through skype. Which I was pleased with it because if I couldn't handle her ridiculous beliefs, then I could make it possible to 'lose connection'.

After doing all the necessary research, and outlining all the appropriate questions for Mary, I was ready for the interview tonight. Exhausted from preparing everything, I decided to lay on the couch with my dog, and take a nap.

Slipping into the dream world, I found myself walking through my home. This was new. I walked through my interpretation of what my house looked like. It was odd… everything was the same, aside from my work that I had spread out along my kitchen table. It wasn't what I had written… The words on all my notes, and post-it's was the same word written repeatedly, *STAY, STAY, STAY!!* The handwriting of each word seemed different, as if hundreds of people took turns writing. Feeling eerie, I justified to myself, it's just a dream. Don't be stupid, Anne.

Something dark moved in my living room out of the corner of my eye. Assuming I was dreaming of my dog, I looked over and saw my dog was sitting next to me, halfway under the kitchen table. *What the hell is going on right now?* I thought to myself. My bedroom door slammed, making my mind go blank. I had to shake this fear overcoming me. It was only a dream. *It's my mind, I control what's going on!* I stood in front of my bedroom door, and tried to steady my hand so I could grab the door handle. Grabbing it caused my ear to start vibrating uncontrollably, tickling my face. I took my hand off the handle and began to itch and shake my ear lobe. Suddenly, I realized what was causing this annoying irritation. I'm sleeping on my phone, it's my alarm, which means it's almost time for Mary's interview. I should wake up. I shut my eyes in my dream state, and felt my body waking up. Opening my eyes, I was back on my couch, I grabbed my phone from under my face to shut off the annoying alarm.

Grabbing a beer, I make my way to my bathroom to freshen up my appearance for Mary. I need to look professional rather than having bedhead, and drool crust along my cheek. I look like a complete train wreck with my eyeliner smeared down my cheek appearing as if I'm ready to be in the next Marilynn Manson video. I need to grab my makeup bag and fix this mess. Rushing to my room for my bag, I notice my door was shut... *Was my door shut before?* Being the only person that lived in my house, I always kept my doors open. I could see into every room in my living room and that made me feel safe being alone. I didn't have time to remember if I shut it, or if there was a burglar hiding in my closet. I opened the door, grabbed my bag, and moved on to the bathroom.

Chugging the last quarter of my beer I burp out the carbonation in my stomach, then click to call Mary.

"Hello Mary, it's nice to officially meet you, well, virtually," I chuckled, feeling a little buzzed.

"Hello Anne, lovely to meet you as well."

"So, if you're okay with it, I will be recording the interview to use as reference points for the article."

"Oh, that's fine, dear, I've been recorded, and interviewed numerous times in many ways. Do what you need to do. You have my consent."

"You are extremely famous in the nonfiction paranormal world and highly knowledgeable when it comes to the unknown. Now what is your interpretation of lucid dreaming?"

"Thank you, and why yes I am. And as for a lucid dreamer, it's someone who can travel throughout the dream world and understand that they are in this surreal setting that is in their complete control. They have the power to wake themselves up when they're ready."

"Why is it that only certain people can be 'considered' lucid dreamers?"

"Why do you say considered? There is no considering, one either is or is not a lucid dreamer." Mary's warm tone, instantly turned cold

"Same as mediums, correct?" I pushed further.

"I don't understand how mediums are relevant in such topic. But… yes same scenario."

"Do you claim to be a lucid dreamer the same way you claim to be a medium." I must not have slept as long as I should've because I was having too much fun pushing her buttons.

"Yes. Anne, I don't claim to be, I am what I say I am. I figured a fellow lucid dreamer would be a little more open-minded when discussing this subject." Mary's voice was flat, as if I shouldn't be surprised by her statement.

"I'm going to take that as an assumption. By definition, yes, I am 'considered' to be a lucid dreamer, but I know it's all rubbish." My hands started to sweat. I had the feeling she was looking right through me. Mary could tell I was getting nervous.

"I have never been interviewed by someone with such stubbornness as yourself. I want to believe that you don't believe, but from your last dream, I know you're really beginning to question it. Why don't we continue this interview another time, when you aren't so shaken up?

Better yet, how about when you figure out what 'stay' means. Don't forget to keep all your doors open. Talk with you soon Anne." Mary smiled at me through the screen as if she won some kind of debate, then hung up on me.

"Wait, Mary!" I tried redeeming myself by apologizing, but I failed horribly. I can't blame her hanging up on me, I would too if some cunt was talking to me like that.

I've got to be nicer. Being social was never one of my strong points... that's why I'm a writer. Only thing I hate about journalism is that sometimes I must attempt an interview... I'll try to skype her back. I should apologize for my lack of professionalism. Making two failed attempts to skype her back, I gave up. I'll work from home tomorrow and research a little bit more. Having an opened mind, more knowledge, and less sarcasm might help.

I closed my computer, ignoring the mess, and plopped on my couch. I turned on my TV, but watched nothing. My mind couldn't escape the things that Mary had said to me... how did she know the word 'stay' was in my dream?

Waking up this next morning, I skip the coffee and crack open a beer. I check my phone, 1:07 P.M. Holy shit, I haven't slept in that late since I was a teenager. Looks like I'm a no call-no show for work today, but looks like my breakfast is a little more acceptable. Calling work, I went on explaining that the details of this article were a little more complicated to put together, getting caught up in it, my concept of time had completely fell by the waist side. I pretty much fed them whatever bullshit excuse that would get me off the hook.

Okay, so I'm not some kind of alcoholic, I had a rough night last night. My dream last night played out the exact same way as the dream I had during my nap yesterday. I kept reassuring myself that it's all a dream. It had to be Mary's fault... Saying that last night's dream was the same as the nap dream, is kind of a lie. Not having my phone to alarm me that I needed to wake up wasn't stopping me from opening my bedroom door... I did open my bedroom door! And what I found sent chills down my spine.

I was annoyed with Mary, she was the reason why I was redreaming this. Normally controlling what happens in my dreams is a 'gift' I have. This time I couldn't and it must have been a mental block from Mary. That mind fuck she played on me got my head all messed up. Opening that door to prove her wrong was my biggest mistake... I saw a huge black bulky figure standing in front of me. It had white eyes... looked to be about eight feet tall. It slowly lifted its arm, and pointed at me. Belting out the loudest scream my body would allow, I was able to wake myself up...

Five beers later, I call Mary.

"I've been waiting for your call, Anne. A lot sooner than expected. Did you figure out what stay meant yet?"

"What the fuck was that thing? How did you know about the word stay? You can't be a real medium, Mary." Skepticism still bordering my questions.

"Honey, I'm not a fake. I don't know what you're looking for, but all I can say is if you want real answers. Get serious, and stop questioning what you don't understand. Ask the right questions, Anne."

I reach in my fridge for my sixth beer. I need a little more alcohol in my system if I'm going to listen to this shit. "Okay, I don't know what 'stay' means, but I did see what was in my bedroom." Mary let out a sigh of relief. I think she was relieved that I wasn't going to fight her on this.

"This 'thing' you saw in your bedroom was something considered to be a watcher. All black, tall and white eyes?" My first reaction was wanting to lie to her, but I knew Mary would look right through it. Plus, when I'm drunk I have absolutely no filter.

"Yeah! Did you plant that in my dreams with your mind tricks?" I said, hoping this was all fabricated

"Anne, come on. Don't play games. Do you want help?" Mary replies, becoming annoyed

"Yes."

"Every lucid dreamer has what is called a watcher. They follow the dreamer to keep everything in the dream world… let's say running smoothly. A lucid dreamer is never actually supposed to see their watcher. They're very good at making their presence unknown to the dreamers they are assigned to. But yours revealed himself to you, purposely… and has made contact with you."

"He never touched me."

"Maybe not physically Anne, but he successfully sent you a message. It's almost impossible for watchers to speak to their dreamers. He broke the rules."

"So 'watchers' can talk to us, but it's just against their rules? Who sets the rules?"

"That I don't know… I've never gotten deep enough into the lucid dream world to find out everything. But I have been able to keep a conscious eye in the dream realm. That is how I knew Anne."

"How was it able to contact me?"

"That I don't know… All I do know is that your watcher is adamite about keeping you in his realm."

"Well, what the fuck am I supposed to do about that? Just never sleep?!"

"No… figure out why. I can help you if you want Anne. If you trust me."

"I need to go… I can't process this bullshit right now."

"It's not bullshit Anne! It's real, and if you don't deal with this head on, I'm afraid that- "

Click. This is bullshit! How in the hell am I supposed to expect this to be real? So, I have a 'watcher' that isn't allowed to talk to me or reveal himself to me. But… he did, and now I must trust this woman who may or may not be a huge fake! This is just too much. Why does this have to happen to me? What if I never got this article assigned to me? Oh well… it did. So, I must either never sleep again, or I should deal with this. Obviously, I know what I need to do… I just wish there was another way.

All night I stayed up writing my article, emailed it to the editor, and then emailed my boss saying I'm using my three-week vacation starting now. I have never taken vacation before, I always just racked up my days for when I'd really need them. Mary is so far away… but I'm going to fly out to her… figure out how to get rid of this watcher or turn off this lucid dreaming shit.

Calling Mary was extremely difficult. I was on thirty-eight hours of no sleep, and feeling uneasy about the situation, I decided to bite the bullet and get it over with. Mary was very persistent about coming to me rather than me flying to her. I told her I had no problem traveling… and in all honesty, my house was beginning to freak me out. However, Mary stressed that I need to stay in my own environment. She explained that dreaming in my house gave me control. I can't go in blind with zero understanding of my surroundings. If I'm going to face my watcher, I need to have every advantage I can.

Mary was able to book a flight and get to me in eleven hours. Seeing her face to face was almost a joke. I couldn't believe this is what my boring life has come to. One day I'm complaining about having zero social life. Now I'm teaming up with a medium to enter a lucid dream world and take on what could possibly be a supernatural being that is getting ready to beat my ass.

I was trying to be all host-like for her, so I cleaned up my place, set out finger foods, supplied the spare bathroom with plenty of toiletries, and got the spare bedroom together. I figured small talk would take place, but I was highly mistaken. When Mary arrived, she dropped her duffle bag, and kept her bookbag on her back.

She walked over to my kitchen table, slammed her bag down, and said, "well are you just going to stand there? Or are you ready to do this?" Having no idea what she meant when she said, "do this", I knew not to respond or ask questions. There was something about the way Mary held herself that I can't describe. She was under control, the uneasy feeling left my body. I felt as if she were my mom or some type of fairy godmother that was ready to fix everything. For some reason, Mary had my absolute trust. I was ready.

I sat down ready to go with whatever she was about to throw at me. Mary started emptying her bookbag. Sitting there silently, I didn't offer to help. I just watched and waited for her to give me instructions.

Mary set up a voice recorder and a tall, red candle. Lighting the candle on my table, she started chanting in another language. The moment she finished her chant the flame of the candle went black. She looked to me.

"Are you ready?" Mary asked. As if it was more of a demand.

"Yes, what do I have to do?" I was barely able to get the words out.

"This candle is your safe spot from any harm you are about to experience. When it gets too much for you, I want you to run to this candle and blow it out. This will wake us both."

"Wake us both?"

"Anne, I'm going to have you lay down on the couch and enter the dream realm. I will be in a meditative state by the candle. Now I can't walk this with you, but what I can do is guide you with my sight and with my voice. It'll sound like an echo, so I need you to pay close attention to my words. I will be seeing with you through your eyes. Can you do this?"

This can't be happening... I shook my head, stood up from the table, clapped my hands, and yelled, "Yes". Mary nodded her head to me and gestured to the couch. There's my que. As I laid down, she sat at the table like she said she would, but her next instructions were difficult.

She slowly whispered, "Close your eyes, Anne. Now focus on your breathing... breathe with me." I was terrified... what if I breathe wrong and that fucks up the entire process?

"Clear your mind Anne, it's easier to breathe if you aren't letting your mind run so crazy." Wow... she's already in my head. "Concentrate Anne!" I snap my eyes shut and start breathing. The only way I can clear my mind is if I count... You'd think it'd be easy for me to sleep, since it's been days since I've slept. One, two... three...

"Anne, hear my voice." Mary screams. Barely able to hear her.

"Am I here?" I said, frozen.

"Yes, open your eyes."

Once I open my eyes, I see that I'm in a depressing version of my home. Written all over the walls, is the word 'stay'.

"Mary... What does this mean?"

"I don't know, but I promise we'll figure it out. I need you to call out to him Anne."

"How?"

"Let your guard down, feel as vulnerable as you can. Think of something that makes you feel safe, and then I need you to say, 'watch me'. Can you do that?"

When have I ever felt safe? The only time I've felt safe and comfortable was in my dreams. I controlled everything in my dreams; none of it was real ... Now it's the place I feel the least safe in. I have no control. This is impossible.

"Anne, there's no place you feel... Wait a minute... do not move."

"I can't do it! I'm going to the candle!"

"NO! He's coming to you. Stay put."

"Fuck you! I can't!"

My skin starts to crawl as if there are a million maggots under my skin. I can feel him getting closer to me. Trying to be fearless, I tried to look out of the corner of my eye. He's just... standing there, pointing his finger at me. Same as the last time. I get the strength to turn towards him and Mary cuts into my thought process.

"Don't speak!" Mary whispers to her.

"I have to." I say through my teeth, "What do you want from me?"

"I am your watcher." The voice so deep and muffled.

"Why are you messing with me?"

"You need to stay here Anne."

"No! I belong in the real world. I don't want to be here anymore so just leave me alone."

"I can't. You don't understand. You need to stay here. Open your eyes and look at me."

"You're a liar! Leave me alone! I'm leaving now."

"Don't, Anne, you will regret it!"

I open my eyes and sprint as quick as I can to my safety candle. Suddenly Mary's voice is so loud, screaming at me. "Anne! You need to stay! I'm blowing out the candle!" Betrayer! She was working with this watcher the whole fucking time. She set this whole thing up! Punishing me for not being a believer! No fucking way! I will beat this! I will beat her!

"Fuck you, Mary! I'm not going to stay trapped in your stupid illusion!"

"Anne, listen to Mary. You need to stay."

"What the fuck do you mean?! I'm not staying!"

Standing by the candle, I hear Mary yelling, "Anne! it's... don't do it! You need to stay! It's not safe! This is your only way-" I chuckle... What a performer! I look to the watcher and boldly say to him "Fuck you." I blew out the candle. I felt my mind gravitating back to my body. I lay there with my eyes closed. I take a minute to catch my breath, prepping to get this bitch out of my house. I open my eyes. I... see a man standing over my body. Trying to get up he whispers to me, "Time to die." He stabbed me in the chest over and over. The pain at first is excruciating, but then fades to a cold numb feeling as my senses shut off.

After what I can only assume is death, I now find myself sitting in a white chair, in an all-white room. Looking down at myself, my body looks unharmed. Is this heaven? Hell?

I paused for a slight second, then yelled, "that bitch had someone fucking kill me!"

"I told you to stay Anne," the Watcher's voice, seeming like it came from all around me.

"Watcher... how are you here?"

"I told you to stay... You could've stayed in our world."

"Where am I? How did you guys plan this?"

"Anne... Mary didn't plan this. She didn't see it coming... I did. There was a break-in, you and Mary were murdered."

"I don't believe you. This is a mind trick."

"No trick, Anne. You had so much potential. You could've stayed with me. Safe. Now dear... You're, as you would say, fucked."

"What are you talking about?!"

"Goodbye, Anne."

"What did I do to deserve this?!"

My Watcher said nothing. I felt long, cold hands wrap around my ankles. Before I could scream, the arms pulled me from behind, slamming my body into the marble feeling, white floor. I choked out, "is this hell?"

The Watcher's voice had a subtle demonic change in its tone, "you could say that, Anne."

I don't know where I am, or what I'm meant for. I don't know what potential I had, or what I've done to deserve this after-life. But... moral of my story, *stay.*

Killer Boyfriend

"Why does it have to be 90 degrees today of all days?" Maggie complained to herself wiping the melted eyeliner from under her eyes, and fanning her armpits. "It always makes everything reek!" Today was a special day for her, she was finally going out on a date with her life-long crush Jake. Maggie has had her eye on Jake ever since he moved across the street from her ten years ago, they had grown up as childhood friends, going through all the awkward kid stages together. Always trying to ask him out, Maggie could never deliver. She never wanted to ruin the friendship... eh, that was a cop out. Her real reason was that she feared rejection. No one ever told her no. Maggie always got what she wanted. So, having Jake, the one boy who meant everything to her, say no would absolutely devastate her.

As Maggie stands in front of her closet, giddy about picking out the perfect outfit for her perfect date with the perfect guy, she couldn't help but replay the way Jake asked her out. Grabbing her third outfit to test out, her thoughts couldn't help but spill out of her mouth. Maggie turns to her cat on the bed, laying under the covers, "Butters, you've got to hear this one more time! He is so handsomely and perfectly clever, Ah! I'm just too excited!"

She plops right next to Butters. "Okay, so you know how I always like to sit in my car and set up my playlist for the drive to work? Well Tuesday, same routine... Picking songs, just minding my own business and then SLAM!" Butters gave no reaction to Maggie's sudden surprise shout. "UGH! You're no fun! Anyways, I freak out! I look behind me and I see nothing. Check to see if I was still in park, and there he was! That asshole scared the living shit out of me. I couldn't even roll my window down before catching my breath! Then I hear his beautiful voice. Every time that beautiful face starts talking, I just clench up, Butters!"

Jake waved almost embarrassed, blushing and trying to generate enough spit to swallow down his dry throat. Choking out from what he assumed were words, he said "H-hey, sorry about that..." Maggie was a little taken back. Why was he apologizing? He always played little jump scare pranks on her without even a light hearted sorry. "So... any plans for the last weekend before school starts?" Jake asked, fiddling his toes in his sandals, and his hands digging in his cargo shorts.

"Um," Maggie said, confused, "Nope! I'm actually off work this weekend."

Jake perked up a little bit more, and gained a sterner tone. "I would like to take you out this weekend. If you want?" She was still confused.

"Um, okay? What are we going to do? I don't want to go bowling. We did that twice last week." He realized she didn't get it. He needed to elaborate. Why was this so hard for him? It's just Maggie. He's known her for ten years... He's loved her for ten years. He bided his time, so this should be nothing.

"I meant on a date, Mags..." Stunned, Maggie's hearing became clouded, and butterflies began to manifest in her stomach. This was really happening. She couldn't believe her perfect guy was finally asking her out. "Mags?" Not realizing she had never answered him, her throat closed at the same time... Her heart fluttering like a hummingbird, she was able muster up a fast head nod that looked as if she was convulsing. Clearly, Jake took that as yes, grinning from ear-to-ear, he exclaimed, "okay! I'll meet you outside Friday at seven! See-ya!" Running off, both of their hearts were beating with excitement. What seemed like a simple teenage date meant so much more for Jake and Maggie.

"Ah... I just love the way he asked me! Perfect story for our future grandchildren! Don't judge me, Butters! A girl can dream!" Maggie stands up and tries on her third outfit: a pair of overall shorts with a white tank underneath and her lucky red chucks. Fluffing her hair and reapplying her deodorant, she was finally ready. Checking her phone, it was one minute until seven. "Shit! I'm going to be late! Don't give mom too hard of a time, Butters! Love you!" Running down the stairs, she knew, after tonight, she would have Jake's heart forever.

"Later, Mom! Love you!"

"You look so pretty, Maggie Renae! Don't do anything I wouldn't do! Be home by curfew! Hey! Have you seen Butters? He hasn't eaten his food I set out for him."

"UGH! Mom, you're obsessed! He's sleeping in my bed! Goodbye!"

"Bye, Hun! Tell Jake I said -"

Maggie knew what she was about to say. She wasn't about to waste another second inside that house knowing Jake would be out there waiting for her. She walked down to the edge of her driveway where Jake was waiting for her. Feeling timid, she wasn't sure if she should say something first.

"You look beautiful," Jake interjected, breaking the awkward silence.

"You look cleaner than usual." She gracefully slipped in a wink after her little jab of a compliment... And there it was, his million-dollar smile. "So, what are you wanting to do tonight?"

"I was thinking we could have a proper date. Dinner and a movie?" Jake asked.

"Sounds perfect. Since neither of us had to travel too far, which car are we taking?"

"Um. uhh…." he stammers in place.

"Let's just keep this real old school. Phones on silent and take the gentleman's car." Maggie felt so clever.

"S-sure, yeah, that'll be alright. I set reservations and already bought our movie tickets, so we don't need to check show times or wait to sit down to eat. So, we have to just pay attention to the clock."

"Well then let's get going then!"

Jake held out his arm to clasp along with hers. Maggie's mind started racing. She just pictured being an outsider seeing them as a couple. The reverse Barbie and Ken. Maggie with her long black hair, olive tone skin complimenting her hipster outfit. Jake wearing a nice pair of gray shorts with a maroon V-neck and his black vans. She always loved seeing him in maroon; it made his eye color look grey and even complimented his brassy blonde hair. They looked perfect together.

He opened the car door… more nervous than usual. "My lady…" Blushing uncontrollably, Maggie slipped inside the passenger seat. The car had a nasty odor. Almost as if something was rotting.

"You leave your socks in here, buddy? It smells like ass in here." Jake shut the door and ran to the driver side and hopped in.

"Sorry! I must have left my work shoes in here… They have grease all over them from the fryer! We can take your car if you'd like!"

"No, it's fine… I was just messing around." She laughed only partially kidding. "We're already in, and I don't want to ruin your schedule. Hey! Your phone on silent?"

"Yup!"

"So, where are you taking me this evening, sir?"

"Surprise... You'll see."

"What if I don't like it?"

"Mags, I've known you for years. Give me some credit."

Maggie's mind started going a mile a minute, wondering if this is was the real deal. *What's going to happen tonight? What if I don't like what he chose? Is this going to be a deal breaker, should I lie or give him a second chance? One step at a time.* She took a breath and whispered again into her chest. "Just breathe, Mags."

"We're here." Jake pulled his little white Camry into the parking space, turned off the car, and leaned towards her. She closed her eyes, too nervous to see what he had picked. "Since you hate surprises, it's that little Italian place that makes your favorite shrimp alfredo."

"Wow, you really do know me."

"Yup, don't underestimate your best friend. Let's go." Opening the car door, he grabbed her hand. That was when Maggie noticed the dark red dirt under his fingernails.

"Did you cut yourself?"

"No, why?"

"Your nails?"

"Oh, nothing. Must have picked an old scab I didn't realize I had. Hurry, it's so hot out here, I need some AC." Taken back by his demeanor, Maggie just pushed it out of her mind and figured he picked an embarrassing zit or something. She smirked to herself. Jake could do anything, and she would find it to be absolute perfection.

Being seated in their little romantic booth, they were served their drinks and their appetizer. He ordered mozzarella sticks and Dr. Pepper for her. Before Maggie could even acknowledge his awesome pre-ordering skills, he stood up.

"I have to go to the bathroom!" Jake announced abruptly. *Shit, shit, fuck. I must have embarrassed him. He's a guy!*

Of course, he's not going to check every little detail on him! Especially his fucking nails! Please don't ruin this date! Just be nice, she thought.

"Okay, sorry. Had to wash my hands," Jake said, returning to the table.

"You are totally fine, hun." *HUN?! Now I'm his mom?! Shut up!*

"You like the appetizer and drink? I pre-ordered so we don't have to wait forever... you know since curfew and all. I wanted to give us enough time for after the movie."

"You don't have curfew," Maggie responded, confused.

"But you do."

"I'm not surprised that you've got my food and drink down, but I am surprised you FINALLY remember I have a curfew!"

"Hey, I can't help that it slips my mind sometimes."

"Funny how it slips your mind only when my curfew isn't convenient for you." Maggie flicked her straw wrapper at him while he flirted back with a sly wink. After eating their favorite meals and splitting a piece of chocolate raspberry cake, they were ready for the check. Small talk for their first official date was at its finest. "Man, I can't even finish everything. I'd hate to see it go to waste," Maggie belted out in a burping voice. Jake smiled as if that was the cutest thing he'd ever seen her do. Then a flush of paleness flooded his face. He began to blink uncontrollably.

"Well, I can ask for a box if you want?" he offered.

She was so confused with his drastic mood changes. Nervous or happy, Jake needed to pick one. "Thanks, that'd be great."

"Hey, ma'am?" Jake waved at the waitress standing a couple tables down from them, "May we please have a couple of boxes?"

The waitress smiled, "Right away."

Maggie scrunched her eyebrows. "You know they always say right away, and it ends up taking a half hour!"

"Yeah... but the food is worth it, right?"

"Right, hey, are you OK?"

"Yeah, why?"

"You just seem off... that's all."

"Well I am taking out the most beautiful girl in town. So, what'd you expect?"

"It's just me, Jake... But I can relate... I am on a date with the most handsome guy in town." They both gazed into each other's eyes, forming smiles when all the sudden Maggie thought of the perfect question.

"So... What is one thing you've always wanted to do, but you were too scared to actually do it?"

"Well... I already did it tonight... You ever get so excited and want something so bad, it just happens without even consciously deciding?"

"Yes."

"That feeling after... The satisfying thrill... the enjoyment, such a rush, best decision I ever made."

Maggie knew he was talking about her. She was filled to the brim with butterflies. Thinking of how to respond to such an amazing compliment, the waitress popped up with the boxes. She dropped them on the table then rushed off. "I think she realized she was interrupting something." Jake chuckled.

"What a bitch. Still doesn't give her the right to just throw them down like that. Let's just pack up the food and go. I don't want you tipping that snobby asshole." He couldn't help but laugh out loud at Maggie. Every time some stranger was rude, she couldn't help but go off to herself and the ones around her about respect and manners.

"I love when you get like this," he said.

"Well I don't. She's lucky I am on the perfect date, or else I'd be following her ass all the way to the back to call her out in front of everyone she works with."

"Perfect date?" he jokingly asked.

"Um. yeah... so far so good..." Maggie responded nervously.

"Well then let's escape out of here so we aren't tempted to ruin our perfect date."

"Agreed."

Getting back in the car, Maggie couldn't help but blurt out. "It actually would be the perfect date if we took my car. I'm sorry, your car is just getting worse by the minute! Phew!"

Jake blushed then snapped back at her in a joking manor, "Well I'm a guy, what do you expect? Why do you think we always take your car?"

"Because mine is clearly nicer in every aspect," she flirts back.

"Whatever you say, babe. Just throw the food in the back. We're going to be late thanks to the waitress."

"What movie are we seeing?"

"Finding Dory."

"I've been wanting to see that!"

"I know. Seriously Mags…"

"I know, I know, don't underestimate the best friend."

Getting into the movie, Jake got all her favorite snacks and pop. Maggie was so full that the pure thought of food should've made her sick, along with Jake's greasy car smell on her clothes. However, she couldn't help but splurge on every movie snack they had. The date was pure bliss. Maggie got her favorite foods, snacks, and now seeing a movie with her best friend (and hopefully soon-to-be boyfriend).

Halfway into the movie, Jake had to excuse himself. Maggie would've been worried and followed him, but she just couldn't. She had been dying to see this movie. She didn't think much of it. Engrossed in the movie, Maggie had realized when the credits screened that Jake wasn't back yet. "No fucking way…" Furious, she grabbed her things. Power walking out of the theatre, she passed the bathrooms. There he was, out of breath and rushing out of the bathroom.

"Maggie, I am so sorry. That Italian sausage did NOT agree with me."

"It's okay, I'd be pissed if it was just any other movie. Don't do that again, though."

"I'm sorry, I would've text you, but I left my phone in the car… no distractions, remember?"

"Me too." Her anger immediately disappeared, and they were back on with their perfect date. Holding hands while they walked through the parking lot, Jake started pulling her slightly to the left.

"We parked over here," she said.

"No, we didn't it. My car's right here, Mags."

"Oh, I swear we parked by the light pole with all the gum on it."

"Nope, come on. Time for the last surprise!" He rushed her back to his car. As she got in, the smell had escalated to an absolute disgust.

"If we are going anywhere together again, I swear. We will never take this damn car again. I don't even want my leftovers anymore."

"If you say so," Jake chuckled. He pulled up to the town's public playground. It was so romantic at night. The trees bordered the park, blocking the town and making them feel like the only two people in the world.

"Why are we here?" Maggie asked nervously.

"I thought maybe we could end the night playing our favorite… swing jumping wars. Remember?" After he replied, she let out a huge sigh of relief. Which was a little alarming to her. Was she nervous?

After playing a couple of rounds, Jake ran out to his car to roll the windows down, and air it out for the sake of Maggie's nose. Sitting alone, she began to feel edgy... Something seemed off with Jake but she just couldn't quite put her finger on it. It wasn't nerves. She knows how he is when he was nervous. No, something felt wrong... especially in his body language.

"Car is airing out for you."

"Thanks, come sit with me."

They held hands as they swung back and forth with each other. Maggie couldn't find any words. Jake just sat there, dazed, like he was lost in worry and thought.

"Jake?" *Crack, Crack, Crack.* They both shot back, looking towards the woods. "What was that, Jake?"

"I don't know. It sounded like someone was stepping on sticks."

"More like crushing branches! What if it's Bigfoot?"

"Come on, Maggie... That's just idiotic."

"Let's go check it out!"

"No." Before Jake could continue with the reasons of not going, she pulled the lanyard that carried his keys out of his pocket and ran for his car. "What are you doing?" he yelled, chasing after her. She was so much faster than he was.

"I want to check it out. I'm getting the first aid flashlight out of your trunk! The one our moms gave us after we got our cars. It'll be perfect! Grab our phones!"

"MAGGIE, NO!!"

As she flung open the trunk, Jake came to a halt. Maggie couldn't believe her eyes… It was their neighbor, Mrs. Holtan. Suddenly, it all clicked for her. The behavior, the parking, the *smell*.

"You killed Mrs. Holtan?"

"Yes, but just let me explain."

"Are you going to kill me next?"

"Of course not, Mags! I could never hurt you! Please, just get in the car. Let me explain myself. It's eleven-thirty, and I should get you home soon. Please just hear me out."

"Okay."

"Okay? Yes, Okay!" Jake jumped to get her door on the passenger side, handing her phone and his keys to her to make her feel more comfortable. "I didn't want you to see that."

"Why?"

"Because dead bodies are disgusting. The way they stare at you…"

"No, why'd you, do it? Why her? Why not me?" Maggie asked stunned, just staring at the dashboard.

"You know how at dinner, you had asked me what I've always wanted to do? Well, I've had this… need… well, more like a hunger… Monday night, I saw Mrs. Holtan drinking on her back porch, smoking her secret cigarettes that she hides from her husband, and…"

"Why were you in her yard?"

"I was walking back from here. I come here a lot and stare into the woods... I've been dealing with this for a long time... I normally can calm myself down, but seeing her hide out in her yard, I just knew it was a sign. The perfect moment... I just ambushed her... Crushed the bones in her neck... She didn't bleed until I put her into my trunk. Her body just threw up blood. Which made the smell worse. I-"

"So, you killed her Monday and then asked me out the very next day?"

"I just felt so alive, Mags. I finally grew the courage."

Maggie was in utter disbelief. She was trying to wrap her head around the situation when she heard her phone vibrating over and over. She was getting an assembly line of texts from her Mom. Glancing down she read the first three.

Where are you?

Come home.

Maggie please.

Her phone started to ring. It read "Mom". She ignored it. Jake was still talking, trying to explain and justify what he did. He looked at her, complete terror covering his face.

"A-are you going to tell anyone?" Before she could answer, she gets a few more texts. As Maggie went to check her phone, Jake choked out one last plea, "I wish you could understand Maggie... Please try to understand..." Maggie said nothing, her face still blank. She peeked at her phone.

Mom:

Maggie, I found Butters.

You are absolutely sick!

He's torn to pieces!

Come home now!!

Maggie, I am going to call the police!

ANSWER YOUR FUCKING MOTHER!!!!

Maggie grew a haunting grin across her face. She looked over to Jake who looked like he was about to be sick. She went in and kissed his beautiful, pale lips.

"I completely understand, my love," she whispered.

Clinic

Just a taste, just a taste is all I need. Then I'm done. For good. I'm done. But how am I supposed to be done? How am I going to differentiate what is real or not? It's like a medicine. My medicine. I need my fucking medicine. How am I supposed to save lives if I don't save myself? I'm calling Rosa, she will help me. Where's my phone? I can't find anything, these bottles clanking are driving me insane. God damn, it's so dark in here. Do I really live in this shit hole?

These days... everything is either clear or hazy. What if it's all hazy? What if this is all just a dream? Fuck, I'm getting too deep. Where's my phone? I've got to call Rosa.

Six rings... "Damn it, pick up!"

"What Doctor Marshall?"

"Rosa, please."

"No, I can't keep doing this.

"Then tell me, tell me I'm better than this *NURSE, ROSA*!"

"..." She says nothing.

"ROSA"

"I'll be in at noon. I have a meeting with my kid's teacher. Wait until noon."

She hangs up before I can even say goodbye. God, what a bitch. So back and forth, What a joke. Fuck, it's 8:30 AM, I'm going to be late.

No time to shower. Find your keys and go. I Smell like a brewery, but no one will notice. That place smells like an infectious shithole with rotting bile everywhere. Hah, what a privilege to be working at such a classy establishment.

I'm walking slow this morning, wondering what the day will entail... coughs and colds that never tangibly exist, prescribing pain meds to nonexistent pain. This condemned clinic in the middle of Chicago is like a squatting watering hole for the pathetic homeless, and I am their water awaiting to quench their thirst. Fucking losers.

All I can think of is overdosing them purposely... It'd be too easy. Watching them slowly disintegrate into nothing but carcasses, empty lifeless shells buried deep, molding inside the ground. There is something majestic about seeing life slowly leave the body... I wonder what it'd be like to watch a body fully decompose naturally. The smell, the beauty, hmm, what a wonder.

It's extra windy today. I need to open my coat up, hopefully the cold breeze can clear out this wretched stench that is my life. I need to at least put some effort into remaining superior to these scum bags.

Walking into what I call 'work', the same damn thought passes through my mind every single time. This place is so fucking depressing. As soon as you walk in, your eyes need a minute to adjust to the yellow, dim lighting. It's almost like stepping into an alternate reality... Brown walls that are slowly fading into a green, tan slum. How is that even possible? There are these appalling off white chairs in the waiting room. You couldn't pay me to sit in those things. Not even natural light can spruce this place up. I walk through the clouded glass doors, which clearly shows that it's been at least twenty years since they've been touched by a cleaning rag.

Normally doctors entering work go through the back, avoiding their patients for as long as they absolutely can. I personally like to walk through the front entrance to see the pathetic lives before me. It's like my coffee, sort of a breath of fresh, stale... sad air that boosts me. Sick you might think, but everyone has their own quirks.

As I slowly walk through, looking at the damage for the day, I see straight ahead... reception. Beckett... Eighteen-year-old aspiring doctor. Really wanting to make a difference. Top of his graduating class. Why does he looks up to me? I will never understand.

The long oval desk at the back of the waiting area stands so high that all I can see are his little eyes, wide and bright, peeking out at me, waiting for me to bestow wisdom upon him. Poor kid... I literally have nothing to offer him, except don't practice medicine. This career is worse than any addiction out there. It promises you the world, then you find yourself reaching your peak, then sitting there with all this knowledge and your thumb up your ass, doing the same old song and dance repeatedly. Not to mention, you are physically and emotionally sicker than your patients. Strung out to your whit's end for people who just selfishly want nothing from you but to have you 'fix' their problem. Sucks the fucking life right out of you, isolates you. Why did I hire him? Kid is wasting his life. He could have a normal job, wearing an amusing uniform, at some teenage hot spot with better pay and all his friends. But no. Beckett is here, always with a copy of my article... *My* article. From when I was a God. Best medical surgeon of all time... pushing the limits. Saving lives. Fuck. Too depressing.

"Hey Beckett, how are you doing this morning?" I attempt small talk.

"G-good sir... um, how are you, do? Doing? Good morning... hi." Beckett said Nervously.

"Hah, just another day, man. What's the schedule looking like so far?"

"Um, um let me see..."

I'm going to fuck with him. "Come on son, there are thirteen people here. I hired you to know things, not to make me wait."

Beckett flashes his big brown eyes at me. His eyes lose all sense of hope and his tear ducts begin to fill, ready to spill with the slightest blink.

"I'm so sorry, sir, I dropped the ball sir. I'm so, so sorry, um we have-"

Okay, I can't keep doing this. This is the seventh morning in a row. Kid just isn't that quick.

"Calm down, Beck, I'm just kidding."

His eyes drop as he gasps for air. I can tell he's trying to secretly wipe his tears with his sleeve.

"Oh yes! Sorry s-sir. Funny Doctor Marshall. Rosa called, she won't be attending until noon."

"Yes, I know."

I say just that three-word sentence with such wisdom and grace as I lay down my empty briefcase and hang my bathrobe on the coat rack... Damn it, that's the third time this week, mistaking my robe for my coat. Come on, Doctor. Get your shit together! How in the hell does this kid look up to me? "I need a few minutes Beckett. I'll start the first patient at 9:50" He jumps at my words like a deprived little puppy waiting for a treat.

"Yes sir, absolutely, sir. I'll have Shelly get the patient ready for you at 9:50 sharp."

I can't even reply to that kid. So, sad. If only he knew... If only he could really see my bathrobe as a clear symbol of absolute failure, the stench of booze seeping through my pores, and the empty briefcase that I carry just for the look of importance, but really, it is only a lie. One big lie.

Come on Rosa. I know you said noon, but at least answer your fucking phone! Selfish bitch... that's all she is. Why did I hire her? Why did I hire any of them? Whatever... I...

"Doctor Marshall?" Shelly peeked around the corner into my office. Well, more like a dim, small closet attempting to have the status of an office. Of course, little miss mousy CMA here to ruin my fucking train of thought. I hate her. Her little scrunched face, long, blonde braid. I swear that girl has never looked in front of a mirror a day in her life. If so, she would've killed herself years ago, do us all a nice, little favor... Standing there in her black scrubs, looking at me like I'm a hideous monster ready to gobble her up. She's facing death as she stands before me. There's something more to her, I know it.

"Yes, Shelly?" I grimace, swiveling my chair back and forth, trying not to look too hard at her cabbage patch doll features.

"Your first patient is ready. 300 lbs. 5'10 Caucasian male, age 36. Complaining of constant pain radiating through his bones. Saying it's so crucial, he can barely stand to breathe." I shrug... Looks like it's my first addict of the day. 300 lbs., there's something new. Wobbling his fat ass all the way down here for a fix. Now that's dedication. I glance at the chart and look at Shelly.

"Get me 40 milliliters morphine, and an alcohol wipe please." She looked at me confused.

"Rosa is supposed to dispense?" she said questioning my authority.

"Well she's not here, looks like you're promoted for the time being. Problem?" I scowled. She looks disgusted, yet entitled to do it.

"Yes, Doctor."

I enter the exam room and realize entering meant submerging myself into the atrocious odor of what had to be rotting roadkill. I look around and see nothing. I immediately start breathing strictly through my mouth and try to introduce myself as professionally as possible.

"Hello, I'm Doctor Marshall. You must be Carl?" He sits up on the examination table, his skin peeling loudly off the bed as he pulls up. It surprised me that this fat fuck could sit up so quickly. Wearing a pair of red basketball shorts, and what I think used to be a white tank top, and off-white sandals to match. I'm not surprised by his attire with the weather being so cold, dude radiates so much heat that you can feel it six feet away from him. He wiped his hand through his half balding matted greased hair, then brushed off what I assume are old crumbs from his untamed, smelly beard and went to shake my hand.

"Why yes, I am, you goanna fix me up, Doc?" Who in the hell is this character? We live in a city with more concrete than grass. Where's this mock southern accent coming from? This is going to be a long day. Play along, Marshall.

"Why yes, I am, sir. Going to fix you right up. Where is, the pain located exactly?" Too much, Marshall. Knowing he just wants his fix. I'm willing to give him some pain relief, but I can ask all the doctorly questions just for fun!

"Everywhere, Doc! It starts in my heels and shoots all the way through my body. Even my hair hurts, Doc."

"Did you ever think about maybe losing weight? You are a tad overweight for your age and height."

"Hey now, Doc, I may be a tad overweight, but I still can get all the pussy I want. So why lose weight? Can't ya just give me something for the pain?"

Ugh, now all I'm able to picture is a stale, bug-infested vagina searching through that fat lard's rolls, trying to find his chode of a dick. Focus! Doctor mode!

"Why yes, sir, I can, but first I need you to lay back to make sure everything is in order. Do you mind laying back, please?"

"Waste of time, Doc, I know what my problem is. I have constant pain... maybe it'd just be easier to prescribe me some percs or something?"

His upper lip twitches as he says it, and I can hear his saliva glands filling. Like having a parasite inside of him dying of hunger. The look in his eyes was almost animalistic. A part of me wants to just say yes, but then, what do I get out of it? Never having to deal with this crusty pathetic excuse of a human? Nah, not good enough. What if I can make this parasite inside him grow? Just let it completely take over... I do have the power to do that. I hold this man's fate in my hands. I decide his present, his future. Mm, I remember this. This is the fun high. Life, death. My choice. What a rush... What am I to do with him?

Let's torture him! Let's keep him! Feed the parasite, watch his body disintegrate while the life just slowly fades in his eyes... Come on Marsh! We haven't played in so long! We could even keep him. Finally have what we've always wanted. He's the perfect candidate. You know we can get away with it! No one will miss the guy. Look at him, we'd be doing those hookers he pays a favor!

"No, I can't..."

"What, Doc?"

Knock, knock, knock... "Doctor Marshall, may I enter?"

I just cringe at the sound of her sweet and innocent tone. Her loaded question. I just don't trust her. "Yes,

Shelly. Exam is finished. This is Nurse Shelly. She'll be assisting me today. We have the perfect antidote for your chronic pain." As I turn for the syringe, I see the smug look on her face. I know why... Go ahead, Shelly, relish in that temporary "nurse" title. It's the closest you'll ever get to a real job.

"Uh, what's this for, Doc? Is this going to be a permanent fix or just a temporary? Because I don't got the time to just keep comin' back, and I'm not a huge fan of needles ya see..."

Oh God!! Knock him on his ass, Marsh!

"Well Carl, this is only a temporary fix, but I will also prescribe you a pain medicine to take twice a day."

Now that's my guy!

"Shut up, I can't do this with you blurting in my head." I hissed into my shoulder.

"Excuse me, Doctor Marshall? I didn't get that."

"Well, NURSE Shelly, let me repeat myself. Can you please go into my office and fetch me my prescription pad?" She looks at me like I just pissed in her lemonade. Ha, if only.

She should be next... There's nothing to her. Little miss Shelly would be so easy... like a little snack... We would have so much fun with her if we just slowly start-

"That's enough!" Another hiss into my shoulder. Great.

"You alright, Doc?" Carl asked, nervously.

"Yes, just allergies."

As I explain the milligram dose and the cautionary speech about painkillers, my mind starts to trail off, and my mouth switches to autopilot. I feel my eyes gloss over. What am I? Do I have a monster inside of me? Am I nuts? Am I the one with the parasite? Feeding this sick monster, it's death taking cravings. I need my fix. I need Rosa here, she'll get it for me. I can't write myself scripts, but I can for her, and I know she'll rush to get it for me. She knows I need it, I need to cloud this voice in my head. Rosa doesn't want to clean up my mess again like last year.

Last year... oh how sweet she was... she reminds me of Shelly... We should do Shelly next, in tribute of Molly... Let's color her hair red like Molly! Then it'll be a true throwback tribute!

I shake my head uncontrollably, blame it on a bug. Not hard to believe… I'm sure he has a maggot nest under that armpit roll. Come on, Rosa, I need you!

"Carl, do have anyone that can drive you home?"

"Nope! Don't know no one that drives."

"OK, do you have someone to walk you home?"

"Nopers! I'm a lonely man, Doc. Maybe that nurse of yours could-"

"Okay, that's not necessary, you can stay until your morphine shot wears off." Even though I would love to see Shelly try to carry this fucker all the way home!

"Sounds good! Got any food while I'm here?"

"No, but trust me, you won't be able to function, let alone eat, after I inject this into your system."

"Well, I'll be damned! Let's do this!"

"Alright, you're going to feel a slight sting." Fuck, I forgot to sterilize his arm! Oh well… In his condition, I'm pretty sure this asshole could fight off the plague.

He'll be a fun challenge!

"Get out of my head man… I can't keep doing this with you!" I snap my eyes close, trying to push the voice deep into myself. Not worried about Mr. Carl Stank over here… Guy's seconds away from being in lala land.

I come out of the room and immediately bump into Shelly, reeking of old lady, I can't help but take in a big gasp of the musky scent. Lesser of two evil smells attacking my nostrils. Ah, such a sweet and sour breeze of old lady. What a relief from rotting roadkill.

"Um, here's your pad." As soon as she hands it over, I hear the back-door slam. I know that slam. I hear it up to four times a day. That's Rosa's slam. The sound of annoyance, yet eagerness, to help save lives, such a conflicted slam. I love it.

Perfect timing! "Shelly! What do you think you're doing?! You know you're not supposed to touch my script pad! You're a CMA! For goodness sake do your job! Go up front and get the next patient ready. Put them in exam room 8. Can you manage that?!" She looked at me in shear shock. She won't say anything, she's too afraid of Rosa. Not sure why, but I don't mind it. Gives me nothing but utter amusement throughout my day. Shelly scampers off and does exactly what I tell her too. At least she's quick.

I glance at the clock: 10:30 am. Yep, that's my girl. Always early. Always here to save me from myself. I'd die without that beautiful woman. She is pretty much the only reason I have for being here. I hate to love her so much.

It'd be an honor to make her our finale... Just slowly die with her. Then we'd all three be bonded together. What a love story!

I bang my dead watch (another fancy prop) against my temple, and I power walk straight to her, anxious to have the chance to briefly smell her perfume.

"Oh no, I knew that's why you needed me. You know I had to leave my little girl's conference out of fear of what you'd do? Not only am I the mom and dad of two kids, but I must take you on as a third child... What'd you do? How many patients have you seen with him blabbering in your damn thing you call a brain?" I just stare into her face.... Focusing on every detail. Even mad she still has the most angelic face... caramel skin, midnight hair, lips that just portray beautiful waves crashing into each other with every word she exclaims... So, majestic... She must be more than human.

"I saw one patient a while ago... writing him a script, and I have... well, I haven't given him his morphine shot yet... The fucker just passed out on me. Figure I'd wait until he woke up before I prick him." My ear twitches to where it jerks my head to the side. I play it off like I'm cracking my neck and top it off with a subtle yawn."

It's so hard for you to lie to her... how cute!

"Well, that was extremely generous of you. You're not like that. What's wrong?" Her eyes widen and her beautiful face transitions into skepticism. I look at her with my charming brown teeth smile.

"Nothing, Just a damn good day! Hey... so can you get to the pharmacy today?"

"How bad is it Marshall?" I look at her... Not knowing the expression on my face, I don't even get out a single word before she cuts me off. "Okay, I'll get it, write it." Wow, I wonder what my face looks like for her to just spring into action... zero convincing needed. She rushes off to go get my oxys. I like to switch it up occasionally. Whatever kills these interrupting, sharp, head pains, or what I like to call him my true self.

Rosa gets back by the time I'm done with my third patient, and I just feel my body unclench, feeling a warm, soft rush through my body. Rosa always takes the edge off. So, full of life, even on her tired, strung out days. She just illuminates this light of life... I feel alive with her. Best feeling in the world, even if it's only for a moment.

"Thank you, love. I truly appreciate your dedication to me." Said Marshall with a grin on his face.

"Shut up. Just take it and get back to work... and don't call me love." Rosa demanded.

"Sorry, love."

Rosa just rolls her beautiful golden eyes at me and struts away. I'd say I love her, but I can't. Love isn't a strong enough noun to describe what I feel for her. She's my oxygen... my....

Stop getting so fucking sappy and get back to old Hoss!

"Shit, I forgot Carl!"

"Doctor Marshall? Doctor? MARSHALL?"

"For fuck sake Rosa! What?!"

"Are you giving that 36-year-old male pain medication?"

"Yes, why is this relevant?"

Rosa just looked at me with such a disappointing, yet still captivating, look.

"He's a textbook addict, we should get that man some help. He probably passed out because he got blown out before waiting to get his next fix."

Don't you fucking tell her! Keep your shit together! Don't take this away from me!

"Bah... yes, I know. But, instead of getting him help, I planned on giving him a high dose of morphine and then a prescription to take home. I'll keep dwindling the milligrams down, so, I'm weaning him off. I'm secretly helping him, see? Doing good, taking one fuck up at a time!"

Smooth, buddy.

"I'm not your fucking buddy!"

Look at you! Moved up to talking in your head. Baby steps! We're getting there!

"No steps, I just can't have Rosa see how bad it is."

You keep calling me "it" ... What exactly do you think I am? A figment of your imagination? A "split" personality? I'm apart of you. I am here for a reason... why haven't you recognized that yet?

"Are you real?"

What do you think Marshy?

"Marshall!" Snap! Just like that, Rosa brings me back. Back in the hallway of the exam rooms, staring at me. "Where'd you go, Marshall?"

"Um, just replaying my plan in my head. Awaiting your approval." She saw right through me. I can't lie to her.

Not on your own... let me.

"That's a pretty good plan Marshall. Go do your thing. Do you need me to dispense any medications?" There it is, The ultimate question... This is my only chance. Don't make her a part of it, Marshall.

Keep your angel's hands clean.

I strap on a false smile and instantly slip out a "no". Rosa grins the most breathtaking corner grin that reminds me of the beginning of sunrise. So, astonishing. "OK, Marshall. Take your medicine and get back to it."

I get my morphine. I don't record the dose I'm taking. I know there could be possible problems. I don't care, I'll blame it on Shelly. She already did one illegal thing today. It'd be so easy to pin it to her.

Back into the swing of things!

"No, I'm not back. After I pop four oxys you pass out."

Don't do it. We've got this plan in motion. What are you going to do without me? You can't handle this alone. You need me, Marshy!

I choose to ignore what he's saying. I can back out now. Inject myself and take a nice solid break. That's what is best. I can do it. As I walk into check up on good, old Carl, it hits me. Goddamn it! How could I forget this stench? Retrain your breathing. Strictly through the mouth... whew... Okay.

"Carl, Doctor Marshall here. How are you feeling?" His eyes roll from the back of his head and try to focus on I think is me... And if I'm correct, a fuzzy version of me. I don't think he's completely out of it yet.

Hit that fucker again! He can take it. Plus, it'll speed up the process.

"Now just hold on... I haven't decided if I'm keeping you yet."

"Carl, I'm going to write your prescription now and place it in your hand. Would you like another dose of morphine? Carl?" Before I knew it, he shot up like a bat out of hell.

"Doc! What is this trip? It's like I had me a damn wool blanket over every part of my body but on the inside. Yes, another round! Is it safe with me still having this trip? I want to ride this gravy train as long as I can, dude! Because of the pain... you know my, as you call it, fancy chronic pain." I look down at this asshole and just think to myself well, what might be myself.

87

Do it.

"I assure you it's 'doctor approved'" He raised a gleaming grin as fast as if I put a candy bar right in front of his pathetic face. "Oh, and I'll do you one better. Here is your script, here is another bottle of oxys, and I'll stick you with one more shot to ride out until tomorrow."

Lovely.

"Sounds good, Doc. But just one question, am I just supposed to spend the night here or what?"

Set it up.

"How about this: when I'm finished with my patients, I'll drive you to get your prescription and then take you home. That way you can come down from your high and be able to pop those percs you love so much. You know? Just to beat the chronic pain." It looked like this was the happiest moment in his life!

Perfection.

"Oh, Doc! That's mighty fine generous of you sure! Thank you much! Ya know what, anytime you feelin lonely, I'll hook you up with one of my finest ladies. Pussy made of gold, I tell ya what! My body just cringed in ways I didn't even know it could.

Play along, Marshy.

I swallow hard, slightly suffocating myself, because breathing through my nose is not an option. "Mighty kind of you, Carl. Why don't you lay back and get your morphine dose in? Don't want that chronic pain to creep back up now." He lays back, ready to hop right back on that cloud of euphoric bliss. Slightly jealous of this fat fuck. Such beautifully constructed gifts. Happiness on a fucking platter. Such a waste.

Oh, don't think that buddy. It's going towards us. We get the ultimate high! We manipulate God's creation! We wither down his greatest achievement. We conquer! You and I, we ARE.

"Okay, I get it. Hop down off that soap box of yours there, 'buddy'"

Aw, you love me. The voice getting more and more frequent.

"Don't get ahead of yourself."

He's fucking knocked out… I just want to say, thank you, thank you Carl! Thank you for getting my boy back into the game!

"I'm not back!!" Rosa throws open the door to the exam room. Shock on her face.

"What is going on, Marshall?! What's wrong with his back?" She said, confused.

Better come up with something good.

"He-he asked me to stick it in his back, insisted really, so I raised my voice harshly and stuck him in the arm. I'm sorry if I startled you." Rosa's shocked expression dwindled and quickly transitioned into a disappointing grimace.

"I'm going to have to stay here until he wakes up." I immediately perk up and squeak out.

"I'll stay until he's up! I've got some paper work I must do. He shouldn't be out for long. I only gave him 10ml morphine." Lie! She raised her sunken head and started going on about our nonsense bullshit patients. Blah blah blah. So, boring yet still so full of life. They're all just scum of the Earth.

"And Beckett cashed out the last patient. Front and exam rooms are shut down. Closing early for the holiday."

"Holiday?" She looked almost sad for me... wanting to console me while breaking the awful news.

"It's, um, Thanksgiving tomorrow. Remember? I figured the hanging paper turkeys in the office was a subtle reminder, yeah?" So quippy this one!

"Yes of course! Go on home then! Anything left to finish I'll handle it. Go home to those kiddos of yours."

She nodded her head to me and turned around on her heel. Before she took that step out the door, she turned to me. "Beckett and Shelly already left. Are you sure you don't want to me to stay and help?"

"No, no, no. Go, don't worry. I've got it... love." That little pet name I gave her for the day set off a reaction I least expected. A smile... A genuine, unloaded smile.

"Hey, if you don't have anywhere to go for the holiday... My door is always open. People talking loud, spitting food, booze. Kids running around making obnoxious sounds. It's going to be so exciting."

That's not the plan, Marsh.

"Well, as enticing as the offer is, I'll have to pass. I kind of have my own holiday tradition." Curious, she tilts her head to the side, her hair brushing back, exposing her flawless skin and the most perfectly placed beauty mark right under her jawline. I blink, dazed. Barely able to hear her tease out, "oh yeah, what might that be?"

Oh, prepping this asshole for all the fun we're about to have!

I stutter, pushing the voice back so I can carry out a thought long enough to spit out an excuse as to why I won't take her up on such a generous loving offer. "I, I c-call my dad and have a drink with him over the phone and just reminisce life before my mother passed away." Wow, that's not true. My father is dead. Left me. Right after mom.

Left us, Marshall. That mom of ours offed herself and daddy followed suit. I'll never leave you.

"I'm so sor-" She cut herself off. She knew better than try to lay genuine pity on me. Rosa couldn't help but throw me a pitiful smile and compensated for it with a classy, flatulent joke "You better leave this room before he rips ass on ya, with the way he smells, I can't imagine. I bet it'll knock you right on your ass." She looked forward, carrying her pitiful but joking smile out with her... I felt the light in the clinic dim. It's so depressing when Rosa isn't here. She can make any atmosphere euphoric... She's that constant cloud of happiness.

Fuckin-A man we did it! She took it hook, line, and sinker! Such smooth lies... They flowed like poetry. Yes, you were made for this! Just rolled right off the tongue so naturally! Jesus Christ, this is just too easy!

"I hate lying to her. When she finds out, she's going to hate me."

No way... She is pitying our pathetic ass. We're her wounded puppy she can never give up on. It's not in her damn nature.

"I hope you're right, I hope I made the right decision."

You did. I'm your person. I'll never leave you. This is what we're meant to do. I can assure you on that, my friend. Now it's my turn. Switch me.

"Okay, only one time though."

Eh, we'll discuss semantics later!

I close my eyes. I walk through a door in my mind, and there it is: him. My carbon copy, passing me by with a polite nod. A simple thank you gesture. Fuck, why can't I stop? Why can't I just clean myself up and swoop Rosa off her feet? Become that knight in shining armor, and we help this city one fuck up at a time? I could like kids, I think?

"Oh, my fucking God dude. Shut up with the emotional banter. Stop torturing yourself, and let's do this shit!"

Fine. Be discrete, don't scare him. He could easily fight back.

"Don't worry! I've got this Marshy! Oh, Carl, wake up, you fat fuck!" Carl, dazed and utterly out of it, flutters his eyes. He can barely hold consciousness. "Atta Boy!! You know, Thanksgiving is tomorrow?" Carl can hardly mutter out a word, but he gets cut off. "I just want to say I'm thankful for you. Thank you for being such a complete waste of life and space. Thank you for leaving not a single paper trail… thank you, thank you for being such a fuck up. You're the best gift I could ever ask for. I feel like it should be fucking Christmas! Now come on, you lazy twat! Let's go play!"

Carl had to have broken one of my fingers. I want to feel it, but I can't. He's made me numb to all feeling.

"I want to ride the pony!" Carl mumbled in his high.

"You will buddy, let's get you to bed first" Marshall said, reassuring Carl.

This is wrong.

"No, it's not. This is what we were meant for, don't puss out on me, marshmallow. I know we're old now, but we've still got it. Haven't lost the touch."

We're going to get caught. Rosa…

"FUCK ROSA. It's you and me. And when you realize what I truly am, you'll understand and feel disgusted with yourself for even thinking of shutting me out. Now say it with me."

FUCK ROSA, WE ARE IN THIS SHIT TOGETHER UNTIL THE BITTER END.

"You're with me!"

I'm with you, this is what we're meant to do, you're right. Let's get him home.

"Almost there, brother!"

He throws the limp lard onto the bed in my apartment, startling Carl. He shouts out a withering howl mixed with a feminine cry.

"Where, where am I?! What's going on? You gonna kill me, Doc?!"

"Oh, no dear Carl. You're too precious for that. We just want to play."

"Play? What kind of play?"

"We'll show you…"

Reverend

When someone finds, themselves hitting rock bottom, they will do whatever it takes to get back on top. Harm, lie, cheat, anything for their selfish benefit. Now, I'm going to tell you about a couple who took their so called 'rock bottom' and turned it around into a true masterpiece of selfish sin and why they deserve to be punished. This is their story.

Trent and Milly Claud started off as a normal happy married couple. He worked at the post office, and Milly was a homemaker. Her strong personality made her the head of the family. Milly took care of everything financially. She gave her husband a weekly allowance, what she thought was a 'generous' curfew, and had him trained to be at her beck and call. Milly constantly made sure that Trent knew his place.

Around Christmas time, the post office gets a bit chaotic, which is to be expected. With packages of gifts being shipped all over, things get hectic quickly. A lot of times after the holidays, some packages get damaged, and some are never delivered due to being lost through inventory. Trent's responsibilities weighed heavy on him every year during this season. Not the work but knowing that Milly would make him pay for this at home. The second post-Christmas season, He found an outlet to get through Milly's scorn. Heroin. No, not the best idea, but what's a man to do under this immense amount of pressure? Trent did the only logical thing he could think of to ease his stress.

Doing the inventory; grunt work; at the office, tended to keep Trent fairly late into the evening. This took away Milly's power and control over him, which pissed her off. She would go to the office after hours and wait in the parking lot for him to be finished. But waiting in the parking lot wasn't enough. She made him call her and keep her on speaker phone while he did his work.

One night after three hours of waiting, Milly couldn't take it any longer. Instead of rationalizing like a normal person and realize what she was doing was completely idiotic, her thought process went another way. Now, understand that her mindset is not what could even be considered as normally insane.

Milly said to herself, "If there is less product, there is less work."

"What'd you say, babe?" Trent replied.

"Trent, I have a grand idea! What if there weren't that many packages for inventory?"

"Then I wouldn't have to be here so late. What's your point?" He began sounding confused.

"Tone Trent." She snapped.

"Sorry babe. I don't understand your grand idea, please explain?"

"What if we lightened the load a bit?"

"Wait, that's stealing, Milly."

"Don't look at it that way. Think of it as funding your little habit. So that way you don't blow your weekly allowance in a matter of a day Trent."

"You know about that?" He mumbled into the phone.

"Honey, I know everything you do." Milly said proudly.

Two years of funding what became Trent and Milly's 'little habit'. Trent was finally caught at work. No charges would be filed if he left gracefully without any issues. Milly wanted to wreak havoc to what she considered 'shitty management', but Trent convinced her that if she did, she would be arrested. Being arrested would mean that she couldn't keep her eye on Trent, which was what held highest priority in her eyes. Calmed down, and working through their budget. They saw that they had at least eleven months before they would become dead broke.

Living the vacation life, Trent and Milly didn't make it to the full ten months. Their addiction grew stronger. Only making it to four months, they were down to zero. Not a single cent to their name, they decided to sell everything in their home, not to make the mortgage, but to feed their fun addiction.

Down to nothing, Milly started coming down from what she knew would be her last 'rush' for a while. Suddenly she had an epiphany.

"Trent, snap out of it and listen! What free places get money from everyone? Even donations!"

"I don't know?" Trent drooled. Eyes still rolled in the back of his head.

"Church!!! Nice to meet you *Reverend Claud*." Milly said with a fake smile.

"What the fuck are you talking about, Milly?"

"The ultimate scam! Where we never have a want for anything again! It's a perfect plan. We'll become a new religious church of living 'minimal'. It will be in our house, and with us not having shit to our name, it's totally believable!"

"How are we supposed to do this? I can't just be a 'reverend', can I?"

"Well of course not you, dumbass! But who would dare question a fucking REVEREND?!" Milly then smacking Trent in the back of the head.

"Okay, say that we do this. If we live 'minimal' than how are we supposed to take donations?"

"You annoy me. Shut up, be the Reverend, and I will do what needs to be done."

"Okay Milly… What's my job as the Reverend?"

"Make flyers and pass them out in the 'ritzy' neighborhoods. We're going to offer 'prayer mediation'. This will help people lead a more simplistic, less materialistic lives. Make sure you clean your nasty ass up. Ask for change around town, then take the change and make the flyers. It should be easy. I'm not going with you, so you better behave, and don't fuck it up. Understand?"

"Your mind scares me, babe…" Shaking his head.

"Don't start whining and just do what you're told. It's the perfect plan. When you're leading prayer meditation, I will go into their belongings and steal their shit. It's flawless."

Letting Trent go off and do what Milly had instructed him to, he was confused by her not going with him. Shrugging off the confusion, he decided to finally enjoy going out without his nagging wife. He hoped that maybe he could get a fix, of not have to give it to Milly, while he was out.

Milly let him go by himself for her own reason. She had another part to this plan that Trent had no knowledge of. She had been having an affair with their drug dealer since she met him one year ago and decided it was time to be with a real man rather than the pathetic child she had chosen. Calling the dealer over, Milly knew that her man would be generous enough to give her the perfect fix she would need to make it through the night. As soon as he showed up, Milly filled him in on what was getting ready to happen. Her big plan was flawless this time compared to the post office plan. Instead of falling with Trent, she knew she could leave him to be the one to blame, and duck out with everything, and leaving her dealer to swoop in like some coke covered super hero.

The dealer insisted that she do this just right. He'll take all the belongings that Milly will steal; and he'll pawn them for her. Now one would think if this dealer loved Milly enough, he would just take her right then and there to live 'happily ever after.' But, this is a drug dealer you are reading about. He never truly cared for her, but he was the ultimate con. He led Milly to believe that as long as she proved herself to him and earn her way, he would rescue her. He made sure that Milly would ride this out until Trent would be caught.

When Trent printed the flyers. He was proud. There were one-hundred flyers printed and handed out to every rich neighborhood Trent could walk to.

Reverend Claud and his wife invite you!

Please join us for prayer meditation.
We are a non-denominational.

Church that specialize with living minimal.

Come check out our way of worship!

Tuesdays and Fridays.

6pm-8pm.

Ready to worship?!

Milly was unimpressed with Trent's so called successful flyer. "You better not have blown this for me!" Trent knew not to upset Milly. He loved her with all he had, because he knew why Milly was so controlling out of fear of losing him. He could never hurt her or make her unhappy. She'd break, and he never wanted to be the cause of something like that. So, he learned to take the word, no, completely out of his vocabulary when it came to her.

After a month of people joining this prayer mediation, Trent became a real professional and even began believing the bullshit he was feeding to these poor people. He forgot what Milly was doing in the background. He never saw her officially steal anything. Guests would bring him food offerings, medicines, money, and clothing. Trent felt like he was doing honest work. He stopped referring himself as just Trent. He was officially Reverend Claud. Provider of the people.

The way prayer meditation worked was very simple. He called the people that would attend his "children". When they sat on the bare wood floor, and his reason was that the less you have the more grateful you become.

"No longer must we be stuck in the product they call modern living." Reverend Claud would say this every session. For the rest of the first hour, his children would explain what they're giving up and what they're struggling to live without. Then they would all tune in their breathing and then breathe as one. For the last hour, Reverend Claud would hum, and they would sit in silence with their eyes closed, just listening to the relaxing hums. After it was over, they would all hug, kiss, and say no words, just walk out with feeling immense peace.

Milly, started to get good at taking what she could without being caught. Milly and 'Reverend Claud' started living separate lives. She was gone every night and he would only come home to do her conning, and would focus on other meditations. He even began writing a book about his new way of life. Everything was perfectly normal to them.

At every prayer session, there always was a quiet, woman. She was a widow. In her mid-sixties, and prayer meditation was a way of coping with her husband's recent death. That woman was… me.

Now how do I know the story of dear Trent and Milly? Simple… They crossed me. How? They took something very precious to me. I had to do what I had to do to get it back. Here's where their story gets more interesting, so pay attention.

Tuesday prayer meditation, I had noticed that my husband's most prized possession, his watch, was missing from my hand bag. I instantly knew. The other people and I would talk about never seeing Reverend Claud's wife when we were there. Some people have said that

101

they've noticed that some of their belongings have come up missing, but they learned to let go of their need to have it. It was just talk, but they figured it was Claud's way of teaching us a lesson. I went along with it for a while. But taking something that was so precious to my husband and myself was the biggest mistake they could've ever made.

Friday's meeting was the perfect time. I was completely aware of Milly's little plan to split with her druggy boyfriend. Greedy bitch kept giving him more and more just to keep him at bay. But he was going to leave regardless. It wasn't worth it to him. Her knight and shining drug dealer decided today that he was done. Which meant, this is my perfect time. After prayer was done, I did not move, I did not even open my eyes. I was waiting to be approached. They both deserved what was about to come. Claud tapped on my shoulder, bending down, face-to-face with me. Perfect.

"Child, we are finished, focus on your breathing and come back down to reality." Trent falsely preached.

Eyes still closed I replied, "you took something from me."

Claud looked confused, "excuse me?"

Opening my eyes, I pull two knives out and sliced both of his alkalis. After he timbered down like a tree, I quickly got up, dragged him to the stairs, and handcuffed him to the banister. Yes, I was prepared. After getting that piece of shit settled, I went for Milly. I knew that she was waiting on the back porch for her 'man'. I opened the door, grabbed her greasy ponytail, and dragged her to her precious husband, handcuffed her right next to him. She was screaming uncontrollably. I carved out her tongue and told her that her teeth were next if she didn't shut the fuck up. Badass? I agree.

Any ways, I chose to reveal to them what Mrs. 'Reverend Claud' took from me was. What they didn't know is my husband's watch had a special bond with him. Once he passed, that bond grew with me. Any time the watch leaves my presence, it eventually makes its way back to me, no matter the distance. What they also didn't realize was that the watch was capable of creating time traps.

"What are time traps?" Reverend asked me. Watching the look in their eyes after answering his question was priceless.

"Good question, I guess you guys should know what you're in for."

I sat down in my prayer mediation pose, laying my two knives in front of me. "A time trap is only given when deserved. You see, you guys have done some unforgivable things. Faking a religion in my eyes is the ultimate crime. You are stealing from these people that love you and would be willing to give you anything you ask. You go as far as calling them your 'children'." Taking a breath and giving them a warm smile, I went further with my explanation. "This watch is very special to my husband and me. Once one has formed the bond with this watch, it creates time traps for whoever I see fit. Now, they can be happy time traps, they can be torturous and anything I want trapped, I get."

"My husband is dead in this particular life. But, before he passed, he left a wonderful gift: a watch. He said I'd know what to do with it. My husband remains in his time trap with our last moments. He'll relive it for all of eternity."

"How is that possible?"

"Good question! I'm not sure on how it all works, but I do know that a figment of myself is able to stay in a time trap if I choose so. Today… I choose to do just that."

"Please, please don't do this. We'll return everything, we'll leave town, turn ourselves in. Whatever you want! I'm so sorry on behalf of Milly and myself!" Trent pleaded.

"You're so naïve Trent. Here's what's going to happen. I'm going to cut whatever parts I want, slowly, until you fade into nothing. Then, as soon as you think the pain is over and think you get to rest easy, time will take you right back to this very moment, and we will proceed with as we are right at this moment. Ready?"

"NO! PLEASE DON'T DO THIS! I-" Milly Cried.

"Hang on! Setting my time trap now. OK! Here we go!"

I started with the flesh and muscle, then slowly started sawing through the bone until there was nothing left to these horrible people. Their blood had a foul stench. Their souls were tainted. Wiping disgusting people out of this world is what I am meant to do. Trent and Milly thought, just like many others, that they had hit rock bottom. Let me tell you something. I am their rock bottom.

Behind You

My name is Becca Peters. I am eleven years old. I have lots of friends. I have an amazing mom and dad and a fun, older sister. My cousin, who's my best friend, is on the gymnastics team with me. I'm normal. Except for... what is behind me. I can't look in a mirror. I can't look at pictures of myself. I can never look back. There is something that is behind me. It never leaves. I don't know what it is. But I know I can never find out, because if I do, it will take me. Since I was three, I stopped looking behind me. I'm writing to you hoping that you can help me get rid of it. I'm starting to get so scared that one day it will be in front of me, and I won't be able to run away from it. Help me please.

– Becca

Rebecca Peters' parents had her write to me in hopes that I could find a way to help her. I'm Dr. Angelica Rothman, one of the top therapists in the world. I'm located in Chicago, Illinois. I specialize in unique cases with children, and I have a more natural approach. I don't use medication. Some of the exercises I perform with my patients seem unconventional to many, but having nothing but positive outcomes from what I practice, I feel that my methods of practice outweigh the negative opinions.

105

In some cases, parents can't afford to bring their child to me. Depending on how severe the case is, I choose to help the families for betterment of the child. Some think it's because these kids are my "lab rats", but that couldn't be farther from the truth. Children should not have medications forced upon them if there is a possibility to prevent it and find a better solution for them. I feel that Rebecca writing to me is a true cry for help, and her parents have written me several times. So, I believe it's time to send them to Chicago from their home in Iowa and give this little girl the help she deserves in order for her to live a normal, happy life.

It took two weeks for the Peters to settle business at home before they could travel to me. Today, Rebecca is finally coming in to have a one-on-one with me. After meeting with her, I will set the schedule that I see fit for her and her issue that she is facing, and I'll continue to keep this journal to document her journey.

Session 1: Rebecca was extremely nervous when talking about "it". Steering away from the subject, we discussed a little bit about her life. She enjoyed her family, her school, gymnastics. Rebecca said that her friends call her Becca. She insisted that I do so as well; in return, I told her my friends and family call me Angie, and I would be honored if she would call me that. Starting off on a real positive note. I really feel that I can help her. Without a doubt, I know medication won't be necessary in her case. For tomorrow's session, we will continue to build our bond; hopefully, I will be able to gain her trust, and she will allow me to try a few exercises with her.

Session 2: Today's session was a little like the first. I began with asking Becca how her and her family were liking Chicago. She began saying it was "busy", and she missed her home. Taking that little piece of information, I began talking about "it". Her body tensed up, and she immediately said, "That's not what I want to talk about," her body language immediately turned stiff. I proceeded to inform her that she was going to have to face "it" sooner than later, and the sooner she trusted and opened up to me, the sooner she would get to go back home and live a normal life. Becca's leg began to fidget. Not waiting for a response, I asked her, "Does it bother you more at home or here in the big city?" Becca replied with "It doesn't matter where I'm at, Angie. It's always there." Today's session wasn't as productive as the first, but we'll get there.

Session 3: Giving Becca a week-long break, I decided to dissect everything in her life. I will be doing this in every session until I can find something that I believe would trigger this "it" figure that she claims is behind her. I was searching for anything in her life that may have caused such severe paranoia. I will be seeing Becca two times a week. I decided to send her parents home and put her in a children's home with other kids that are struggling with similar issues. Becca will be doing group therapy at the children's home and will not be on any medications. Since a diagnosis hasn't been made, I'm making her my top priority. I already reassigned the rest of my patients to other therapists so I can solely focus on her. Also, she will be keeping a journal and have no contact with her family and friends. I will be speaking with her parents about her progress. I'm trying to isolate her by taking away all familiarity, and maybe this "it" character will disintegrate.

<u>Session 4</u>: I believe Becca is struggling with scopophobia. She isn't necessarily afraid of people staring at her, but she feels like there's someone constantly behind her, watching and waiting for her to turn around. That's the closest diagnosis I have thus far. It doesn't exactly explain her refusal to look in mirrors or photos of herself, but I'm not ruling out this diagnosis yet. There's a chance this could just be a unique case of scopophobia.

<u>Session 5</u>: NO PROGRESS.

<u>Session 6</u>: NO PROGRESS.

<u>Session 7</u>: NO PROGRESS.

<u>Session 8</u>: NO PROGRESS.

<u>Session 9</u>: NO PROGRESS.

<u>Session 10</u>: NO PROGRESS.

<u>Session 11</u>: According to reports from Becca's temporary home, she refuses to help with her daily chores. She no longer participates in group therapy. Every page in her journal is blacked out with ink. Becca has become extremely angry with me. She says "it" tells her things about me. I started to tape our sessions so I could thoroughly analyze her every word and action. At the end of today's session, she said that she'll never see her family again. There was also something else she said that really worries me. She's isolating her own mind, and she may become dangerous to others and herself. I will write this part of the conversation for written record.

"Becca, will you share with me what 'it' is?"

"You need to stop talking like he isn't real."

"My apologies, Becca. Help me understand."

"He says that you want to send him away. But… if you do that, then you'll kill me. I'm not ready to die, Rothman."

"What happened to calling me Angie?"

"My friend wouldn't want to kill me… Rothman, you're not my friend."

"Becca… what if I promise you that I can get rid of 'it' for you, and everything will go back to normal. You can go home to your family."

"I will never see my family again."

Session 12: Earlier in the morning, Mr. and Mrs. Peters called to tell me that they'll be here tomorrow morning to pick up Becca. They want to find a more productive way of helping her. If they could just see what I'm trying to do will work, they could just wait a little longer. I didn't make any progress in this afternoon's session. Her last words of this session were the same as the last's ("I will never see my family again"). I need to keep trying. I'll have one more session with Becca before her parents pick her up. I know that I'm the only one that can help her.

Session 13: I set up the last session later in the evening with Becca. I truly wanted to help her! I wanted to try one more thing on her. I wanted her to face her fear, and hopefully, this would resolve it instantly. The exercise I tried on Becca was too drastic for the stage she was in, but, with her parents coming in tomorrow, desperate times called for desperate measures. I didn't realize the repercussions would be this severe. I keep watching this session's tape repeatedly, and I still can't believe it. Maybe if I write out what happened, it'll feel more real.

"Becca, this will be our last time seeing each other. Your parents will be here tomorrow morning to take you home. I know earlier today you didn't want to talk to me, but are you at least excited to see your parents?"

"He says I don't get to see my parents, remember?"

"Yes, I remember, but what if I told you there was nothing behind you?"

"I would say you are lying."

"Okay then. What we're going to do right now isn't something I think would be appropriate, since this is only your sixth week here. However, with this being your last session, and you are such a smart girl... we're going to try something, and I need you to trust me. Can you trust me, Becca?"

"No. But do I have a choice?"

"Always."

"No I don't. I know what's going to happen... so let's get it over with. He got me ready for it."

"Becca, sweetheart, there is *nothing* behind you. I promise. Everything you think that's going on is all in your head. Now, I need you to take a deep breath, and close your eyes."

"Okay..."

"Trust me, Becca." What she said next sent chills up my spine.

"You are next, Dr. Rothman."

"Becca, open your eyes."

I placed a mirror in front of Becca. When she opened her eyes, she would see that there was nothing behind her and thus proving that it was all in her head. A phobia that had grown into an obsession; an obsession that controlled her life. I wanted to show her how beautiful she was and that there was nothing to fear.

Revealing Becca her own reflection is the worst thing I've ever done. As soon as Becca opened her eyes, she froze, standing as still as a statue. It was like her breath was stolen from her as her hair turned white. Instantly, she was "scared to death". What have I done? My desperation to fix her cost Becca her life.

I called for an ambulance and then called for the medical staff from the children's home she was supposed to be leaving tomorrow. I felt nothing but immense guilt. I selfishly killed this little girl. I gave her no real chance… and she knew it. "It" knew it.

<u>Four years later</u>: I have not looked at this journal since my last entry. What happened to Rebecca caused me to quit my practice. Everyone was right about me. I took time for myself to try to follow up on previous patients, but no one responded. I tried publishing a novel about the six weeks I spent with Rebecca, but her parents said they never wanted to hear from me again. They wanted nothing to do with the monster that murdered their daughter. I can't blame them. I have no children. I can't imagine the pain I caused. The guilt is always there. Sometimes I selfishly think about her; I wish I would've just sent her away.

When Becca died, not everything went with her. Her "phobia" was not what I thought it was. It transferred in some sort of way. I don't know how... but I can feel it. Maybe Becca was right. I remember when she told me "You're next Dr. Rothman." Did she know something that none of us did? I can feel "it". I can sometimes hear the whispers in my sleep. I fear every shadow, every noise. I found Dr. Marshall at the downtown clinic, who prescribes me whatever I need just to get through the hours. I'm truly scared... Am I crazy? Was Becca, right?... I don't know... All I know is that I don't want to die.

The Baby

First time pregnancies can be one of the scariest, yet one of the most thrilling, experiences anyone could ever face. The excitement of bringing a life into the world that you have created is such a wonderful experience. Making sure that mother and child are healthy and safe throughout the nine-month process is the scary part.

Steven and Christy had been together for only three months when they found out they were pregnant. Thrilled and in love, they decided to have a courthouse wedding and started to look for a house to rent immediately. Both sets of parents were happy for their kids and their soon-to-be grandbaby. They supplied the happy couple with plenty of hand-me-down household items for their new home and bought them everything for the baby. Steven and Christy were ready for the adventure.

With Steven being twenty-one and Christy being nineteen, being young made them feel invincible. They had the perfect, little life. Steven worked as a mechanic and went to night school to get his criminal justice degree, while Christy stayed at home and tended the house. She wanted to dedicate all her time to being a mother to the baby growing in her belly and any other children that could follow shortly after. Steven wanted to make sure she had everything she could ever want.

Normally in a woman's first pregnancy, it's more than likely she won't deliver until her due date has passed. Christy was a very healthy and strong woman; so, all throughout her pregnancy, everything was right on track. Baby and mother were happy and healthy.

One night during Christy's thirty-sixth week of pregnancy, she woke up with sharp pains shooting from her back to her belly. She stood up to walk to the bathroom, thinking that maybe she just needed to use the toilet, when she felt a warm liquid rush down her legs. She quietly groaned, annoyed that she might've peed herself again. She leaned over to turn on the lamp on her bedside table and looked downward, finding herself standing in a pool of blood.

"Steven, babe," Christy said, trying to suppress the surge of panic she started to feel, "I need you to wake up." Christy knew she needed to stay calm for Steven's sake. If there was anything that could possibly threaten the safety of Christy or the baby, he'd freak out. Steven opened his eyes and saw Christy standing by the bed, looking over at him. Seeing the shock in her eyes, he hurled himself out of bed and instantly knew what to do. Steven threw some jeans on, grabbed their to-go bags for them and the baby, and headed to the car. After starting the car, Steven ran back inside to Christy, scooping her up as gently as possible, when he noticed the blood and immediately began to cry.

Christy looked into her newly husband's eyes and almost felt guilty. The first thing she could think of was providing some kind of comic relief. Even though she was bad at jokes, she attempted at one.

"Wow, when did you get this quick, babe?" she asked. Christy knew that wasn't even a little bit funny as she pressed her head into his chest. Steven always loved when she would try to make an effort for him. Even though it wasn't remotely funny, he gave her a sympathetic chuckle.

"Everything will be okay, babe. I promise," Christy whispered and pressed a small kiss on his neck. After gently placing her in the car, Steven pulled out his phone and ran to the driver's side. The first thing he could think to do was call 911 and rush his pregnant wife to the ER.

Nurses were already waiting outside for them with a wheelchair as Steven pulled into the hospital. He rushed Christy out of the car and into the wheelchair as gently as possible, and he grasped her hand, refusing to let go. After she was evaluated, doctors escorted Steven out of the room, telling him that an emergency caesarian was necessary and that they would have a nurse come out to keep him updated with how his wife and baby were doing.

After four hours (which felt like four years) of waiting, Steven called both of their parents and told them they needed to hurry out to the hospital as soon as they could. While on the phone with his mom, the doctor walked out Christy's room. Without saying anything to his mom, Steven immediately hung up.

"How are they, Doctor?" Steven asked. The doctor took his surgical cap off, and his gaze fell to the floor, seeming grim.

"I'm so sorry," the doctor started and then hesitated, "We did absolutely everything we could." Steven dropped to the floor, unable to process what he had heard, and his legs weighed what felt like tons. After a few moments, he slowly got up and made his way to the operating room, where his lifeless wife lay. As he walked in, the nurse handed him his newborn daughter and apologized for his loss. He didn't say a single word, just held his daughter and left his wife, dead, on the table. He couldn't see her. Christy didn't look the same. Her soul was gone; what he loved about her was gone. Steven knew that her parents were on their way, so he knew he could just take his baby girl and leave.

She looked just like her mom. She even had Christy's light about her. Taking her home was the hardest thing Steven had to do. He dreamt of this moment. The surprise of finally finding out if they had a son or a daughter, taking his wife and child home, caring for them both, seeing Christy holding their child as Steven held them both. Everything was wrong. He had to leave his wife and drive alone in the middle of the night to bring his daughter home.

"Christina." That was all Steven could call his beautiful daughter. He turned off all communication with the outside world. He already had everything he needed for Christina, thanks to her grandparents. Steven didn't want to cut himself out, but he just couldn't handle mourning Christy's death. He knew that his wife would want him to focus all his energy on their daughter, Christina, and she became his only priority.

Christina was extremely colic. Steven couldn't do anything right with her. He hadn't had the chance to eat, sleep, or check his messages. Hell, he didn't even have time to brush his teeth. Finally having enough, he called the pediatric office that Christy had chosen for the baby before she had passed away.

"I need help! My daughter has been crying for three months straight. I have tried everything. She needs to see a doctor as soon as possible, just to make sure there's nothing wrong with her. Please," Steven desperately asked.

"Okay, sir, please calm down. Have we seen your daughter before?" the nurse asked calmly.

"No," he blurted.

"Okay, name, date of birth, and what kind of insurance does she have?"

Steven was giving the nurse all the proper information. As hard as it was, he also informed the nurse about the baby's mother passing and how he has been on his own with Christina since she was born. The nurse sounded alarmed and stand offish. Her tone sounded almost sympathetic, which made Steven's stomach turn.

"Um, Sir, we can't schedule a time for you to come in. Might I suggest another doctor for you? He's a mental health specialist."

"My daughter is not MENTALLY DISABLED!" Steven snapped. He hung up and did the next best thing he could think of at the moment: search the internet. He found out that he wasn't feeding Christina enough, so he made her one huge bottle that instantly put her to sleep. Laying her down in her crib upstairs, he heard a knock at the door. "Who in the hell?" he hissed to himself, feeling pissed off, "If they wake up Christina, I'm going to fucking lose it!"

Rushing to the door before the inconsiderate uninvited guests could knock again, he flung the door open, squinting at the bright sunlight behind them. Before he could focus on their faces, he heard his mother's voice call to him.

"Steven, finally," she said, sounding relieved.

"Mom? What do you mean 'finally'? I opened on the first knock," he replied.

"Are you kidding me?! I've been knocking every day for the past three months! You refused to answer. No one has heard from you. I know losing Christy was hard, but you didn't even come to the funeral? I was a couple days away from calling the police." Steven could tell how stressed she's been by the newly added wrinkles on her face.

"No offense, Mom, but keeping in touch with you isn't really at the top of my list. I've been doing what I know Christy would have wanted."

"Honey… what are you talking about?"

"Taking care of my fucking daughter, Mom!" As Steven was making his point obvious, he noticed an unfamiliar man standing behind his mother, and his dad was sitting in his truck, looking through the window.

"Mom, what's going on?" he asked, frightened and confused.

"Can we come in, Hun?" his mom asked politely.

"I don't know. I finally got Christina asleep, so I really don't want anything to wake her up."

"How about we promise we'll stay quiet? Please? It's been so long since I've seen you, bud."

"Who's this behind you? Why is dad still in the car?"

"Well, you know how loud your dad talks. I didn't want to risk him waking up... Christina? Is that her name?"

"Yeah. So, who is this then?" he asked defensively.

"This is Doctor Mathis. He's here to help with Christina. That way you don't have to leave with her anywhere."

"Well sorry, Doc, but I really don't want to wake her up."

"Uh, that's okay... I can wait if you'd like?" Dr. Mathis smiled kindly.

"Sure," Steven agreed. He gestured them to come in and led them to the living room. "Sorry for the mess, it's been rough with Christina constantly being cranky." Looking over to his mom, he noticed her eyes were looking watery. To reassure her, Steven quickly added, "Mom, it's not as bad as it looks. The house has just been a little unorganized since Christina came home. I'm sorry I've been away. I've been trying to just do what I know Christy would have wanted me to do." His statement clearly didn't give his mother any reassurance. She instantly burst into tears. "Mom, I'm sorry. Please stop you'll wake Christina." His mom stood up and looked towards the doctor.

"I can't, I'm sorry. I will be outside." She kissed Steven on the cheek and then ran out the door, slamming it as she left, which woke Christina up.

"Well, I guess her nap didn't last long. Let me go get her for you," Steven said.

"Let me ask you a few questions first. Have a seat for me, Steven," Dr. Mathis demanded.

"I'm going to get my daughter first, Dr. Mathis. I can't just leave her up there to cry."

"Did you know that self-soothing is extremely beneficial for a child this young? Have a seat. I assure you that she will be just fine," he said sternly.

"Are you sure about this?"

"Positive. Have a seat, and we'll get some questions out of the way before you go up to her."

"Okay?" He didn't trust the situation. Steven sat down hesitantly. Unsure of what was happening, he sat without arguing. "What kind of questions do you have for me?" he finally asked after a minute of awkward silence. Dr. Mathis cleared his throat and pulled out a tablet, which Steven assumed would be used for notes about Christina.

"Can you tell me exactly what happened the night that your wife, Christy, passed away?" Suspicious, Steven came back with another question.

"How does this pertain to Christina's physical health?"

"I'm sorry, Steven. I know this ca be hard for you to talk about. You have been isolated since that night, and to know what has happened day-by-day since that tragic incident will help me find what could be wrong here."

"Wrong? My daughter is crying. She can't do anything without crying. So how does that night, or any question I know you are about to ask me, pertain to my daughter's issue?"

"Tell me about that night, Steven," he demanded again.

"Fine. My wife went into labor thirty-six weeks pregnant, and she had an emergency C-section. I called our parents.

Christy died, so I grabbed Christina and brought her home. She's been crying ever since. I called the doctor's office and tried setting up an appointment with them, but they've been no help. I've been taking care of her by myself."

"What kind of formula does she drink?" the doctor asked, looking at his tablet.

"Whatever my parents purchased for her before she was born."

"So, you don't actually know?"

"Sue me, alright?! I'm doing the best I can!" Steven felt himself reach his boiling point.

"You don't know her diapers either?" Dr. Mathis assumed.

"No, just what my parents bought," Steven replied, annoyed.

"They must have spent a lot of money buying more than three months' worth of baby supplies," he lightly chuckled.

"Your point, Dr. Mathis?"

"Will you go get me a tub of Christina's formula? Maybe she's on the wrong formula."

"Now you're asking the right questions." Steven went into the kitchen to grab the formula. On his way to the kitchen, he grabbed every dirty bottle he could find, trying to tidy up the place. He knew that Dr. Mathis was judging him, but how was he supposed to be cleaning the house, caring for his daughter, and tending to the outside world by himself? Especially with Christina constantly crying?

He dropped the bottles in the sink and went to the cupboard to grab the formula. Annoyed with the doctor, his heart started breaking. Christina's cry reached to an all-out bloody scream. "Go get her right after this," he assured himself. Steven knew he didn't have to listen to what Dr. Mathis was saying. He was going to get his daughter help on his terms, like he has been doing since the night she was born.

Grabbing an almost empty can of formula, Steven made a mental note that he needed to get more, since it was the last can. He walked back into the living room and chucked it at Dr. Mathis. Heading upstairs, he didn't care to hear what the doctor had to say about the formula. He was going to get Christina and then ask Dr. Mathis to please leave his home.

"Wait, Steven, do you have an open can?" The doctor's question confused Steven.

"What are you talking about? That can is almost empty," Steven replied. Steven stopped dead in his tracks on the stairs and turned back to the doctor. He looked straight at the formula can that Dr. Mathis held up. It was unopened.

"Would you sit down and talk with me, Steven?" After he asked, Christina's cries came to a halt.

"No." Steven sprinted up the stairs to his daughter's room. Running in, he noticed that Christina was gone. "What did you do with her?!" He rushed downstairs and stood in front of Dr. Mathis, ready to rip his throat out. Dr. Mathis calmly looked at Steven and asked him one more time.

"Will you please sit down and talk to me, Steven?"

"What's going on here?" Steven asked, his voice shaking.

"Steven, I'm going to explain something to you, but you have to promise me you will not try to interrupt until I am finished. Can you do that?"

"Do I have a choice?" he said, trying to steady his breathing.

"That's fair," Dr. Mathis replied.

"Will I get my daughter back if I listen to the shit you have to say?" Steven asked desperately.

"Steven, listen to what I have to say. The night that you took Christy into the hospital didn't play out the way you think it did... The night that Christy passed away is the same night your daughter passed. They did an emergency caesarian, and neither of them made it. After they informed you, they saw you run off, and apparently, you came back home."

"That's impossible." Steven was stunned, his face feeling numb.

"A few people have spotted you once at the liquor store, alone, purchasing boxes of alcohol in town."

"No, that's not accurate. It had to be somebody else they saw. I would never leave my daughter home alone. Ever."

"Steven, I'm sorry, but your daughter never left the hospital that night."

"This can't be right. How do you explain all the baby bottles I just picked up?"

"What baby bottles?" Dr. Mathis said.

Steven walked into his kitchen to retrieve the baby bottles out of the sink to prove his point. When he grabbed for them, he realized that they weren't baby bottles… Instead, they were all liquor bottles.

"No… this isn't real… Where the fuck is my daughter?! Who the hell are you?!" Steven yelled out. Dr. Mathis came into the kitchen. Standing in the doorway, he replied, "I'm not a pediatrician… I'm a therapist. I'm here to help you, Steven." He reached out for Steven, but he refused to believe what the doctor had to say, shaking his head and saying, "NO, NO, NO!" over and over again.

"Steven, please. You never attended your wife or daughter's funeral. Everyone assumed you were mourning in your way. Once you called to set up 'Christina' an appointment, they immediately notified my office. I called your mother, and now we are here." Doctor Mathis was trying to be as sympathetic as possible. He could tell that Steven was being blindsided and truly believed he had been raising his daughter for the past three months. He knew that the other issues leading up to that night were not ready to be discussed. "Steven, I would like you to come with me to my facility and talk more. Will you come with me? Your parents are willing to come with you as well."

"I can't leave. Not until I see Christina," Steven replied. Doctor Mathis shook his head.

"How do you think you've been surviving? How is Christina real, and you've been caring for her all this time, yet you haven't opened a single pack of formula or diapers, for that matter? Your house is full of liquor bottles. How have you been able to live here, paying no bills and not working? Your parents. You've been alone, Steven. We need to get you help. If you won't come to my facility, at least come and continue talking to me at your parents' home. Let's get you out of this environment. Please?"

Steven's head was spinning. "NO! How am I supposed to trust you! I'm not crazy. I've never been crazy! I'm going to wait here until you return my daughter to me!" Doctor Mathis took out his phone and made a call.

"Hello? Yes. No, he is not willing. Bring them in... We will take him back to his parents' residence." Steven stood up and looked down at the doctor.

"You will not take me anywhere until you give me Christina!" He ran through the house and screamed for Christina, checking every room. He found nothing. In a matter of minutes, he was taken down by two men and felt a stinging sensation in his neck. He slowly faded into blackness, fighting against every blink for his daughter.

Waking up for what felt like days later, he found himself in his childhood bed. He went to sit up and saw Dr. Mathis sitting at the edge of his bed.

"What are you doing here? Where is my mom?" The doctor looked at him with sympathetic eyes.

"Steven... We're going to start from the beginning. You aren't going to like what I am going to be telling you. But you will sit and listen to every word. Remember... I'm here to help you."

Lover's Quarrel

Falling in love can be a dangerous thing if you're not careful. To love someone is to fully devote yourself into one another, to trust one another. Once there is a form of betrayal within loved ones, it is almost impossible to gain it back. Love can be beautiful or it can be a cruel bitch. Be careful who you choose to fall in love with…

Hannah Miller and Dean Novak have been together since their freshman year of college. Making through four years of hell and still be in love, they were ready to conquer the world side by side. Both became teachers, Hannah majoring in band and Dean in English. They were hoping to get a job at the same school. Unfortunately, that was next to impossible. Hannah got a music position at a local middle school, two blocks down from their newly purchased home. Dean was only able to find work clear across town as a study hall teacher. Not the best offer, but they knew the area they wanted to live in were slim to none.

Hannah and Dean had the entire summer to vacation at home before the school year started up. The summer was spent in absolute bliss. They had remodeled their home and spent some time attempting DIY projects that failed miserably but made fun, loving memories. The loving couple went to Costa Rica with Dean's family where he purposed to Hannah. Newly engaged, home and settled, they were ready to start the school year.

Hannah was beyond excited to start her new job. She wasn't a fan of singing but she was still open to the idea. She loved meeting all her students and their parents at registration. Dean wasn't thrilled. He didn't need to attend registration for his school. He only received a letter notifying him the date and room that will be holding all seven periods of study hall.

"Yay." Dean said as he tossed the letter on the coffee table.

"I'm so sorry, babe. I'm probably not making it easier by talking about my job." Dean looked at Hannah and could tell she genuinely felt guilty.

"Not at all, babe. We both knew that it would be difficult finding work here. At least I was able to find something. I'm just surprised you got your dream job so quickly." Hannah stood up from the couch and wrapped her arms around Dean.

"I wouldn't say dream job. You know I can't carry a tune to save my life. They might let me go after the first week due to being tone deaf!" Dean smiled, kissing Hannah on the forehead and he pulled her in and said, "you always know how to make me feel better. But yeah, fingers crossed for you. Your voice is like nails on a chalkboard!"

She slapped Dean in the chest and pulled away. He started tickling her, mocking her tone def tune. They had that loving, playful relationship. No matter which one was down, the other was right there to pick them up. They both chose the perfect person to fall in love with. Or so they thought...

After the first semester, Dean starting to grow resentful. Not enough to start picking fights with Hannah, but enough to make it obvious that something was wrong. Hannah knew what it was right from the start. The only thing she was surprised by was how he was more envious of her than supportive. Dean never wanted to hear about her day. Was always annoyed when she brought work home and spent most of his time out in the garage, chain smoking and playing whatever free games he could find in the app store. As they spent less and less time together, Hannah tried to come up with things they could do together. However, Dean immediately shot down anything she came up with.

Hannah's next step was to try to post memories from college and the summer they moved into their home on his social media page. She tried not to look too much into it, but it did hurt her feelings that he 'liked' everyone's posts except hers. Getting fed up with his attitude towards her she decided to confront him. She went out in the garage ready, to go to her last plan: tough love.

"Dean, what's going on with you?" Hanna said, firmly.

"Nothing," he muttered.

"Seriously? Don't be short with me. You barely talk to me. You don't want to do anything with me. You don't care to talk about wedding plans. You're annoyed whenever I bring work home. Are you jealous?" Hanna said, knowing she overloaded him.

"Are you really that self-centered, Hannah?" Dean chuckled.

"What are you talking about? You don't talk to me, so what do you expect, Dean?!"

"Why are you yelling?"

"I'm yelling, because you refuse to give me a fucking answer, Dean!"

"I'm not talking to you like this. Go inside."

"Fuck you, Dean. I'm going to bed. Sleep on the couch!"

"You're going to bed? What about dinner?"

"Make your own fucking dinner you, asshole!"

"Get your rest! It must be so tiring getting little snot nosed brats to be able to sing words off a piece of paper!" He smirked to himself.

Hannah slammed the garage door and locked him out of the house. She spent the rest of the evening crying in bed. She couldn't believe how heartless he was towards her; it was never in his nature to be that mean to even his worst enemy.

"He was such a dick." A woman's voice said right behind Hannah. She quickly turned around.

"Hello?" She said staring at nothing.

Hannah could've sworn someone was behind her. The woman's voice sounded like it was coming from right behind her, as if this woman was laying in Dean's spot. The fear instantly faded when she heard the garage door open. Hannah got up to look out the bedroom window and saw that Dean had left. *Where is he going?*

The next morning, Hannah woke up to discover that Dean was still gone. She still went about her normal routine before leaving work. When she was walking out the door to leave, Hannah even turned toward the living room and said to herself, "love you, babe, have a good day." Knowing that Dean obviously wasn't there, she just felt the need to say it for her own comfort. "Hopefully he'll be home later…" Hannah wasn't talking to anyone specific, but she had no one to talk to. Getting into her car, she heard the woman's voice that had spoken to her the night before. "Let's go out." Immediately whipping her head and frantically looking around her car, there was no one. Putting the voice out of her mind, Hannah drove off to work and decided to just forget about the whole morning. Refusing to call Dean for how he left.

Dean sat in his parked car around the corner of their house, waiting for Hannah to leave. With the coast being clear, he pulled into their garage. After walking into his house, he realized how bad he smelled of a rotten hangover. Dean knew going to work in the state that he was in was not an option. Calling into work, he tried to decipher the hazy flashes of last night's festivities. Nothing was adding up.

After Dean remembers saying her 'bitch fit', he decided to say fuck it and get out for a bit. Enjoy reminiscing the highlights of what he had said that night. His first memory of what happened last night was confusing. Dean doesn't say things like 'single time', and 'bitch fit'. "Why would I say that?" With no one to answer, he started questioning how much he had to drink. Remembering the bar wasn't far from his house, maybe a five-minute drive and he had six shots as soon as he walked into the bar. After that, nothing else was clear. It was like wax paper was covering the sight of every flash of what he thought happened last night.

He gave up trying to remember. Dean took a shower trying to wash off the left over booze his body was carrying. Before he could even get dressed, he passed out on the bed. Dean's dreaming was somewhat filling the gaps of last night and he began to carefully remove the wax paper from each flash of memory.

Dean remembered bitching to some guy about Hannah.

"Everything works out in her favor. Everyone loves her. Bitch does no wrong. Whatever Hannah wants, Hannah gets. She is so fucking lucky. I can't stand her. It feels like even her presence can suck the life out of me. I've lost all ambition, dreams, or want for anything. I must live for her, accommodate to her. As long as I stay with her. I lose."

Dean slammed another two shots after his little rant. Looking to the man that listened to everything, the man smiled at him, "kill her."

Dean woke up sweating. "Kill her? No way that was real…"

"Dean?" A familiar voice trailed into the bedroom.

"Hannah?" He questioned, still in a fearful gaze.

"Hey, good to see that you're home." Her tone shifted, sounding annoyed.

"I didn't realize I slept this late." Scratching his head with confusion.

"You reek of alcohol, what'd you do last night?" Crossing her arms with disappointment.

"Leave it alone, Hannah."

"Dean, you can't just expect me to not want to know what happened with you last night."

"And you can't expect me to feel the need to tell you about every little thing in my life. It's not always about what you want, Hannah."

Hannah couldn't hide her stunned face. "Don't look at me like that." Dean hissed to her as she was getting dressed. Hannah looked down to the floor.

"I don't know what's going on with you, but for you to think that you can talk to me like this is absolute bull shit. You are obviously going through something right now that you don't feel like discussing with me, and that's fine. But, I'm not putting up with this shit. Figure it out, and talk to me when you're ready."

He laughed to himself and said, "Yeah, okay, I'll talk to you the way you want me to when you're ready to hear me."

For the next few weeks, it was like the couple were walking on egg shells around each other. Hannah couldn't stand it and Dean just isolated himself. They did nothing together. They treated the sleeping arrangements like two frat boys calling for 'shotgun'. Whoever got into bed first would easily just fall asleep while the other waited to come to bed. It was an unorthodox way of avoiding animosity, but that's the way that they did it.

Those nights when Hannah would slip into bed she would stare at Dean, missing their relationship. Missing the man, she chose to spend the rest of her life with. The man she was lying next to was a stranger. On other nights when Dean would be the second to sneak into bed. He would run his fingers through her long black hair. He couldn't understand where all this hostility was coming from. Dean didn't want to feel this way about Hannah, but he couldn't let it go. The hatred was growing like a fungus inside of him. There wasn't anything he could do to rid of this nasty hate.

"How can I love you, but still hate you more?" He whispered as he leaned in to kiss her on the forehead, Hannah woke up confused. She decided not to fight it. She yearned for his touch, as she embraced the moment, she took it one step further. Signaling that she wanted more than just a kiss, Dean immediately picked up on it and fought the urge to choke her. He pulled her in. They never felt closer.

After a long night of making up, they both decided that they wanted to stay home and continue this little honeymoon. They spent all day reading, dancing, and cooking together. Everything fell back to normal. Hannah felt completely at ease.

"Just our first marital rough patch." She felt proud to say that . It almost proved to her that there wasn't anything they couldn't get through.

Dean sat up from the couch and headed towards the bedroom to put his pants on.

"Where are you going?" Hannah asked confused.

"Going out for a smoke, babe. Don't worry, I'll be right back." Leaning in to kiss her.

"Just one, right?" Hannah childishly pleaded.

"Yes love. I promise just one."

"Miss, you!"

"Ha, miss you too, babe!" Dean winked at her.

Dean knew Hannah was trying to be cute. She always did little things like that. As he lit what he promised would be his only cigarette, a smile grew on his face as he thought about Hannah. Every time he or she would leave, Hannah would kiss him like it was their last. She would be so dramatic, when Dean would take even a step away from her she would always yell out "Miss you! Or I love you!" When they made up, Hannah would kiss him like it she hadn't kissed him in years.

"Fucking cunt..." Dean looked straight ahead, checking his peripherals and trying to see who said that. It sounded eerily like the guy's voice at the bar. The one that had said, "kill her." Dean reacted offensively.

"Fuck you! Don't talk about my fucking fiancé that way." Looking around he was waiting for this man to reveal his face.

"You let her dictate how many fucking cigarettes you have! You've bitched so long about her, and now everything is good now? Are you kidding me? So much for caring the title as a fuckin MAN." Dean had no response. He put his cigarette out in his ash tray, and standing silent. Nodding his head, Dean sat back down, lit another cigarette, and looked down at the floor.

"Tell me what your take on a man is." Dean asking curiously.

"A man tells his woman what is and what isn't." The voice becoming closer.

134

"Keep talking." Dean replied.

"You give her everything. No real man would ever let his woman be more successful than him. I thought I saw real potential in you. Bitching about Hannah. Saying everything you said. Reminded me of a true man. Not like those bun wearing, skinny jean, pathetic pukes."

"What I said about Hannah wasn't me. I never talk like that." Dean admitted.

"What were you on, your man period or something?" The voice lashed back.

"Fuck you, dude. Get out of my house." Dean yelled, feeling ashamed.

"Who said I was in your house? Look around. Do you see me anywhere?"

"No? Come out, then... if you're man enough."

"Turn around," the voice whispered from behind him.

"Holy shit! Who are you? Why do you look like that?" Dean was stunned by the man's appearance. He was covered in burns all over his body. It looked like fleshed craters, glossed over with a shiny transparent coat of skin.

The man stood there grinning at Dean, "This... this is what happens when you trust a woman. I'm going to tell you a story... and hopefully, by the end of this story, you'll know what needs to be done. You remind me of myself, Dean. I'm here to help you." Dean knew, judging by the way this guy talked, that he had to be the one that put those words in his head at the bar. Wanting to know his story, he decided to accept this man's help.

Hannah grew restless in the house. She knew it didn't take longer than ten minutes for Dean to smoke one cigarette. She began to think that maybe he was playing a game, and just lost track of time.

"No, he's not." The same voice she had heard before chimed in bringing her thoughts to a complete halt.

"Hello?" Hannah sat up from the couch, "who's in my house?!" She didn't wait for a response. Hannah shot off the couch and headed towards the garage to get Dean. As she reached for the garage door, she saw a mangled woman, badly burned, standing between Hannah and the door.

"Holy shit. Who are you? Why do you look like that?"

"Hannah, consider me as a friend. This is what it looks like the one time you give your man control. I'm going to tell you a story… and hopefully, by the end of the story, you will know what needs to be done. You remind me so much of myself, Hannah. I'm here, because I just want to help you. Please, sit."

"Okay…"

Two hours had gone by without Dean or Hannah even realizing it. Hannah mentally felt like she was in a daze, yet her body felt physical rage. She found herself smashing, and ripping up everything that belonged to her fiancé. Dean was having mutual feelings towards Hannah's. He rushed into the house and instantly went after Hannah's belongings. After twenty minutes of physically bashing each other's things, the couple started to argue.

Dean was in a blind rage, saying things that weren't even true accusing her with these off-the-wall assumptions, knowing that it would get a rise out of Hannah. *Why am I doing this? Why can't I stop?* Dean thought to himself.

Hannah wanted to yell at him to stop. She was continuously punching him in the chest. She felt the need to stop, but her body just wouldn't let her.

"Kill her, Dean," the man's voice called out.

"Kill him, Hannah," the woman's voice hissed.

Within a matter of seconds, Hannah and Dean had each other by the throats, wrestling, and thrashing into everything. Dean could hear in his mind, *Be a man Dean. Show her. End her.* Dean didn't want to kill Hannah. She was his fiancé. Why would he want to hurt her? He tried to pull his hands from her neck. He begged Hannah to stop and tell her that he loved her. Why was she wouldn't stop.

"Don't be a pussy! Stand up to this cunt," the man's voice roared.

"I c-can't," Dean cried, defeated.

Hannah tightened her grip. Digging her nails deep into the skin of his neck. "Atta girl Hannah," the woman's voice cheered.

Hannah looked Dean straight in his eyes, "you think you're a man? You are nothing without me." That's when Dean knew. This wasn't Hannah. Fumbling in the kitchen, he realized what he needed to do. Her mindset was to fight to the death. Whether she truly wanted to, or if she was trying to resist, he didn't care. There was no way he was going to continue this any longer. He tore one hand away from Hannah's arm and grabbed the grater out of the sink. It wasn't a knife, but he knew he could do the job with that.

Dean grinded the grater across the hand that was wrapped around Hannah's neck. Blood splattered everywhere, but it didn't even phase Hannah. She was fully submerged in this sick manipulating game. Dean knew there was no way he could reason with her. He had to grate his hand all the way to the bone before he could physically let go.

"Pussy," the man said, disappointed. Dean was screaming in agonizing pain. He fell to his knees and yelled out to the man.

"Fuck you! I am a man! I'm man enough to love my Hannah and refuse to leave her or cause her any more harm than I already have. You do not win! Do you fucking hear me you piece of shit?! You can't control me! You are the pussy!"

"Do you hear him Hannah? He doesn't love you enough to fight with you. He thinks he's better than you. Hit him where it hurts. Take the upper hand here. Take away what is so precious to him," the woman manipulated her.

Hannah looked down at Dean. "Done." Her smile was menacing. Dean knew what she was going to do. Before he could bring himself to his feet, Hannah already had the knife to her throat. "I thought I was with a man."

"The fuck you talking about, Hannah?! I worship you. I always took care of you. I stood behind you, even sacrificing everything in my life to make you happy. Please tell me how I'm not a FUCKING MAN, HANNAH!"

"You weren't man enough," her voice sounding flat.

Hannah slit her throat and fell to the ground. Whatever possessed her body, was gone. She started to cry, reaching for Dean. "Dean… I'm, I'm, I didn't mean…" Hannah couldn't speak with the blood pouring out of her.

"Babe, no! Don't say anything… I love you… Hang on for me Hannah, please! I'm calling 911!" Dean could barely see, his eyes couldn't focus.

"I'll love you after death."

"You're not dying on me Hannah! Stay with me!"

He watched the life fade from her eyes a few seconds later. "Where are you, you sick fuck?! You want to test me as a man. Come out here asshole! I'll show you what kind of man I am!" He appeared around the corner, smirking at Hannah's dead body, as if this were his plan al along.

"Didn't play out exactly the way I had hoped, but this will do."

"BASTARD! You were in Hannah's head, just like you were in mine. Weren't you?!"

"Maybe…" He smiled.

"What did you want from us?! We were happy. We lived a normal life. What kind of sign did we give that this could happen? Little bickering cost my wife her life. Why?!"

"Because I like you."

"That's it, you like me?! No, I need more answers!"

"Pack your shit Dean. We're leaving."

"No way in hell am I going anywhere with you."

"Hmm… it's funny how you think you have a choice."

"What are you going to do with me?"

"Give you a job opportunity, of course."

The Transfer

My mom disappeared when I was six years old and when Anthony – my older brother – was thirteen years old. For three weeks, my brother and I had to fend for ourselves. We would walk around, asking her friends and work colleagues if they had seen our mom. Nothing. I was so angry with her. Before she disappeared, she was always working as a RN at the city clinic, and when she wasn't working, she was constantly leaving us to help Dr. Marshall. Every time that asshole called, she would go. The only one there for me was Anthony, who practically had to raise me.

For a while, we got by on stealing cans of ravioli and SpaghettiOs. Anthony and I took turns taking grocery trips, and he was so smart about it. He would scrape up change to go in a quick-stop-and-shop store, buy a candy bar, and then steal as many cans as he discreetly could. We knew that stealing was bad, but it was the only way we could eat.

The third week was my turn. My brother told me it would be easier for me to grab more cans, because no one would ever question a little, six-year-old girl. Wanting to contribute, I grabbed double the number of cans I normally would, and that was where I fucked up. I tripped on my shoe lace and dropped all twelve cans that I had hidden in my coat. I could never forget it. The manager grabbed me by the arm and called the police. It all just snowballed after that. They found out that Mom was missing and that my brother and I had been alone. The manager decided to not press charges; all we received was a stern warning from the police officer, and we thought we would be able to go home. The officer took us home, gave us fifteen minutes to grab what we wanted, and had a Child Protective Service worker pick us up.

But then CPS separated us, and it became the most devastating day of my life. The only person I trusted and the only family that had never walked out on me was taken away. They sent me to an all-girls foster home, and those bastards sent him far away, leaving me completely alone. Wouldn't even tell me where he was going. They pretty much made it impossible to have any kind of contact with each other. For the next eleven years, I was left to fend for myself.

The foster house I was sent to was a joke. This place wasn't for girls to be adopted. This was a place for the unwanted. Living there felt like a prison, with its strict rules and isolation from the outside world. The other girls, who ranged from six to seventeen, knew that cliques were the only way to stay safe. If you weren't accepted into a clique, you were scrap meat. You were treated like shit. Nothing belonged to you. Every clique had the power to take whatever they wanted of yours. Being a loner meant you were chosen to do the grunt work for whatever clique that owned you for the week. When the week was through, they passed you on to another group.

I was considered a loner. You would think that the other loners would report to the "house moms" what was going on, and trust me, they did numerous times, but those "mom" bitches could give two fucks about them. They used the loners just as much as the foster cliques did. It was a flawless system if you were on the right side.

After eleven years of being what they called a "grunt bitch", I couldn't handle it any longer. I snapped. I stole a fork from the kitchen and stabbed at any cunt that looked at me the wrong way. Not going to lie, it was the best feeling in the world. Taking out all the anger I felt from being left by my mom, from being separated from the one person that truly had my back, from being stuck in this place where children were forgotten, from being treated like a personal maid to whatever clique I was assigned to that week. I was done. I let it out. I honestly didn't think I had it in me. But knowing that I was capable of it, I never felt more powerful.

After severely injuring five girls and minorly harming two house moms, I was arrested. After my confession and my reasoning on why I had done such violent acts, I got nothing but another stern warning. My case worker tried to have a heart-to-heart with me, but little did she know that my heart had been taken away eleven years ago.

"Kylie, you know you can't go back there," my case worker said, folding her hands together.

"Your point?" I asked while I crossed my arms.

"You can't even go grab your things. They'll pack up what they can and –," she started, but I was quick to interrupt. She never understood.

"Anything that actually meant something was taken from me years ago. I want nothing from that place. So, can

143

I go now? I'm one year away from being eighteen. Can't you just send me out early?" I snapped.

"I'm afraid it doesn't work that way, honey," she said, looking apologetic.

"I'm not your 'honey'," I replied coldly. She pressed her lips together into a thin line.

"I know this is hard for you. Please, talk to me," she pleaded.

"You don't care. Just do your job and be done with it. Where are you sending me?" I asked, trying to appear nonchalant. The case worker wore a sympathetic facial expression that I almost felt bad for the woman. But before I considered opening up to her, I remembered what they took from me, and my mood soured once again.

"We're sending you to a foster home in Vermont."

"Vermont?! Why the hell are you sending me to VERMONT?!"

"Kylie... it's the only place that will take you. You won't be sent to a foster home for obvious reasons. The only set of foster parents in our program that agreed to take you in are in Vermont. I'm sorry... but you have no choice."

"So, you're telling me, even after reading my case, they still want me?"

"Yes."

"Huh... Tell me about them."

"Mr. and Mrs. Adams are in their late twenties. They only have one foster kid residing with them at this time.

His name is Ryan, and he's thirteen. His case is delicate like yours. I think that's why they volunteered to take you in. They're a sweet couple. I think you'll enjoy living with them."

"So, I literally don't have a choice?"

"Right."

"Well… let's do this. It's one more year. Shouldn't be too bad."

"That's the spirit! I think you'll enjoy Vermont. Overall, it's quite calming. Not so busy like the city."

I only had the clothes on my back when my case worker and I arrived in Vermont. When we pulled up to the Adams' house, it was definitely not what I had expected. I figured I would see parents with a sad-looking, tween boy standing in front of their cookie cutter home, and they would all be in matching plaid outfits with sweaters tied around their shoulders. I couldn't have been more wrong.

I could tell the house was built like any other house, but the Adams put a different spin on things. With it being October, I assumed they would have brightly-colored, child-friendly Halloween decorations. But no, I felt like I was walking up to a serial killer's home. There was fake blood everywhere with the scariest statues I had ever seen. The one that stood out the most to me was this little school girl statue. Her head would spin three times, and then she would puke up green-pea-soup-looking shit. I looked to my case worker.

"Seriously, I'm going to die here," I said. I didn't even know if I was joking or not. She looked at me and laughed.

"Don't be so dramatic, Kylie. They're just really into Halloween," she responded through her laughter. She was an idiot.

"Clearly!" I replied, walking with her to the front door. As my case worker knocked, I couldn't take my eyes off all the fake blood. How did they make it look so real? It smelled awful, and I hoped that it didn't smell like that inside. I'd puke more than just fake green pea fucking soup.

"Come in!!" a woman's voice called out from inside the house. The case worker looked at me, shrugged her shoulders, and opened the door.

This inside did NOT match the outside. It was... normal. Really cute inside. Every room was a painted a bright color. Decorated by classy posters and collectables. Shelves and shelves of music, movies, and video games. There was an entertainment system that was filled with every type of game system imaginable. This place looked like it was owned by kids who had money.

"In here!" the same voice yelled out. When I heard her voice again, my palms started to get sweaty. Was I nervous? After passing all the hallways in the one-story house, we walked straight to the back door. I could tell that the case worker already felt awkward; she couldn't even hide the weird look on her face. I laughed to myself, because what the Adams were doing in the yard only intensified the look on her face. The couple and the foster kid were in their backyard, making something out of a green substance.

"Hi!" Mrs. Adams exclaimed, who was covered in green slime. She walked up to us when we stepped outside, holding out her hand for the case worker to shake. My case worker grimaced but then quickly tried to hide it with a fake smile and hesitantly shook Mrs. Adams' hand. Their hands were stuck together for a good minute.

"You must be Kylie! Did you bring your bags inside?" Mrs. Adams asked after turning towards me with a grin.

"Don't have any," I answered.

"Well, that's no good, because the clothes you have on now look like shit. Come here!" she said and pulled me in for a heart-felt hug. After two squeezes and about a pint of slime later, she finally let go. "I have some clothes for you to look presentable while we go shopping. Come on, let's go inside." She grabbed my hand and headed for the house.

"Mrs. Adams, I have some paperwork for you to sign," my case worker stated, pulling out a file from her bag as she followed us into the house.

"Call me Maggie. And have my husband do it. Jake!" Maggie said, "He and Ryan will come in a minute. We're making this booger ghost to put with the rest of our decorations in the front yard, but this slime is a real bitch!"

"Um, I can see that," I added, looking out at the green blob. While my case worker waited for Mr. Adams in the living room, Maggie took me to her room and pulled out a cute outfit.

"You a size two?" she asked, holding the outfit up.

"Uh, yeah…" I answered.

"Awesome! Nice to put my Jeans of Hope to some beneficial use!" she grinned, handing me the outfit.

147

"Jeans of hope?" I asked, confused. Maggie started to get naked in the attached master bathroom. I quickly covered my eyes.

"Kylie, don't be weird. We're both just girls. Oh, and Jeans of Hope. Every woman has a pair of jeans in their closet that they hope to fit into again but know that it'll never happen. But I can see how you wouldn't know that. You don't have anything but those dirty clothes. Which I hope you're not attached to, because I'm burning them. That okay?" The only response I could mumble out was a "sure". This bitch had to be on something.

Maggie took a shower, put on some clothes, and grabbed my hand to go back to the kitchen. Mr. Adams and the case worker were sitting at the kitchen bar, talking over the paperwork.

"Kylie, go in the living room and meet Ryan. Oh, and don't get anything on that shirt. It's my favorite. Jeans of Hope, I don't really care. I'm probably going to have to sign some shit, but once I'm done, we're going shopping." What was this woman's deal? Why hadn't Mr. Adams introduced himself yet? *Whatever, onto Ryan,* I thought, walking into the living room. He was sitting on the couch, watching YouTube on the TV. Uninterested in talking to me.

"Hey, I'm Kylie," I said, trying to be polite.

"Hey," Ryan answered, his eyes still glued to the screen.

"So, how long have you been here?" I asked.

"Few months," he replied, glancing at me for a moment before he paused the video. He then gave me his full attention, probably understanding that I was just like any other foster kid, defensive and looking for some answers.

"How bad is it?"

"Not bad. They homeschool, so it's nice that I don't have to deal with school bullshit."

"Why do they homeschool?"

"They believe that the school structure is pointless, and it doesn't get you prepped for the real world. Something like that."

"Ah… so, what's your story, Ryan?"

"Got put into foster care when I was four. Apparently, my nanny brought me in. Said my parents went missing… I have no memory of anything except for staying at the foster home and calling myself Braxton. But they constantly corrected me, saying my name is Ryan. I guess I must've been put through some shit to not even know my own name. Anyway, I was moved from home to home, and finally, I came here on a request from Maggie and Jake. And now here I am. What's your story?"

"Mom left when I was six. Brother got sent away. I was in all-girls home, and then I was accepted here. Have they ever had any other foster kids besides us?"

"Nope, we're the firsts."

"Why'd they request us then?"

"Hell, if I know. They're nice. Normal. They give me my own space. So, I'm not complaining."

"I guess… I only have to stay here for a year, and then I'm out on my own."

"Lucky."

"You from Vermont?"

"I don't know. You?"

"Chicago." The adults came into the living room after my case worker signed my rights away to sketchy people.

"Hey! Did you guys get acquainted?" Maggie asked, smiling warmly.

"Yeah, Ryan was just filling me in on the way you guys do things around here," I responded as I tried to fake a smile back. Maggie plopped herself next to Ryan and looked at the case worker.

"You can go now. We'll take it from here," Maggie told my case worker. The case worker looked at me and nodded.

"You guys have a good day," my case worker said as she walked towards the front door. Shutting the door behind her, Mr. Adams looked at me.

"Hey Kylie! Welcome! Want a tour of the house?" he asked, walking over to where I sat on a couch.

"Sure," I answered, standing up from the couch and straightening out my borrowed T-shirt. He took me throughout the house, and he also showed me where my room was and where my personal bathroom was. They had decorated the room for me, which made me start feeling excited. Even though the drawers and closet were empty, they managed to make my room really cute. It wasn't too girly, and it was decorated maturely. I had a desk with school books and a special shelf with teen chick-flick movies, books, and magazines. I had a huge flat-screen TV mounted on my wall, and the top of the line was a Blue-ray player.

"Sorry to ask, but are you guys rich?" I bluntly asked.

"In a way. Let's just say we're entrepreneurs. Do you like the room? Mags worked really hard on it."

"Of course. Thank you, Mr. Adams."

"Please, call me Jake. Why don't you go get your shoes on? You and Maggie have some shopping to do." Shopping with Maggie was surprisingly fun. She didn't act like she was trying to be my mom. She was simply being friendly. It didn't feel like she had a private agenda. She spoiled me; she had to have dropped at least a thousand dollars on everything for me. Makeup, shoes, clothes, jewelry. She went all out.

As soon as we got back to the house, the guys came out and carried in all the shopping bags. Maggie helped me put everything away in my new room, while Jake and Ryan were cooking what I said was my favorite food: steak and steamed broccoli. I wasn't sure why I said it was my favorite. I never had a steak in my life, and I thought Jake figured that out when he asked me how I liked my steak cooked. I didn't care. I never had a fancy meal before, so I planned on riding out this gravy train for as long as possible.

Living with them the first week was amazing. We did school whenever we wanted to. I had all the freedom in the world. We worked on crazy projects. There were no rules.

Correction, there was one rule. There was one room that was attached to the garage that we weren't allowed to go in to. Maggie had explained to me that in that room was all their one-of-a-kind collectables that were priceless. Maybe one day she'd take me in there. I didn't care for it. Yeah, these toys were cool, but it just wasn't my thing. I had my bedroom, and it was my favorite place in the world. I had no desire to go in that forbidden room. I felt like maybe that room held all their sex toys or some shit like that. Jake and Maggie would be in there for hours. So, what else would they be doing besides fucking? Playing with toys?

I almost felt guilty. I really clicked with this family, but I still had my brother in the back of my mind. Where was Anthony? Did he get as lucky as I did? Was he even alive? I know I needed to go look for him. He was probably waiting for me to turn eighteen so he could find me. I couldn't give up on him. He had never given up on me. I didn't want to leave though... Maggie and Jake talked about future plans for me after I turned eighteen. I knew they wouldn't boot me out as soon as I was old enough. Maybe if I told them about my brother they'd help me find him? Maybe even take him in too? They had the space for it, and he'd love it here. Ryan reminded me so much of Anthony. Jake and Maggie were such good friends; they were more like older, wiser siblings that understood what we had been through. I wondered if they had been through what Ryan and I have been through? Were they fucked over by the system and never wanted that to happen to anyone else? It would make sense, I guessed.

Halloween was Jake and Maggie's favorite holiday. Originally, they made plans for us to hang out as a family and stay in and watch all the classic Halloween movies. But the plans changed. Maggie and Jake brought us into the kitchen and showed us this prize invitation they had received in the mail. They were given a free stay in one of the six VIP suites at the five-star Oliver Sweets Hotel on opening night. Jake and Maggie were so sweet. They were asking our permission to break plans. They promised that they'd make it up to us, and if either of us would be disappointed about canceling plans, they wouldn't go. However, Ryan and I were excited for them. If anyone deserved to win a free night stay in such a luxurious suite, it should be them. We assured them that we were totally fine with the idea, and we'd be fine to just stay home and pass out candy.

Halloween night arrived. Maggie had me go shopping with her to get her an outfit for every possible occasion.

"It's only one night, Maggie. Why do you need two sets of silk pajamas? It's going to cost you a hundred and sixty dollars for just these," I asked, point at the sets she held on her arm.

"Kylie, you have got to learn. It's better to be overly prepared, especially going to a place like this. What if they have a midnight Halloween pajama party? I need Halloween jammies! And if they don't... then I'm going to look damn good walking in these to the ice machine!" she replied while giving me a cheesy grin. I loved Maggie. She always had a rebuttal for everything. She always knew how to turn everything into a joke.

When we arrived home and as I helped Maggie pack, Jake was occupied with putting together my and Ryan's surprise. He had made all our favorite foods, including steak and broccoli, and pulled out a playlist of horror movie classics for us for the night.

"Now, are you guys sure that we can go?" Jake asked one more time, expecting to hear a different answer.

"Just go already!" Ryan and I laughed out.

"Okay... oh! Before I forget, I bought you guys extra candy. Don't forget, keep your phones charged, doors locked, stay home, and call if you need ANYTHING!" Jake replied.

"Just go you guys! Don't worry! Have fun. Love you both!" I responded with a smile, ready to push them out the door myself if I had to.

"Okay! Try not to fall into a sugar coma, and please don't scare the shit out of each other tonight. I don't need any calls from any hospitals, because of a prank-gone-wrong between you guys!" Jake added as he followed Maggie out the door. Giving him no verbal reassurance, I slammed the door behind them. For the rest of the night, Ryan and I passed out candy and watched movies. As sad as it was, Ryan passed out before the first movie was over. Which was fine with me. I couldn't wait for Jake and Maggie to get home and tell us how their night went. Maybe they'd love it so much to go again with Ryan and me.

Six Keys to Hell

This is what I'm meant for. I conquered my inner demons. I was chosen. Well we were chosen... to be fucking bellboys. I don't know how a dog could be tested, but he did, and now we sit, waiting patiently for *his* guests. He calls them his children. Bullshit. These people are scum. Weak scum. He shouldn't even waste his time doing this. He should've just killed them, save us the trouble. I look down at the mutt, with a reassuring tone, "what we're doing is honorable." It's not fair. I am his child. I am strong. I'm the only one that could make it. He liked me above all others... Right? I'm here, helping him. Playing, as a voluntary crucial piece, setting up his pawns in the game. A mutt is held at the same importance as me though? His children are so precious to him, but they don't have what it takes. I lost my beautiful fiancé, Hannah, but I still willingly embraced what my meaning in this life is.

Room one. Right on time. "Hello! Welcome to Oliver Sweets Hotel. I assume you are one of the lucky winners?" Assholes.

"Yes, we are! Maggie and Jake Adams!" The woman said excitedly. I had to force my face to look inviting. It took everything in me to not hurl myself over the counter and kill them myself. Weak. Sick bastards.

155

"Do you have your invitation?" I ask with the politest tone I could manage.

"Jake, can you pull it out of my bag?" Maggie said with an annoying tone. It took everything I had to fight my hateful urges.

Fumbling through the bag, Jake pulled out the invitation, and handed it over to me. Taking the invite, I turned around. The wall behind the front desk had slots of keys for every room. All keys were lined up in rows from floors one to thirteen. All floors had at least twenty rooms. Except for the thirteenth floor. Those were considered as Oliver's deluxe suites. That room only held six rooms, one could only imagine what it was like up there. My job was down here. I was following strict orders not to go up there. As hard as it is not to let my curiosity get the best of me. I am the chosen one. Self-control is nothing compared to what I'm truly capable of… I think?

"Everything okay sir?" Apparently taking my time isn't acceptable to these people. I put their invitation in the slot, pull out the black key, and turned to hand it to them.

Mr. Adams gave me a smug look, "You guys don't use key cards? All hotels have key cards." Really? He wins a free night's stay at a high-class hotel, and he must make a snide remark about a fucking key. Bite your tongue Dean…

"Well, the owner of the hotel wanted to keep it classy," I respond through my gritting teeth.

Maggie chose to chime in. "Babe, don't be a dick. I'm sorry sir. We're just excited. We don't get a lot of breaks in our line of work."

Wow... "Oh really? That's unfortunate. What kind of work do you do?" They glanced at each other, and giggled like two school girls laughing at an inside joke.

"We're what you would call, entrepreneurs." Clever cunt. I know what you do. She continued conversation.

"So, what does this night entail?"

"You will be checked in to your room, so freshen up, settle in, and dinner will be in our dining hall in the west wing of the hotel. You will be joining the other guests and the owner of the Hotel."

"Yeah, what's his name?" Jake asked.

"Oliver Sweets," I answer.

"Of course... Stupid question. Weird name though, Sweets, is that his real name?" Maggie asked, judgmental.

"No such thing ma'am. And, yes, that is his real name. Do you need any help with your bags?" How insulting! If only they knew what Mr. Sweets was capable of.

"No, we've got it thank you." Jake said, grabbing the bags.

"You're very welcome. My name is Dean, just call down to front desk if you have any questions. Enjoy your stay!"

"Okay. Hey, one more question. Why are the thirteenth-floor keys black, and the rest are gold?" Maggie persisted. She needs to go.

"Those are the suites, so the owner wanted to differentiate the keys by color."

"Just weird, all keys should be black, and gold fancy." She laughed.

"I'll make note of that for him, thank you. Enjoy your stay." I say with a dead stare. I'm over these people.

Start walking, now get in the elevator, stop asking me stupid fucking questions. Gone. Thank God. "Mutt, I was about to have you bite them. They would not shut the fuck up. If they call down here, I'm going to fucking lose it. Entrepreneurs. I know what they do. They thought they were so clever. Being fake is harder than I thought." Stupid mutt just stared at me. Pointless talking to a damn dog. Black keys weren't fancy enough for them. They'll learn what their key is truly for. Crossing their names off the list, room two walked in, right on schedule. The mutt ran away, before the front door closed.

"Uh… Hello, I received this invitation. Is this right?"

"You are correct. Mr. Multer I presume?"

"Yeah, just Doug please," he responded, timid, while handing me his invitation.

"Well my name is Dean, here is your key. Do you need help with your bag?"

"I can manage, thank you."

"Well alright then, elevator is right over there. Dinner will be at six, with the other guests, and the owner. Located in the dining hall in the west wing."

"Thanks," he said, still looking at the floor.

Good thing that didn't take long. Immediately walking in was room three. Dr. Marshall. Quick in and out. You can easily tell he's a little pre-occupied in his head. Room four, Dr. Rothman… Room five Steven. Paranoid fuck. Steven was the only one to ask why there was no plus one allowed. "The owner wanted to make this a special night, for one to relax and feel rejuvenated when they leave. Being alone, and feeling no need to entertain a guest, you'll be able to really relish in the experience." The answer I gave was able to glaze over his anxiety enough to get him upstairs. Why won't someone have me take their bags? Give me a reason to go up there.

Room six. Megan. I don't know what he sees in her. Megan was so plain. She didn't even do anything wrong. Why does she deserve a key? Walking in she seemed closed off from the outside world. The bag she was carrying looked as if she's been staying in motel after motel for a while. Her face had scratches all over, covered poorly by makeup. The only other scratches were around her wedding ring. I wonder if he'll tell me why she's here, and why he has been keeping it from me. He's filled me in on everything. He's completely let me in his mind. I'm the only one he trusts and yet I'm still not his child. But, this plain jane, timid, sad looking woman standing before me is… pathetic. She's not even capable of looking me in the eyes, and looked devastated when she found out that she was told to attend dinner with the other guests and Mr. Sweets. This should be an interesting night.

Room One

"Classy place we've got, and we didn't have to kill anybody to get here." Jake laughed, and belly flopped onto the bed.

"Stop making it messy! Enjoy the fanciness while we can. And don't say kill. That's so barbaric." Maggie climbed on top him to pitch her 'fun' idea. "What do you think we have some fun tonight?" He instantly knew what she was talking about.

"Did you bring the tools? Isn't this a little complicated, with all these people here? We normally do smaller Mags…" Rolling her eyes, she climbed off him like he couldn't see what was right in front of his face.

"Jake, there are no computer records here. Everything is done the 'classic' way. Which means one copy, which means one record. You know how easy this would be. This is our biggest challenge yet! Makes me kind of want you right now." He pulled her back on him. Kissing her neck, Jake agreed that he was on board with her plan. Jake only had two objections that he needed to be reassured by her.

"Why out of everyone did he pick us to travel all the way out here for one night? It's not like we're celebrities. And who else is going to be here? This just all is a little sketchy, don't you think?" Maggie reached down, licking his lips, and whispered into his mouth.

"Stop talking." She knew she could only calm Jake down one way. Jake wasn't into it. As much as he wanted to, he couldn't shake this bad feeling.

"Okay. What's going on?" Maggie asked annoyed.

"Nothing."

"Jake, you never hesitate with this. And, you *never* have a problem with saying no to this." Maggie was nervous that Jake was growing tired of her.

"Please don't Mags. I'm sorry. But, nothing about this makes you wonder?"

"No. Babe we've been doing this for eleven years. We even have foster kids."

"It's sick that we bring them into our lives." Jake said, guilt soaked in every word.

"Don't. we had to. We needed something to justify us 'working' from home. Just sales, isn't good enough." She snapped, mad that he thought there was another way. Maggie always made sure it was impossible to get caught.

"I know. It's just, for some reason I feel like our time is running out."

"We're invincible, babe. No one will ever compare to what we are."

"Ha, I love your teenage mentality," he chuckled, beginning to feel reassured.

"Shit, what time did we have to be down for dinner?" Maggie rolled off the bed.

"Six. We have ten minutes! Get ready! Put the tools by the door, I don't want to be late."

Maggie put on her best dress she had packed, and fluffed her hair. Jake buttoned up his shirt, and straightened the tie that matched her Navy-blue dress. "You look gorgeous, Mags."

She rushed into her heels, and yelled coming out of the bathroom, "leave your phone up here!"

Jake followed to the door, and bumped into Maggie. She turned the knob, but the door didn't budge, "the door is locked." A feeling came over Jake, that brought him speechless.

"Jake, grab the key. Stupid, 'classic' style bullshit."

"Here, I had it in my pocket," Jake fumbled in his pocket for the key.

Snatching the key, Maggie inserted it into the lock. The key was fully engulfed by the door knob, "What the fuck?" The room quickly became hotter, making difficult to breathe almost instantly. "What's going on Jake." Jake still speechless just stared at the door. Hoping that the key would magically pop out of the keyhole. But, he knew that wasn't going to happen.

"I don't think we were ever meant to leave this room Mags," the sound coming out of his mouth scratched at his throat. Like sandpaper rubbing together. His mouth was so dry, he couldn't generate enough saliva to smooth his throat.

Maggie began to plan. "Okay, we've been through worse. So, we're locked in a scorching hot hotel room. I'm sure there is more than one way out of here. There's got to be. I've got the tools, go look for anything we can use."

Both focused on escaping, didn't realize their bodies began to give out. Suffering the beginning stages of heat stroke in such a short amount of time, Jake dropped everything, grabbed Maggie, and escorted her to the bathroom. "Get in the shower Mags. I'll take the sink! Strip down. Try to do warm water so your body doesn't go into shock." Shear fear grew fiercer when neither faucet turned on. Jake went to the toilet to dunk his face in. Empty. Maggie went for the minibar, empty.

"Jake it's so hot... my eyeballs are melting," Maggie choked out through her dry mouth.

"Don't think like that Mags."

"My skin feels like it's boiling..."

"STOP IT MAGGIE! Focus on getting out."

"Do you hear that?" Maggie quickly stopped breathing, so she could hear the subtle sound.

Jake stopped to listen. It was a vibration noise, like a cat purring. The sound grew louder, and louder. Maggie was terrified, she crouched down into a ball. Naked, vulnerable, and dehydrating more and more by the second. She knew whatever was making that noise was going to be the cause of her death. She couldn't help but think back of her mom. She was their first kill together. The loving couple celebrated their same interest by trapping Maggie's mother in her tanning bed out in the garage, then made love for the first time on the ground, next to their smoldering screaming victim, the same night as their first date.

"Something's coming out of the bathroom." Jake was trying to blink his dry eyes to help him see clearer. Creeping out of the bathroom, purring away... Butters.

"No fucking way. Maggie..."

"Oh, my god. That's impossible," Maggie sat up in shock. "It's a hallucination."

Maggie refused to accept the hallucination. Her body moved from her cowardly position to standing tall and fearless. Her head faced the ceiling, she closed her eyes, and exclaimed as loud as possible. "COME OUT YOU FUCKING COWARD!" She used the last of her strength to shout. Collapsing, Maggie didn't have long left. She fell to the floor, almost appearing lifeless. Her eyes were locked on Butters, who made his way around the room, and sat on the bed. His eyes enclosed on her body, as if she was his prey.

"Mags get up! We have to find a way out of here, I can't do this without you," he pleaded, unable to move due to exhaustion.

Jake reached his arm out to Maggie, and started mustering up the strength to grab her, when all of the sudden he began to feel hands around his neck. He looked up at the culprit, and fell paralyzed of who was standing over him. Mrs. Holtan... Jakes first kill. Mrs. Holtan had her long cold fingers around his neck. The cold felt like scolding hot irons, burning through his skin. Gripping tighter and tighter, Jake felt his eyeballs begin to swell. He tried to signal to Maggie. Peeking out of the corner of his eye, he saw Maggie, being ripped to shreds. Jake knew he lost his hearing, he couldn't hear Maggie crying out to him. Butters sat only inches away from her, staring intently. Wore out from the heat, and losing oxygen, Jake had no strength in him to fight back. His heart was shredded into pieces along with Maggie, so him dying didn't matter. He stared into Mrs. Holtan's eyes with pain and remorse. Mrs. Holtan only said one thing to him before death took over, "welcome to hell."

His eyes closed slowly as he accepted what he knew he always deserved. Brutal death. Waiting to enter of what he thought would be the utter blackness of hell, or some sort of light for a chance to repent to heaven… Jake opened his eyes holding the key in his hand. For a moment, he thought to himself, it was just a day dream fueled by his bad feeling. But, Maggie's expression answered his unasked question.

"Don't put the key in Maggie."

"What do we do?" Maggie replied, worried.

"Break the door down!" Jake yelled. "Grab something Heavy, we'll smash it!"

No matter how many times they tried a new way to escape, they key always made it into the lock… which shortly led to their death. It was somewhat poetic… Her first kill, his first kill, intertwined with their first kill together. It was a beautiful symphony of revenge and karma. Repeating, for all eternity.

Room Two

Doug Multer. Convicted of killing his girlfriend Emma, was sentenced to live in a mental institution, for claiming that a homeless man and his dog killed his girlfriend. Only serving eleven years he worked through his issues. Doug's Doctor, who was assigned to his case, said it should be addressed as an accidental death due to past trauma. He's has worked through the trauma, and should be released, and assigned to mandatory therapy to continue on this healthy, healing path.

Doug did the right thing by doing everything the Doctor instructed him to, not to heal, but to be released. He had to get out. He knew that they were still out there. That it was his job to avenge Emma's death. When Doug was released and his personally belongings were returned to him. He received something new. The invitation. Dead set on declining such a miraculous offer, Doug knew he had no one to call and nowhere to go. All his friends and family had disowned him over the years. He had no choice, but to stay at the Oliver Sweets Hotel. With twenty dollars in his pocket, he called a cab and was taken to the hotel. He'll devise a plan, and start fresh tomorrow. Hell, maybe the owner of the hotel will hear his story and offer to help.

Entering his room. Doug couldn't help but think of Emma. "You would love this room, babe." Having nothing to change into for dinner. He laid across the bed, and began to think. First off, he couldn't help but feel as if he had fallen on a cloud. The beds at the institution were like laying on a bumpy, sharp bolder. It was nice for him to relax and feel rejuvenated before dining with normal strangers. Especially after everything he's been through. He needed a plan. He needed closure. The only way he knew how to reveal that he wasn't crazy was to find the mutt and bum, and prove his innocence.

Checking the time, Doug saw it was ten 'til six. He should probably start walking. With how large this hotel is, he needed to give himself enough time, and mentally prepare himself on the walk down there. Reaching for the door handle, he realized it was locked. "Of course, I get the room with the faulty door." Trying credit cards, and jiggling the door knob every way possible, he went to the hotel phone by the bed to call down to front desk. The call never went through. Doug began feeling panicked. "What if they forget I'm up here? What if they think I'm being rude, and kick me out? Key! Maybe the key unlocks from the inside as well!"

Doug removed the key from his pocket and inserted it into the lock. The key submerged itself into the knob. Shocked of how that was even possible, he was hoping it was just a fluke. Doug bent down to look through the lock. Hoping maybe there was a way he could weasel it out of the key hole.

But what he saw was no key... Looking through the hole, Doug saw his room. Or what resembled his room. He blinked in disbelief. Mistake. After he took a long hard blink he opened his eyes and saw her. Emma standing there, covered in blood. It didn't look like her blood. But,

Doug couldn't really study what was going on, he was just shocked to see Emma's face. He shot back as if he took a gunshot to the chest. He tripped back, and fell into someone's arms. Looking up trying to balance his feet, he saw it was Emma who caught him. "NO! Baby! How?!" Emma smiled down at him and helped him regain his balance. Doug was stunned. *How could be real?* He thought to himself. Happy to see her, He glanced up and down at her. There wasn't any blood on her like he saw in the key hole. "How?! Is this real?! Are you real?!" He embraced her, and kissed her face. Every little wrinkle, engorging himself in her smell.

Emma whispered in his ear, "I am. Surprised?" Doug couldn't even respond, he had to relish in this moment he's been yearning for, for eleven fucking years.

He kissed her lifeless lips. Doug tried to get a physical response back from her, but nothing came of it. "What's wrong?" He pulled his face away, looking deep into Emma's eyes. His hands cupping her face. She continued to smile at him, but it grew into more of a menacing grin.

"Oh Dougy… Why did you do this to me?"

"What do you mean?" Doug was stunned.

"You killed me Dougy, over a dog," Emma hissed at him.

"WHAT?! You sent me out there to go get the damn thing!"

"Still playing the victim, aren't you? God, you are pathetic. What did I ever see in you?"

"Emma, I would never hurt you. It wasn't me. You have to remember."

168

"Oh, I remember, you are the one that doesn't have all the facts straight. Let me refresh your memory." Emma grabbed each side of his face. Smashing his cheeks together, she kissed him with such force, Doug felt his nose crack. Emma replayed for him the truth of what had happened the last night they were together.

He was standing in their apartment, as a third party to their past selves. He watched them unpack. Everywhere she set something up, he immediately criticized her. Doug called Emma the cruelest names, then would isolate himself on the balcony and occasionally poke his head in to yell at her, "you make me want to kill myself!" Doug had no recollection of that incident. Fast forwarding to the first night he saw the mutt, it was almost like Doug was in a trance. He began talking to himself. Staring intently at the dog.

On the last night, Emma couldn't take it any longer, "if you love that fucking dog so much then why don't you just go get the damn thing!"

When he returned with the dog, he grabbed a knife on the way to the bedroom, "I'm going to kill this dog, and then myself. He should never be subjected to this kind of emotional abuse you put me through." Emma rolled over in bed, her back facing Doug.

"Dougy, if you think that I abuse you, you are sorely mistaken. Honestly, I don't even know why I'm with you. I went from pitying you to just hating you," that's when Doug snapped, and brutally murdered Emma.

Doug awoke, and found himself lying flat on the bed in his hotel room, with Emma standing over him. This had to be a trick of the mind. He thought maybe he is fabricating this in his head out of guilt for not saving her. "Mind over matter." He clenched his eyelids shut as hard as he possibly could. Trying to envision his escape from the room.

"It's not in your mind, dear. You're here, this is real. Open your eyes and look at me damn it!" Emma demanded.

"What do you want from me Emma?"

"Why, to help you do what you've always wanted... to kill yourself."

"I don't want to kill myself. I have a job to do. I have to catch the fucker that murdered you."

Emma grabbed him by his shirt collar, and swung him into the mirror across from the bed, smashing his face against the glass. "Take a good look Dougy. There's your murderer."

He kept reflecting on his memories of Emma... He started to see a little clearer. He thought maybe she was right. Or maybe he's doing what he was trained to do, agree to whatever he must, to be able to escape.

"Okay, you are right. Will you let me go? I will go straight to the police station and make sure they put me away for life in prison." Doug subtly pleaded, nervous.

"You don't deserve prison."

"What do you deem appropriate then. Whatever it is, I'll do it."

"Like I said, I'm going to assist your suicide Dougy. I've always made you want to kill yourself, Right? So, I thought we'd take it up a notch and actually pull the trigger. Pun intended, ha."

"So, I have to shoot myself? That's what will make you happy?"

"Oh, no, Dougy. That's too painless. We're going to get creative."

Doug started to tremble. He didn't want to kill himself. Emma was wrong. He just needed to prove he's telling the truth. "Please, Emma, I didn't kill you." She walked to the drawer by the bed and pulled out a knife, the exact knife he supposedly murdered her with.

"Where do you want to start? Small with the shallow wounds? Or do you just want to go for the deep organ piercings?"

"Emma, I'm innocent. I'm not doing this," he pleaded, starting to cry.

Grazing the knife over her finger tips, she sang her response, "Mm… You're going to change your tune real soon Dougy. This is going to be fun. Here. Take the knife." His body was moving against his will. He lost all physical control. Doug accepted the knife from Emma and stood in front of her as she was sitting on the bed. Standing there, tears were streaming from his remorseful eyes.

"Please. Don't." he hoped one more plea would help her see that it wasn't him.

"I know! We should start with my first stab wound. Where was it? Oh, yeah! My right breast. That one wasn't too deep. I'm being generous. This time."

"What do you mean this time?" Doug asked, directing the knife to his breast.

"Just, proceed. Now." Emma instructed.

"No."

"You're going to make me force you. No Fun Dougy!"

Pouting at Doug, Emma forced his hand that was gripping the knife, and pierced into his right peck. Howling in pain, he noticed Emma was bleeding from the exact spot he just stabbed himself. "Emma! How is this possible?!" Giggling, Emma showed how anxious she was, waiting to answer this exact question.

"Well, Dougy. Here's the thing. Wounding yourself just isn't enough. What would really get you? What would really serve as an appropriate punishment? And then it just hit me! In your mind, I'm the only one that you 'truly love'. So… hurt yourself, while you witness what you TRULY did to me! So, let's continue!"

Emma relished in every single stab wound, until they both fell on the floor, choking through their last breaths. To Emma, this is exactly where she wanted to be. To watch this monster torcher himself was all the justice she needed. And to spend an eternity playing this process repeatedly, was her heaven.

Doug let death take over, like a dark drape covering over his body. He was ready to embrace heaven. He was innocent. He would never do such a treacherous act that she is accusing him of. Doug felt the blood in his body replenish. Excited to open his eyes and see the golden gates to heaven, his was sorely mistaken… Doug's eyes were looking up at the ceiling of the fucking hotel room. He fluttered his eyes over a hundred times, praying for a different outcome. His prayer was never answered. Doug knew what was coming next. This is hell.

Room Three

*Why did you come here? This is ridiculous. Can't bring
a guest. The fuck are we supposed to do in this romantic
looking place alone.*

"Shut up. Just shut the hell up. After what you've done,
you don't deserve to occupy my thoughts." Dr. Marshall
entered his room with the clothes on his back, a bottle of
pills, and large bottle of rum. He had no intentions of going
to dinner. All Marshall wanted to do was put his mind at
ease, and pass out in a luxurious bed, and sleep through the
crashing hangover he was going to have after a few hours.

Entering the room, he raised his eyebrows thoroughly
impressed. He laid his medicines, for the mind, on the
TV stand. Sitting on the bed, he gave it a bounce. "Yep,
this will do." Marshall removed his shoes and coat.
Falling back on the bed, he closed his eyes, and drifted
to sleep accidentally.

Every time he would sleep without his 'medicine' he'd
have the same recurring dream. Rosa. She was standing
in the hallway of the clinic and just call to him. "Rosa."
He whispered in his sleep. Quickly Marshall jumped
frantically off the bed. "I need a drink." He reached for
the ice bucket to chill his rum with and went for the door.
The door didn't open. Without having a fearful reaction,
he noticed the other side of the door knob also had a key
hole. Rationally thinking, he put the key in to open the

door. The key sucked into the knob, locking him in to his journey of hell.

"HEY MARSHY!" he heard the voice in his head. Only this time it wasn't in his head, but behind him.

"How?" he turned around, shocked to see the voice had its own body.

"I don't know! But it's pretty fucking awesome! I even look younger!" the voice laughed.

Speechless that he was looking at an exact clone of himself. For the first time in his life, his head felt empty with only his thoughts occupying his mind. He tried to respond with no hint of emotion, "we look exactly the same. How did you manage to do this?"

"This isn't my doing Marshy, if I was able to do this, I would've done it years ago! Would've been a hell of a lot more fun than fighting with you constantly. Speaking of… What are you going to do now that you're alone?"

Marshall didn't even know how to respond to his question. Excitement took over as he started to realize he was free. It's what he's always dreamed of. But, he mostly wanted a chance to be with Rosa. He knew that would never happen… Depression and pain hit like a freight train. Feeling such an immense amount of emotions, being alone was the most painful thing he's ever had to endure.

"Hello? I'm not in your head anymore Marshmallow. So, this tortured silence of in your head nonsense is weird to witness as an outsider, and yes, I'm highly judging you for this."

"Give me a minute. You are always so pushy." Marshall's pain turned into frustration.

"Because I live in the now Marshall. Don't think it, do it. Which reminds me. I need a name. my own name. Something dependable, trusting. Oh! Dave! Everybody wants a buddy Dave. Uncle Dave. Daddy Dave. Works! I like it!" Dave cheered.

"You are more annoying as a person, than you were a voice."

"And you are a more pathetic sight than I ever could've imagined. You should be excited!"

"I would be if you wouldn't have killed my one and only love on this world." Marshall snapped.

"Love? Really?" Dave chuckled.

"She was innocent! Rosa had nothing to do with your sick game." Marshall dropped to his knees, cradling his face.

"Me? Oh, that's real rich Marshall. Sorry... but the 'urge' you have doesn't stem from me." Dave sounded offended for being accused of causing harm to others.

"What do you mean?" Marshall looked up, confused.

"Marshall, I feed on impulse. Your most inner desire. I have a need to help you fulfill your subconscious wants and needs."

"You're lying. I would never want to hurt Rosa!"

'Dave' opened the bottle of rum and took a hefty swig. "Marshy, I never wanted any of this. Truly. You asked for this. You wanted it. Solley. I just gave you that little push to help you. Now, you might as well have a drink. Looks like we're going to be in here for a while." Marshall snatched the bottle from his buddy Dave's hand. Trying to wrap his head around how any of this was logically possible. Was he truly his own worst enemy?

Before he could accept this strange situation, he was put in, another party fell right into frame without warning. Marshall was sitting on the bed facing Dave passing the bottle back and forth.

"You going to share the love guys?" Marshall's heart stopped mid beat. Turning his head, there she was. Rosa. How did Marshall get so lucky? Or maybe unlucky... If what Dave was saying was true, then the want to do it again isn't going to go away.

"Rosa, How?" Marshall asked.

"I'm dead Doctor Marshall," Rosa replied.

"I know... I'm so sorry," he sunk his head lower, putting his lips to the bottle.

"Don't feel sorry for me. Feel sorry for my kids! You ripped me away from Kylie and Anthony with no warning what so ever. No explanation. I felt sorry for you. I should've left when I had the chance, and moved far away from your ass," Rosa was filled with bitterness.

Marshall snapped. He smashed the bottle right across her head. "Oh no. Why did I do that?! Rosa!" He feared his impulses.

Dave was shaking the bottle of pills, contemplating on whether to take a few. "Because this is who you are. This is what you're capable of. Nothing will stop you from the urges Marsh. I just sped up the process."

Tears streaming from his eyes, Marshall searched frantically through the room to find something to suture the huge gash on her head. There was nothing. The only thing he could think of was to grab a towel to apply pressure to the wound. Rosa gained consciousness as soon as he put the towel to her head. She writhed in pain. Screaming into Marshall's face. He was crying to her apologizing trying to get her to calm down. He wanted to relieve her of the pain he caused.

"Dave! Give me the pills!" Marshall cried out.

"Okay… you going to shove them down her throat?" Dave said, still acting calm.

"Just give me the damn pills!"

"Fine, here. Hey, wouldn't it feel amazing to take your precious woman's life again? Just be her blanket, as her body turns cold. Maybe if you try it a second time, she won't puke on you like before!"

"QUIET!" He cried out.

Marshall opened the pills and fed Rosa one after another. Rosa awoke quickly from the chalky textured pill being shoved down her throat. Choking out, all she could manage to say was, "hate you."

Hearing hate come out of Rosa's beautiful mouth was appalling for him to hear. Instead of giving her a number of pills to relieve her pain. He couldn't stop. He started grabbing the pills by the handful instead of one at a time. After shoving down everyone he had. He cried and screamed in pain. "Why did you make me do this? I loved you! All I wanted was for you to love me back. You don't love me? Then you won't get the chance to love anyone else. The last thing you will ever see is the pain in my eyes, caused by you!"

Rosa's eyes rolled to the back of her head. She began convulsing. Marshall looked to Dave.

"This is how you killed her. You didn't do it slow... You brutally hurt her! You are a monster," Marshall accused Dave again.

Dave was stunned, then broke out in laughter, "are you kidding me?! Look at you! You no longer have the option to hide behind me so innocently while I act out your deepest desires. Marshall... you say you have no recollection of how she died. But look." Marshall looked across the bed and saw scalpels, syringes, and every type of medication he's ever used in the past. All labels showed that everything was prescribed to Rosa.

"What... what is this?" He started hyperventilating.

"Marshy, you know what you did. Don't play dumb. You were there. Face the truth. The monster that you thought was me is still inside of you. I'm not at fault. It has always been you."

"This can't be," he sat there in disbelief.

"Marshall! Look! Read the labels. Everything here is what you've prescribed for her. You never took any of it. You just wanted to save it, for her. Because you knew that she truly despised you. She pitied you. And you just couldn't handle it anymore. Show yourself. Remind yourself of exactly what you've done."

Against his will, his body was grabbing different injections, and inserting them into various parts of Rosa's body. He then grabbed the scalpel and began to slice into her precious caramel, silk skin. It felt as if he was grazing into butter. He began to feel euphoric. Feeling her body twitch and drift away. Matching her outer beauty to her inner beauty. If she was as angelic as he thought, she would've loved him. Fucking bitch. "You will die in my arms. I am the last face you will see. You've ruined me Rosa. I loved you. And now, you have no choice but to love me in return. You are mine forever." Rosa took her last final breath…

Marshall, held her close to his body, "What have I done?... I couldn't stop. I couldn't allow her to treat me this way."

Dave decided, now this was the time to interject. "I told you so… now, she's dead. You were never fighting me exactly. You were always fighting yourself. I just helped with the 'urges', and no matter how you feel about someone. Nothing will ever stop you from restraining from *your own* urges. Hold her now, while her body is still warm. It's the closest you'll ever get to physical emotion. Hey, I got to take a leak. Be right back."

"She doesn't even look human. Why can't I just sustain, and be the man you want me to be Rosa? You deserved so much better. I never wanted to hurt you. I love you. Watching you die by my hand is the hardest thing to witness. I removed the most beautiful woman from this world. I sent your body into a coma, and mangled your beautiful skin like my own personal rag doll. I'm nothing but a monster. Depriving others from meeting the most amazing person that's ever walked this earth. I made your children motherless. I should be the one dead." Tears streaming from his eyes, he clenched them closed. Ashamed of himself. Especially for being too big of a coward to do the world a favor and kill himself.

Opening his eyes, everything changed. Rum unopened. Pill bottle full. "What?" He went for the door. Locked. He inserted his key, out of genuine curiosity.

"HEY MARSHY! LOOK!" he heard the voice in his head. Only this time it wasn't in his head, but behind him.

"Fuck." Marshall laughed to himself, he instantly knew what was going on. "At least I finally get what I deserve. Well played Mr. Sweets."

Room Four

Dr. Angie Rothman. A paranoid, strung out therapist who is incapable of helping herself from this psychotic breakdown she's been suffering from for years. After accidently scaring the life out of one of her patients, she lives with that guilt. Rotting in her from the inside.

Angie made it up to her room, she was excited she could successfully sneak up her own food. She had no intention of going down to dinner. Being around groups of people made her extremely uncomfortable. People talked too much for her. Angie liked being in her own head. For eleven years, she has been living with the fear of looking behind her, including walking backwards, reflections, even photos. Angie also refused to look at past photos of herself. All this time she was battling if this was real or if this was a contagious phobia.

Angie went straight into the bathroom. Leaving the light off. Keeping lights off always made it easier to avoid the mirror. She turned on the bath. Removing her clothes, she took her shirt, and wrapped it around her eyes. The only time Angie felt true peace was when her eyes were hidden. Slipping in the bath, it was dark, quiet, and blind. She could finally unwind.

"Complete utter silence…" she gasped, feeling relieved. Not even a minute had gone by before she heard someone walking outside the bathroom. "Hello?" Removing her blindfold, she saw nothing. She glanced at the door from the bath, and noticed a key hole on her side of the door. "huh… maybe I'm supposed to lock myself in?" Grabbing her key off the bathroom counter and locking the door looked like too much work. Angie hated that she left her key right in front of the mirror, she didn't understand how she slipped up like that. Angie got out of the bath, and went for the key as carefully as possible.

Sealing her eyes shut, she focused purely on her feeling sense. Retrieving the key, it took her another three minutes to exit the bathroom. Finally, Angie successfully put the key in. She returned to her bath. Emerging herself, Angie forgot to put on her blindfold. Terrified, she focused on the light in the doorway of the bathroom. She heard something. Or more like someone, rustling through her room.

All Angie could think of was to slip out of the bath as quietly as possible. Grab her robe, and sneak up on the intruder. Success. Peeking her head slightly around the doorway, she froze in fear. She couldn't believe her eyes. It was Becca…

"Hi, Angie," Becca was staring waiting for Angie to come out.

"Becca… What are you doing here?"

"Just want to talk," Becca responded with a sense of sweetness in her voice.

"I've officially hit my psychotic breakdown."

"No Angie, I'm afraid not. This is real."

"What do you want, Becca?"

"You killed me."

"No, you were petrified to death. You didn't realize mind over matter, Becca."

"So, I killed myself? You truly believe that, Dr. Rothman?"

"Becca, I did everything I could to help you," Angie's voice sounding unsure.

"You didn't want to help me. You just wanted to prove that your traumatizing practices worked. Which they never did. I'm not the only one you've done this too, am I?"

"No..." she confessed guiltily.

"Speaking the truth! Sooner than I thought! Good for you, Ange!"

"What's your point here?" She said annoyed.

"How many kids over the span of your career have you 'helped'?"

"Forty-three."

"Good God woman, you were busy! Now why is it that no one found out about the other forty-two?"

"I staged their deaths as accidents. I was never faulted," admitting that out loud felt as if her ribs were beginning to crumble with every breath she took.

"Correct me if I'm wrong, but, you don't think about your other victims do you. In your head, I am your only one."

"The others didn't count..." Angie blurted.

"Didn't count? Other children that instilled their trust in you, didn't fucking count. Wow, really shows your compassion Doctor Rothman."

"They were ready to face their fear. You weren't I rushed yours."

"Is that why you didn't stage my death?"

"No..."

"Good girl. Why didn't you stage mine Angie?"

"Because I didn't have enough time."

"YES! This is way easier than I expected! You're just laying it all out!" Becca laughed proudly.

"My turn, what is this thing behind me? Phobia? Real?"

"Here's what is going to happen. You have been honest about everything. So, to be fair, I'm going to be honest with you. Angie, you will never know the truth of what is behind you. But, what is going to happen, is so much better. You are going to experience every single fear that caused your victims demise. All forty-two. Except mine."

"Why? I've been in hell for the past eleven years! Isn't that enough?!"

"Not even close, Ange."

"Fine, say I allow this to happen. Please just tell me, is this real or not?" Angie was ready to bargain.

"You are in no position to ask for anything."

"Then I'm walking out," she had enough.

"Try, please," Becca was amused.

"The door's locked. Where is my key Becca?!"

"Gone, now… out of kindness I'm going to fill you in on a few things. You will never leave this room. You will never die. You will never discover what is behind you. Lastly, you will feel every ounce of pain each of your victims felt. And, when you die, you'll wake up. Still residing within these walls. Starting the process again, and again, and again. Forever."

"Please, no! I'm sorry, I'm so sorry! Becca please! I'll turn myself in!"

"Not good enough."

Becca began the process. She danced around Angie's body while she was writhing in pain. Screaming for forgiveness. Dr. Angie Rothman… ha, what a joke.

Room Five

Steven checked in. Angry, he wondered why he ever agreed to any of this. He reminded himself that he needed to escape. Escape from his town thinking he was a murderous monster, protected by his parents. They didn't think he was innocent. They pitied him. Thought Steven was crazy. That's honestly worse than thinking he was guilty.

Entering his room. He slipped his key into the inside of the lock, so he wouldn't lose it. Steven opened his bag ready to 'dress to impress'. It had been so long since he could have a conversation with someone who was unaware of his past. Killing your newlywed wife and unborn baby wasn't necessarily a trait people wanted in a person to converse with.

Wearing his best flannel, jeans, and boots. He wanted to go down extra early to have a few pre-dinner drinks, and socialize. He was hoping that the other guests would be down there. Steven was so anxious to meet new people. It had been so long. His parents never released him for anything. Steven couldn't even piss alone. He was trapped and convicted, being smothered to death. Why would he kill the love of his life, and unborn daughter? That was just nonsense to even think about. "Stop." Steven stopped his thought process right then and there. He didn't sneak out and travel all the way out here, just to dwell on his home life. This was a true opportunity for a new beginning.

Reaching for the door he saw it was locked, with the key nowhere in sight. "What the hell?" *BANG, BANG, BANG!* He banged on the door, trying to get help. "Hello! Anybody?! I'm locked in here! SOMEBODY?!" Steven gave up quickly banging on the door, and decided the most logical thing to do was call down to front desk and get help that way.

Steven turned around to find out he was no longer in his room, but standing in the doorway of his new home that he had with Christy. "Huh?" He saw himself coming down the stairs, looking at his other self, standing in the doorway. "Babe! This is so exciting! Go sit down, and rest your feet. I'll take care of the rest!" Past Steven guided present Steven to the couch, and then kissed his other self's forehead.

Steven instantly felt freaked. To add more to the madness, Steven looked down, and saw he wasn't who he thought he was. He was looking through Christy's eyes. "I remember this day…" He continued watching himself move boxes in with both sets of parents. After both sets of parents left. Things started happening that he had no recollection of. He saw himself just walk over and kiss his beautiful wife. And then… Steven punched Christy right in the temple. Causing her to knock out. When Steven, aka Christy awoke, he was in bed. Past Steven was standing over him with an ice pack.

"Here honey, that was a nasty fall you had," past Steven said with a nurturing tone.

"I need to go to the hospital," 'Christy' muttered.

"You don't remember the Doctor was already here love. You're fine. Mild concussion."

"You hit me…"

"What are you talking about Christy, I would never lay a hand on you."

"I'm not Christy…"

"See honey, you're delusional. Here, drink this everything will be alright."

As the days progressed, Steven found his past self randomly abusing him. Never twice. Just one good hit, kick, smack. Sometimes even throw objects at him. Injuring him badly. Every time Steven would try to speak up to his past self, he would always reply, "Christy, I can't help that you are accident prone. For you to think I would hurt you is just simply insulting." After saying that, he'd hit Steven harder than ever. Still, only one time.

The night she died, Steven found himself packing up Christy's things. He couldn't control her body. It was like he was on a virtual ride, interacting through voice, but no action. He was just an outsider witnessing what was going on. Helpless. 'Christy' went to grab her phone of the nightstand when all the sudden past Steven woke up and saw her. He reached over grabbing her phone, and kicked her right in the stomach, then innocently rolled over to go back to sleep.

This hit was not like the others. His kick had immediate consequence. She called to him. Christy knew for the sake of the baby he would get her to the hospital, hearing her thoughts run through her mind, while present Steven was inhabiting her body was the most terrifying thing he had to hear.

Steven saw and felt everything through Christy's point of view. He understood why she never wanted him in delivery. She insisted that he needed to be escorted by security out of the hospital. He finally was seeing her for the first time. He felt her panic. Felt her pain. He was the cause of all of this. Everyone was right about him. Christy's life was dwindling. In what Steven knew were his last moments of life he closed his eyes and pictured Christy and Christina. "I'm sorry, my girls."

Embracing death, Steven wounded up back in front of his hotel door. He rationalized thinking that the change of his normal environment, to somewhere unfamiliar was the cause of this psychotic episode. He wanted to turn around and grab a drink out of the mini fridge to take the edge off. When he turned, he saw himself standing in his house, again…

Room Six

Megan is not like the others. She is something special. Sort of a prized possession of Oliver's. He finds her fascinating. Megan was his first 'child'. He chose her because of her light. She was so innocent. That intrigued him. He pushed her. Did everything he could to try to bring out her inner demons. He discovered that she was pure.

Instead of moving on, he became intrigued by this challenge. After years of choosing his other 'children', he educated himself on hidden desires, nightmares, and things that could make people tick. After six years, he returned to his Megan. He rose to the challenge of what he thought could be her inner demon. Him.

Megan lost everything. Her family, her home, everything. She became obsessed with finding out who E is, and defeating him to protect her children. She's been on a man hunt the past eleven years. Always thinking she was getting somewhere, she found herself at a dead end. This invitation was a sign of hope. She knew that this had to be connected. Him reaching out to her in some way.

She came prepared. She left a note at the current motel she was staying at. It said to search for her in forty-eight hours. Megan packed every cliché weapon she could think of to fight off the paranormal. Checking in, she walked up to her room, and immediately locked the door. "I've dreamt about this E. Don't fuck around, let's just get this started."

"Now you've ruined my fun," E answered, snidely.

She turned around. "Who are you," Megan didn't ask, she demanded, knowing this is probably her only chance.

"Why, I'm the notorious, E."

"No, you aren't. You look nothing like him."

"Well of course not. E is someone you created. I gave you a blank canvas, and you colored it in quite nicely, Megan. I'm thoroughly impressed."

Megan was standing in the front of the door of the hotel room. Sitting directly across the room was someone she has never seen before, and thankful that she never had. Standing before her was a sickly, slender man. His skin was a chalky tan. Wrinkled from head to toe. He was balled aside from three white hair strands that sprouted off the top of his scalp. Bug eyed, long nose, cheeks sunk in, and the tiniest mouth holding teeth that resembled off white tic-tacs that look as if they were found in the dirtiest couch cushions. He had abnormally long fingers with nails looking as if they were bruised. "I dressed nice for you Megan. I see you didn't return the gesture." He had on a cream button up on with a maroon sweater vest, grass green bow tie, and dark khaki slacks with old fashioned dress shoes. Megan felt her mouth salivate. This was it. Her final chapter.

"I'll dress to the occasion after I'm done with you."

"You're so cute Megan, nothing in that little bag of yours will do a thing. We will have no physical contact. But, I will do you one favor. You see, I can't understand you. You are my biggest puzzle, my dear. And, well, the type of person I am, I can't leave something unfinished, Especially my first child."

"I'm not your fucking child."

"Okay now... let's not get off subject. I'm going to allow you to ask me two questions. And then I'll simply let you go."

"Two questions? You just expect me to comply willingly? Just for two fucking questions?!"

Megan went to swing the bag off her back and found herself at a standstill, uncappable of making any kind of movement. "What is this?!"

He stood up, and approached her as close as he could without touching. His breath smelt of dead ash, making Megan's eyes water. She tried to choke out, be he had her. Without touching her. She wasn't surprised. He stared right into her with his yellow eyes. "You have two questions, and I will let you go. For now, choose wisely. This is far from over, little girl." He allowed Megan to have speaking capability, but kept her body stationary.

"Why... What are you?"

"Too vague Megan, but, I'll answer. I am Oliver Sweets. I am something people fear in their subconscious. They face me without even knowing... until it's too late."

"Also, vague Mr. Sweets. What do you want from me?"

"Oh, my dear, I was hoping you would be more clever than this. This is what you've been waiting for. After all this time, I brought you to me. I gave you two questions. Practically made you feel like you had the upper hand. But, you've simply wasted it. I'm highly disappointed… How about this. I will have you do one thing more before you leave, well five really."

Oliver forced her eyes closed. Megan flashed through each story that led his other five 'children' here. Taking her through each painful step of what every one of them are going through, due to Oliver. Barely breathing, Megan opened her eyes, tears shortly followed. "What's going to happen to them? What'd you do?!"

He twisted his head completely horizontal, and grinned a grin that no one could have ever imagined. "You're out of questions. Well I'd say I hate to cut this short, but… this meeting was quite disappointing, Megan. I had said I will let you go, and I will, but I assure you… I will see you soon, my child."

Megan fell to the floor, passing out. Hours later, she awoke. Springing up she grabbed her things, and ran out of her room. She had no need for the key that was lying on the floor next to her. The door to the room was already open. As Megan ran out of her worst nightmare, she was passing the other five suites.

Every door she passed had screams slipping through the cracks of each door. From shrill, to curdled scream. There were screams for help, and ones that sounded as if they were in the most excruciating pain.

Making it to the lobby, Megan grabbed onto the front desk. "Help me! Please! There are people upstairs. It sounds like they are being tortured to death! Call the Police!"

Dean looked to her, flashing the same smile as Oliver. "See you soon, Megan." Eyes bulging out of her head, she did not utter a single word. She ran to the exit as quick as she could, the mutt running closely behind, ready to bite. Slamming the door behind her put the mutt at a dead stop.

Megan pulled out her cell phone and called 911. She insisted that they needed to go to the hotel. That people were being brutally tortured on the thirteenth floor. She gave them names, and informed them on every little detail she could manage. She went for a walk instead of standing outside the hell-hole she just escaped from. By the time, she circled the block the police showed up. Only one squad car that carried two officers.

"Why isn't there some sort of SWAT team shit here?!" Megan ran up to the car. "What are you waiting for?! He's in there! Go get him!" The officers looked at each other trying to hold back laughter.

"Ma'am calm down. What's going on here?" one of them was finally able to ask, sounding amused.

She filled her lungs with air, and blurted, "His name is Oliver Sweets, he invited us all to stay at the hotel to torture us!" Confused, yet entertained, the officer looked the building up and down, and then again at Megan.

"You came here willingly? No one could pay me enough to stay here." Megan turned around at the miraculous hotel and saw nothing but an abandoned building.

"What?... it was right here, I'm not making this up."

"Ma'am would you like for us to search the building?"

"It was here. I swear it!" Megan persisted.

CPSIA information can be obtained
at www.ICGtesting.com
Printed in the USA
FFOW05n1238130517

9 781612 445724

"Ma'am, the building looks condemned, are you sure there are people inside? Are you positive you aren't mistaken with the address or anything?"

After twenty minutes of arguing with the officers, Megan gave up. Chalking it up to maybe she got too drunk and passed out, having some sort of nightmare. They offered her a ride home. She politely declined by saying she didn't live far. As soon as they were out of sight Megan ran into the abandoned building.

It looked as if it used to be some old office building. Everything was different. Old, condemned. The only similar looking thing to the hotel was the location of the front desk. Megan walked over, in hopes to find some kind of clue that she wasn't hallucinating. There, before her was her proof. An invitation laying on the front desk. Addressed to her. Looked brand new.

Megan felt defeated. There were so many years she wasted searching for him. She had lost everything. For what? A name? She slammed the invitation down, furious with what her life has become. Contemplating whether or not she was creatively insane. That's when she saw it, what gave her the drive to keep going. A note… from him. Reading it, Megan's stomach churned. All this time she spent searching, she knew she couldn't give up now.

We hope you enjoyed your stay with us

here at the Oliver Sweets Hotel.

Sincerely,

Oliver Sweets